THE QUICK
AND THE
QUIRKY

STEPHEN F.C. PORTER

Formatting and Interior Design by Woven Red Author Services

"Memories from Heaven" previously published in *Inkspots: A Collection of New Canadian Short Stories*, (Maple Ridge, BC, Canada: Polar Expressions Publishing, 2011)

"This Story Sounds Vaguely Familiar" previously published in *Below the Canopy: A Collection of New Canadian Short Stories*, (Maple Ridge, BC, Canada: Polar Expressions Publishing, 2009)

The Quick and the Quirky/Stephen F.C. Porter—1st edition
ISBN ebook: 978-0-9959603-3-6
ISBN print book: 978-0-9959603-2-9

TABLE OF CONTENTS

INTRODUCTION

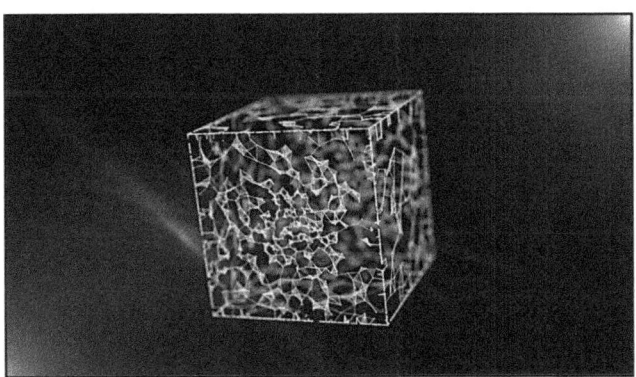

Some folks say short stories are written by authors who can't carry a storyline beyond a few pages, and that most of their readers don't have the time or the attention span to last a full book.

As I have never written a full-length novel, I really can't say what it's like to construct a story which includes an epic, multidimensional plot lasting several hundred pages. Sometimes I enjoy novels for the details and intricacy they paint, and at other times I like the rush provided by a tale told frugally.

I could have taken some of these stories spinning off in different directions, expanding in a verbal spider web until I had a real "book". Usually before I got to that point, for one reason or another I decided to not go in that direction.

The best short stories are like a good meal. You want more, but are satisfied with what you have. When Isaac Azimov wrote his masterpiece short story, *Nightfall*, his longest story at 13,000 words, I must have read it five times, each time taking something else away. Then in 1990 he collaborated with another Sci-Fi icon, Robert Silverberg, and reworked it into a full-length novel which sat at 352 pages. It was indeed more. I read it the same day I found it at the bookshop and came away with the same feeling of wonder and excitement I had with the original mini version. This showed me it isn't the scale, but rather the story, the idea and the characters. A good short story is an art form.

I don't know whether I would classify the following as art forms. They are tales that came from a single idea, reached out to encompass the events and characters I envisioned and then ended at just the right point. Some are longer than others, but I enjoyed creating these mini worlds for as long as they lasted, and I hope you do as well.

THE NICK OF TIME

The first three stories of this collection involve a character I created to bridge my two favourite genres, science fiction and noir. He's an old-fashioned private detective, with a few special abilities. By the time he got to his third adventure, Nick Bannister had developed his own personality, and unique manner of handling whatever came his way.

The Nick of Time

I'm at my desk turning over my business card. *Nick Bannister Integrated Investigator. I Will Travel To The Ends Of Time To Solve The Case*. Well that's not totally correct, there are some caveats. Since access to the Time Skip was discovered, there's been a lot of covert fancy dancing by the powers that be, to keep this from going public. It's limited to very specific situations. We generally try to avoid political issues, but we don't always get what we want. So why is someone like me dashing around time and space? Well, let's just say I have some unique abilities that give me the flair for solving some cases which would have the FBI, MI5 and the KGB collectively throwing in the towel.

As for the business card, goes without saying I don't have it sitting at the check-out at the local diner. My private clientele is very select, but no matter how much security you have, there's always someone saying she heard from some guy in Yonkers who cuts somebody's hair, that you can help her find out where great granddaddy hid his fortune. The government pays me decent money for what I do, but a few private cases help make life a bit more, comfortable. Now I don't disclose my extra-curricular activities to my bosses and if they know about it, they don't seem to be overly concerned, as long as I'm ready and able when they need me.

James

About nine last Monday morning, the door thumps a couple of times. I call, "It's open." and this 20 something kid comes in and offers his hand." Mr. Bannister, DOSARMS sent me. James Tiberius, honour to meet you sir." He reads my face. "Yes, my parents were OTs." He checks to see if I'm with him. "OT's, Obsessive Trekkies, who happen to have been blessed with the surname Tiberius. Anyway, I'm here for...."

"Kinda young aren't you?"

"I think if you look at my CV you'll see that I have more than enough of the qualities you're looking for sir." *Stands his ground, point Tiberius*. While my boss did say he was thinking of bringing in some new blood, I didn't think it would be today.

I offer him a coffee and then I ask why DOSARMS sent him. Sorry, sometimes I forget this stuff isn't exactly available to JQ Public. DOSARMS is the Department Of Spatial And Rift Management Systems. And no, you won't find it on the directory board in the Pentagon Lobby. In fact you'd be hard pressed to find anyone in the Pentagon who even knows we exist. We're the guys they call in to clean-up when the big wigs have messed up bad, and they need someone to blame if it all goes wrong. Anyway, he shows me a couple of citations he'd received doing intern work on a few minor initiatives headed by the Department.

Before I can nod my approval, he starts into one of the capers he had a hand in, nothing earth shattering, but still pretty impressive.

Maybe I should stop and explain a bit more about the Time Skip here. DOSARMS doesn't like the term time travel. Leads to all kinds of misconceptions.

We don't go back in time brandishing swords and leaping into whatever fray is going on. You've heard of the butterfly effect? The stuff we do can be small potatoes. If they're done right, they can be carried out under the noses of the people involved. A Time Skip may involve little more than shifting around a few things in a room, or putting up a simple sign somewhere. In this case, James just had to slip a message onto an official's desk with some plan modifications and bingo, history gets a little nudge. After that, it's kind of Russian Roulette.

He tells me how he managed to slip into the office, shift the paper on to the chief's desk, and get back out without raising an eye, and he isn't being all modest about it either. *I like you James Tiberius, This just might work out.*

The next couple of hours involve sizing him up and filling him in on what to expect, and more important, what I expect. I decide I'll tell him a few tales, just to bring him down to earth; show him this ain't no "Back to The Future" lark. *Yeah, like I could afford a DeLorean.* And there's a lot of scary shit can happen in this line of work.

We seal the deal with a handshake and I tell him I'll call him when I need him. I mean, I'm no Batman and I don't need no boy wonder. I just need an extra hand once in a while.

A few days later, I get a call from the Department. They have a small item needs cleaning up, circa 1992. Now to correct a couple more misconceptions, let's begin with the notion of time travelers bouncing around the past having excellent adventures. The idea of Bill and Ted collecting famous characters and bringing them together is a great premise for a movie. It's also 100 percent bullshit, scientifically speaking. Time travel is mostly restricted to the future. You can go back, but only to the date where time travel was invented. You recall the Philadelphia Experiment? Well the truth isn't nearly as interesting as Hollywood makes it out to be. Let's just say while the government was messing around with cloaking devices, there was a bizarre side effect. They invented time travel. Not in the Doctor Who, Tardis sense, but a few simple items were shifted into the near future, and that was that. In reality, all those brilliant scientists couldn't do much more than move a bottle of coke into next week. So, after a lot of discouraging research, the file was closed, experiment abandoned.

Sixty years later, using all we know about quantum physics and particle acceleration, a couple of physicists in Cern had a Eureka moment and bingo, time travel. At least as far back as 1943. Another thing, and I can't stress this enough. The past is passed. You can't go back and rearrange history by killing Sarah Connor. It just isn't gonna work. But you can make a few tweaks, and see what comes down the pike.

I reckon I don't need the kid. Piece of cake. I'm in and out in ten minutes, and yes ten minutes is ten minutes, no matter how you mess with the timeline.

Did I Get a Wrong Number

I stand scowling at the empty spot on the counter. How could I have been so fucking careless? I'd checked for every contingency, and gone in and done what I had to do. And damn it, it was a successful job. Nobody suspected a thing. I hadn't disturbed anything. Followed all the rules, and then I'd broken the most cardinal one of all. Don't take anything you don't need, and for God's sake if you do, bring it back with you. And I'd gone and left something that could change everything and I had no idea how it was going to play out.

For Chrissake I'm supposed to be a pro. Ten years of crawling down rabbit holes and coming back with barely a scratch. In this business, one slip and the costs can go well beyond the failure of the mission. Like ripples moving across the water. Yeah, the past is the past, but after that, it's out of your hands.

The Sins of the Fathers

The kid is standing at the door, looking at me with this goofy smile, which kind of says "Thanks boss, I knew you couldn't do this without me." I usher him into the kitchen and point to the white cord sitting on the counter. He looks puzzled. "What am I supposed to be looking at?"

"You're meant to be looking at a mobile phone, Tiberius. It's supposed to be attached to the charger, and as you can clearly see, it isn't there."

"Where...?"

"Good question, and I wish I had a proper answer, but I don't. What I do know is, it's not here." I go to the cupboard, bring out the bottle of Wild Turkey, pour a healthy shot. I hoist the bottle slightly as an invitation, but he shakes his head. I take a long pull.

He's looking at me like I'd grown a third eye. Batman is fallible. I'm waiting for something to come out of his mouth, but I reckon he's trying to think of something to express his disbelief at what I've done, while showing respect for the boss. Finally it comes, "I don't understand..." and then it stops.

Poor guy, feel bad for him, so I jump in. "Okay, two days ago I was sent in to try to fix a bit of a political situation back in the eighties. You heard of Oliver North and the Iran Contra Scandal?" Another blank look. "Nah, you're too young. Well, here's a quick history lesson. It was back in the Reagan years. You heard of him? A bunch of big wigs sold arms to Iran, which was strictly taboo, and then funneled the money to rebels in Nicaragua, also not kosher. There was a huge scandal, of course the President and the VP pleaded dumb. Yeah, imagine that, the White House denying a scandal. George Bush Senior was the VP at the time. When he became president, in the 90's, he pardoned a bunch of the players. Stuff passed under the radar, or more likely got buried. But radar blips and backyard skulls have a habit of popping back up at the worst times.

The government decided it would do no good to anybody for them to surface right now, so they called the department, and asked them to do a bit of housecleaning. Make a certain incriminating memo disappear. I just needed to get into the press secretary's office, exchange it with something a little bit more, shall we say, mundane. Getting into the White House, passing clearance, and telling one whopper of a story to security, would take about half an hour. Then five minutes more to make the switch, and soon I'd be back home drinking a Cappuccino, and watching reruns of The Americans on Netflix." Tiberius sits watching me, trying to gauge how serious this really is, I guess. "Why I had my mobile in my pocket, I honestly can't tell you. Wish I could say I was drunk, but we both know that isn't possible. Temporary insanity, hey that's just business as usual in our line of work. Don't know how I did it, but I did. Making the switch was easy, but then I bumped up against the side of the desk and realized it was there. Like a dummy, I took it out to look at it, just as someone came in. Well I couldn't let them see it could I? So I slid it quietly under the fancy leather blotter on the desk. This dude started talking to me about this and that. Didn't seem suspicious, but he kept going on and on, and finally said he'd walk me out. And I guess the time shift kinda had my brain spinning. The next thing I know I'm on Pennsylvania Avenue hailing a cab, phone completely gone from my mind."

I'm grateful for T's silence. Other kids might be peppering me with questions, or trying to fill in the gaps with some *ums* and *ahs* and *I sees*. But he just sits there drinking it in. Finally, he says about the only sensible thing he could, given the circumstances. "So where does that leave us, besides the obvious fact we have to get it back."

"Well, in fact it leaves you in the position of having to go in there, get a hold of it without anyone seeing, and bringing it back before it can do any damage." I'm usually steady as a tree, but I'm scared shitless. I mean this never happened before, so I have nothing to draw on.

Now I'm not being a jerk and giving the kid the dangerous stuff. The fact is, you can't make more than one jump in a certain amount of time. It depends on your health, but the minimum is a week, and even then there are risks.

I can't begin to explain the changes the human body goes through during the process, but suffice it to say you need to be in tip top shape, no drugs, no alcohol for at least a week before, and a few dietary restrictions that don't exactly fit in with my lifestyle.

I really don't understand the whole process myself. This stuff is so classi-fied that if the powers that be thought for a moment that I had somehow discovered how it all worked, they'd either have to kill me or send me on a one-way ticket to Vietnam, circa 1970.

Into the Breach

James Tiberius let the familiar sensations cocoon him. It was an oddly agreeable experience. Pulses of warmth slipped through his field, fixing themselves to every atom of his being, turning his world inside out. Unlike those Hollywood Movies where the protagonist watches time fly by like images on a screen, there was no real indication he was moving. In reality he was not travelling through time at all. Time was looping around him, curving in on itself, taking him for the ride, yet taking him nowhere. This is the paradox of time travel. There's really no such thing. He wasn't going anywhere. Time was shifting, but not moving in the common sense of the word. The only physical movement would be the final maneuver, to put him where he needed to be. To explain any more, would require a smartboard and about three hours of your time.

Slowly the feeling eased, his head began to clear. Then came the waiting. James sat silently. When he had made his first shift, he thought there'd been a terrible mistake. Even though he'd been primed, he wasn't prepared for what he saw. Nothing. There was only a void. You couldn't even call it empty. That implied there was something containing it. This was non-existence. He started to doubt he was there at all. There had to be something. Fog, mist, blackness, anything. But instead, he was saturated by nothingness. That first time he had panicked, and made the crucial mistake of trying to move. That had sent him into a maelstrom of vertigo, only relieved when the world started to resolve itself. Slowly, he perceived shifts in the colours and hues of this abyss. Like a fog lifting under the morning sun, swirling greys and browns now entered his field of vision. He felt his heart nod a swell of relief. His eyes grew steady and sharp, as the shadows resolved themselves into impressions. Then the images refined themselves into pictures.

The haze in his head took a bit longer to clear and as he materialized on the White House lawn, he grabbed onto a branch to keep from falling. It was a marvelous thing. Here he was manifesting on an open lawn, dotted with tourists, and no one paid the slightest notice.

When the Shift became part of the government agenda this issue was one of the first concerns. How could you drop someone into a location without drawing attention? So, a few simple experiments were performed. Skippers were dumped into public places, and people carried on without so much as a "how do you do." In most cases, the crowd didn't even notice. It appears those that did, took a second look, assumed they had missed the interloper, and returned to what they were doing. Obviously Skippers weren't dropped into the middle of Sunday dinner at Grandma's, but for the most part their appearance in public caused less of an uproar than the arrival of a mouse on the kitchen floor.

James started to amble in the direction of the white stone columns, when he started to feel very peculiar. He was light-headed, dizzy, as if he was falling into a deep slippery hole. He looked at his feet. They were fading. He could see the grass through them. His head was spinning. It went dark again. He remembered stumbling on the White House lawn. Now he was in limbo again.

A few seconds later, he felt solidity returning. He began to perceive shapes, walls, furniture, the American Flag. James reached out and touched the corner of a desk. Mystery solved, someone at IT had repositioned his point of arrival.

Liaison Officer Michael Cummings took another look at the smoky apparition near the big oak desk in the middle of the office. It wasn't there anymore. Second time this week something was not quite kosher in the Press Secretary's office. The day before yesterday, he'd entered the room just in time to see a form near the desk. He swore it had looked at him and was trying to conceal something. When he'd shaken his head and looked again, the "ghost" had materialized into a figure. It was an aide, with clearance. He'd talked with the man and escorted him outside. It was strange, but he'd put it out of his mind. Now it was déjà vu again. Was he losing his grip? After all, the hours were long, and with all the political brouhaha going on, security was running pretty high. In the end, he was on the chopping block if something went wrong. Politicians, they got away with murder. No matter what they did, or how much the headlines screamed, after a couple of days of notoriety, the attention of the world wandered to something else. But make one mistake and let someone who doesn't belong, be somewhere they shouldn't be, and next thing, you were handing your resume in to Pinkerton's, praying your little slip up wouldn't reach personnel.

Not that it really mattered that much. Already he felt he was running into a career cul de sac. Michael had finished with an honours degree in Political Science International Relations from the University of Maryland. But he'd made a few simple, yet crucial poor choices. They involved following instincts instead of protocol, something heavily frowned upon in his line of work. It had pretty much quashed his dreams of being a high roller in the world of politics. Unless he found some way of either turning back the clock or scoring a miracle from our Lady of Lost Careers, he was little more than a glorified babysitter to the Press Secretary, albeit with a fancy title.

He moved further into the room and stared as the air became a whorl where he'd seen the strange vision. Michael rubbed his eyes. Was he getting one of his migraines? But what had been a mere shadow was now taking form. A man? Whoever it was, he didn't look out of place. Except for the fact he shouldn't be there. As clarity embraced the scene, he saw the person had a clearance badge and was dressed in the style of an aide. But who was this? He'd never seen this person before, and hadn't received any memo to alert him to any staff changes, or expected visitors. Besides, an aide would never be in here unsupervised.

The man turned and looked in his general direction, but didn't seem to be focusing on anything. He appeared to be trying to get his head around this odd turn of events.

For James, this was no time to think or try to talk his way out of things. Any physical action was completely forbidden, as the consequences to the timeline were still unknown. There was only one response: abort. James reached into his pocket and fumbled around for the small metal disc. A couple of seconds later, he located it and rubbed it in a clockwise direction, with his thumb. This was akin to a diver giving a long tug on his line, when he needed to get back to the surface in a hurry. A millisecond later, one of the techies at DOSARMS would activate the recall mechanism, and in a perfect world, would have James travelling back before he knew it.

But in the time it had taken for James to find and start the recall alarm, Michael Cummings did what his instincts and years of training demanded; stop and disable the intruder. He leaped and sent him tumbling to the floor, spilling a small silver object onto the carpet. Michael scooped it up and held it in his hand. It had begun to flash red and it was emitting a high whistling sound. His hand felt warm.

Meanwhile Back in the Present

This is making me crazy. I mean I'm usually the one in the middle of the action. Sure it's dangerous, but at least I know what's going on. Then I can start a plan. Being on the other end of the timeline, not knowing whether I was gonna be up to ears soon, that's a whole different thing and frankly I don't like it.

I've just about decided to take up smoking again, when I get the message from control. "Nick, Randy. We have a problem. James landed on the White House lawn. So far he hasn't drawn attention. We're trying to get him where he belongs." My heart is jumping. What if he gets swarmed by security? I mean, we've given him all the credentials to pass inspection. On the other hand, if he gets taken into the real Homeland Security boys, it isn't going to hold up to any scrutiny.

I mean it's not like they had any real way of getting to us. We're twenty odd years out of sight. But once one of our boys is caught, we don't know what they're gonna do to him. And then there's the timeline again. Inserting a stranger from the future and scooping him out before anyone notices is one thing. Having him mix with the locals is another.

I'm not what you would call a control freak, but I'm good at what I do and I haven't had many issues with my assignments, the past two days notwithstanding. Now I'm sitting there like the lights just went out, and I have no idea when they're coming on again. And there is nothing to do but wait. The guys in the department don't know any more than me. We're in limbo hell.

When the phone rings again, my heart starts doing the pole vault in my chest. "Nick? Randy. Last time we heard from James, we were picking him off the lawn and putting him in the office where he belongs. Since then, nothing." I won't say my heart sank, but it sure is starting to list a little. Even if nothing's going on, protocol is to check in every half hour. I hang the phone up and entertain a few dozen scenarios in my head, all of them pretty grim. At the one which has him being sent to Guantanamo Bay for a short round of rendition, the phone rings another time. I snatch it up like the last donut on the plate. "Nick, Randy. Better get down here right away." I pick up my jacket, and high tail it out to the driveway.

In the Press Secretary's office things were beginning to heat up. Michael Cummings was trying to get a look at the strange object that now lay in the palm of his hand. James was lying on the floor, just a foot away. He hadn't been hurt when he went down, and now, seeing that the security guy was distracted with the disc, used the opportunity to get to his feet and renew the struggle. If that disc got to Homeland some kind of hell was going to break loose. James had an unquestioning loyalty to the department and his country, but right now his main concern was that he passed his first real test. He knew if he fucked up, there may not be another chance.

The door to the office burst open. Two men dressed in black pointed their guns at James. "Stand back and put your hands up." James glanced at the men, and then looked at the object still lying loosely in the security officer's hand. He couldn't let this happen. He wasn't sure how he was going to do it, but he had to get it back. After that, he hadn't a clue. Ignoring Time Shift protocol and the fire power pointed in his direction, he grabbed at Cummings hand and the disc fell to the floor. It was still glowing and now giving off a high whining pitch.

He heard the men in black shout to a third man, he assumed still in the hall. "Please stay back sir, we have everything under control." *Hardly*, James thought, as they barked their orders at him again.

"I said, put your hands in the air, and move away from what's on the floor. Cummings, move away from the subject." Michael gave a wistful look at the floor and did as he was told, dreams of redemption turning to smoke. The one man held his gun steady at James's head and indicated for his partner to pick up the disc. At that moment, the third man came into the room. He was wearing a grey suit and a red tie.

"Sorry gentlemen, but this looks like a top security issue and I need to be involved. Let me see what you have there son." The guard yielded it to the older gentleman in the suit, just as a series of bleeps pierced the air.

Welcome to the Future

I swerve into my parking spot at DOSARMS, barely stopping the engine to get out of the car. I dash through the main door, straight past security. *Sorry Janice, you know who I am."* My mind is a jumble of ideas and questions, all of them making me sick to my stomach. It's procedure to knock, but this is hardly business as usual. When I get into Randy's office, three DOSARMS brass are standing around a familiar looking gentleman seated in a chair. "Good, you're here. Nick. There's someone I want you to meet. Nick Bannister, this is President George H.W. Bush."

INTO THE WEB

We take so much for granted; things so fantastic a time traveler from the past would consider them to be magic. Yet we use them in our daily life as casually as we would an umbrella or a pen. We switch on the laptop, check our emails, type a memo, and forward it without a second thought. But how many people appreciate the wonder of the internet, and how many could explain what the internet even is? What if we could literally surf the net? My favourite Integrated Investigator is about to visit this magical tool, up close and personal.

Into the Web

Nick Bannister here. A lot of strange shit's gone down since I became a P.I. or more precisely, I.I., Integrated Investigator. Got a flair for going into the crazy and coming out in one piece. Been to space, crossed into other dimensions, even put my mind into someone else's brain, to catch them thinking things which could destroy humanity. I know this sounds like the kind of paranoid conspiracy theory shit that guys who dress in army fatigues and live in cabins in the woods believe. Fact is, it's all true. And that's just the tip of the iceberg. What goes on under the pretext of "Scientific Research" would make your toes curl. And lucky me, whenever they need someone to play in their little government experiments, I'm their boy. It's all been pretty exciting, although maybe once in a while I'd like a real P.I. job, like tailing a cheating husband.

Just thought you might like a little perspective, because that other stuff can't hold a candle to what I'm about to tell you.

So I'm having some down time. What I do isn't exactly dime a dozen. Sometimes I don't work for weeks. Not good, so much time, too much boredom and bourbon. Then I get a text or call and it's zero to sixty. I go from watching reruns of NCIS, to hearing the boss tell me what fresh hell he intends to put me through. But I love what I do. Who else has visited the Whitehouse while George H W was at the captain's wheel? Or strolled by the Berlin Wall as it was torn apart brick by brick? It's totally surreal and I have to pinch myself sometimes.

Here We Go Again

The call comes, and a half hour later I'm getting my eyes scanned at security, giving Janice the most un-PC gesture I dare in a room full of people, and making my way into the boss's office. Randy is looking a bit like the dog who just chewed your slippers, and motions me to sit down. A couple of nerdy guys are sitting in the room. I'm getting a funny feeling about all this. He starts in. "Nick Bannister, this is Doctor Theodore Cunningham, and Dr. Henry Chang." We do the glad handing thing and he continues, "As usual what we say here is not going outside these walls." Of course he's just saying this for the sake of the docs.

I'm a bit taken aback. "Randy baby, did we just meet? You've trusted me with the most covert operations the department has to offer, and now you treat me like a total noob. I am deeply wounded."

The nerds shift about awkwardly in their chairs. "Yeah, like you could be wounded if I ran over you with my van. Okay, look Nick, seriously, what I'm going to tell you now has such enormous implications that if even one word gets out of this room, we'd have a hard time getting a job as a greeter at Walmart." I hear the words enormous and implications, and my curious lobe shifts into overdrive. With everything we've gone through, what could be so huge he has to use the disclaimer? "Here's the scoop. I can't mention any names, because we're still trying to see how big this thing is, and believe me it's huge. Two of the world's biggest corporations are about to apply for the merger from Hell. If it's approved, the effects globally will be disastrous, economically and environmentally, and the human rights toll will be staggering. It has to pass a tribunal who are not in favour of the nuptials. But the fact is, if they're going to nix it, they need ammo, before the fancy corporate lawyers get into the act. Now it looks like our two goliaths have been doing some lobbying that could sway the vote. But the bigwigs in charge have a lot more balls than brains. Some very incriminating emails were sent in the past couple of days. If we can get our hands on them, it'll put an end to the marriage."

Well the only such devil's deal I know is Monsanto-Bayer, and that's so full of lawsuits they'll be still sorting it when cockroaches rule the Earth. Other than that, I honestly don't know who he's talking about. "So what's the prob...?"

Randy does one of those little hushing motions that's always so annoying. "Before you even ask, obviously if we were able to retrieve the necessary data, we'd either have done it, or be in the process of doing so, and you would still be splayed out on your couch. Maybe these guys aren't geniuses, but they have people working for them who are, and they've made sure the emails haven't just disappeared, but for all intents and purposes, were never written or sent." I can't hold my tongue anymore.

"Okay, lay it on. Which mine shaft are you sending this sparrow into now?"

"How do you feel about surfing the internet up real close and personal."

"Rand, baby, the internet isn't a place like Cincinnati, it's just a name for a bunch of things we do. But, now that I've said that, I got a feeling you're gonna tell me something I don't know, and wish I never did."

"Okay, first of all, the internet, as it turns out, is a very real place. What that is and how we're going to get you there, that's a bit beyond this civil servant's brain. That's why our friends are here. Dr. Chang, if you don't mind."

Dr. Chang lifts his lanky body from the chair, and tilts his glasses down ever so slightly, an affectation I reckon is a carryover from years spent intimidating university frosh.

"Listen, Doc, just so you don't waste a lot of breath and time on me, I'd appreciate the idiot's explanation. I'm a bit ADD, so the long version is gonna get lost in the wash. What I am good at is picking things up as I go and keeping my ass from getting burned once you guys dump me into the fire."

"Fair enough Mr. Bannister. So let's start with the basics. Do you know what happens when you upload from your computer?"

"Short of going to another computer, not a lot."

"Okay, well the simple version is that when you upload information, it gets sorted into a packet. If the size of the file is too large, then a second packet or bundle is needed. In the case of the human consciousness..."

"Hang on a minute doc, I think I get the picture. You're going to send me in little bits. Now if I might be so bold as to ask, when all is said and done, how are you gonna put Humpty Dumpty together again?"

"Mr. Bannister there is nothing to worry about as far as your physical well-being is concerned. You've seen the Matrix I assume. Just like those people, you'll be safe and sound here, while your consciousness is going for the ride."

"Okay, and for God's sake stop calling me Mr. Bannister. First of all, I can't say I find your Matrix analogy very comforting. Secondly, I've been in more danger than you can even imagine. I go into this shit of my own free will, knowing I may not come out. It's my mind I'm talking about. No point in coming back alive if my brain is like a scrambled egg on the grill. So without all the technical lingo, just give me the basics, and then I'll let you know whether I'm in or not." I give Randy a sly wink. He already knows my decision.

"Okay Mister...uh Nick. Let's start with the fundamentals. What do you think happens when you press that button to send a video or a file, or an email?"

"Well, I have kind of done the computers for idiots thing, but really, other than what you told me about the packets, I've got no more idea than a goat how it all works. But listen, lots of times you get a file and it's corrupted, or pixelated, or sometimes blank. Where does that leave me? None of those possibilities is exactly my cup of tea."

"With all due respect, you of all people know the perils of your profession Mr. Nick, but to answer your question, I think we've managed to eliminate the chance of mishap."

"But with all due respect to you doc. Every time I get dragged in here, the boss tells me some hair brained scenario he wants me to star in. The tech boys explain a bunch of stuff I really don't understand. The scientists give me all kinds of reassurances and platitudes, and I ask a few questions and shake my head a lot. Next thing I'm in the Twilight Zone without a GPS."

Truth is, when all the doubts and objections are countered, I'm always in. I have no choice. Much as I relish the idea of laying on the couch, watching baseball and drinking whiskey, it's no way to live for the long haul. When everything is said and done, it's all about the rush, and if I don't get that rush, I may as well hang up my holster.

The call had come in the night before. I needed to be in at 0900 hours. No caveats, except a small lecture about the importance of a good night's sleep.

The alarm goes off at 7:30. I shower, preen a bit more than usual and pick out some nice duds. How does one dress for a trip into the unknown? I smile at the mirror, wondering who I might be trying to impress.

I'm pretty cool with all the trials they put me through, but I have to admit I'm feeling a few butterflies trying out their wings in my stomach as I walk through the familiar office.

Doctor Matrix is standing in a lab coat, with a face mask on. Not the most comforting welcome I've had. "Good morning Mr.... Nick." I catch the small smirk on Randy's face. "Oh, don't worry about the mask. Just standard procedure."

"Yeah, I bet that's what they say in the infectious airborne pathogens ward of the hospital. Listen Dr. Matrix, this is uncharted territory. I'd like the bottom line about all of this."

He does that glasses thing again, and I want to ask if he needs a new prescription, but as my ass is kind of in his hands, I resist. "Okay Mr. Nick, now as I have already said, there's almost no risk to your body. We've checked all your vitals and despite your rather questionable food and drink choices," *Again, shut up Nick, don't say a word.* "You seem to be in surprisingly good shape." *Does he know he's doing this?* "Barring anything unforeseen, you'll be fine. Of course that applies on any dangerous mission. It's the mental aspect we have to focus on. Now as you so succinctly said, we are in uncharted territory here, but all the cognitive and psychological tests we've done are very encouraging. You have obviously come up against some daunting situations before, so I assume you are able to work your way through them. *Is he giving me a compliment here?* Did you practice the meditation techniques we gave you?"

Yeah right. "Very relaxing, I'm sure they'll come in handy."

"Their purpose is to help you maintain balance. Think about what's floating through the internet Mr. Nick. You're going to see some very disturbing images; hear and witness things you can't even imagine. When this happens you must move beyond your mind, away from what you think you are seeing and move to a calm place."

Well, it's a bit late now, but flying by the seat of my pants has always seen me right before. "I understand Doc." *You lying bastard Nick.*

"So, if there are no further questions right now, we'll go into the UCC, that's Uploading Consciousness Chamber. You can get acclimatized, and then we'll give you a final rundown.

"Lead the way doc, before I change my mind." Randy gives me a "good luck" look and I return my best "aren't you coming with me?" face. We go down a long corridor, until we reach a black metal door. Matrix pushes a button and it slides open to reveal a simple silver elevator.

He gives me a bit of a *Are you sure you don't want to back out?* smile. God, I'm starting to loathe the man, and the funny thing is he hasn't done anything wrong.

Well, I'd hardly say my first glimpse of the room puts me into shock and awe. Just looks like a computer hub, except for this very comfy looking easy chair in the middle of the room. No pods containing bodies, but there are a lot of wires attached. Not a cheery look.

Doctor Matrix tries to steal a quick look at my reaction. As far as I can tell, I'm not giving him the pleasure of having any.

Surf's Up

"So, Mr. Nick, there isn't really a lot to see here. Most of the mechanisms are at the other end of those wires, in the Cyber Café. Haha, just a little joke we have around here, but seriously, everything in there is not only privileged, but except for computer geeks like yours truly, incomprehensible. All you need to know is on this side. The chair is where your body will be sitting comfortably, while your consciousness is experiencing the ride of your life. We'll be monitoring your vital signs, and if we sense any abnormalities, we will bring you back immediately. Other channels will be performing the actual downloading and studying your activities."

"How much freedom of choice and movement will I have?"

"Mister Nick, everything you do will be your own choice. Also, your responsibility. But remember, you are in a foreign world where the rules you are used to don't apply. Every time you make a decision, your intent will instantaneously travel to the main hub. At the same moment, you will be given the necessary information you need to proceed."

"Wow, can you fix it so I can do that when I get back into the real-world doc? Keep me out of a lot of trouble."

"Mr. Nick, perhaps you are using humour to cover up your misgivings, but at this point you need to be serious and concentrate on what I am about to tell you."

Oh, here's an idea, while I'm in there, how about I find you a sense of humour?

"And again, with all due respect to you, Dr. Matrix, this sense of the absurd is what helps me carry out my job as well as I do. Believe me, I am taking in every word of wisdom you have to say, and when push comes to shove, I'll remember all of it, and do you proud." *Wow, that's odd, I think I actually mean everything I said there.* It's in my DNA. I do all the wisecracking, ignore the training, disregard everything that's said to me, and yet once I'm in the pool, I swim like an Olympian. Sinking just isn't an option.

"First of all, we need to give you a fit for the chair. Remember, despite what we are going to do here, the body and mind are still sides of the same coin, and if you aren't comfortable, then it can affect what happens when we send you in."

Well that makes sense. "Okay doc, size me up, think I'm a ten." *Did I see a bit of a smile there?* I lift my leg over the chair, saddle style and then sink myself in. Oh my god, if Lazy Boy had chairs like this, I'd never leave my living room. It's as if I melted into a giant pool of velvet. "Oh yeah doc, fit for the king of crazy capers."

"I'll take that as a yes then." Doctor Matrix gives me a little nod and then makes his way toward the door. I assume he wants me to follow. I'm sorry to give up my throne, but I force myself to go after him.

"Is that it Doc? Is that my briefing?" He does a thing with his hand that kind of says, keep your pants on dude, you'll find out soon enough. Only he wouldn't say it that way. We get back to the lab and Randy and a couple of the other grands fromages are there.

"Well, what do you think?" Randy is looking at both of us.

"I think this brain needs more input, that is if you don't want it to go floating off into the final frontier."

"Well dude, that's why we're back here." Randy motions to Doctor Matrix, who turns on a screen and launches into a sermon.

At the end, I think I am suitably befuddled, but at the same time I get the general idea. But I have one question. "Okay, so while I'm trudging through all the mental waste of mankind, how will I know when I've found what I'm after? I take it there isn't going to be a little bell and a voice saying, *You've got mail.*"

"Excellent question." *You trying to butter me up doc, in case I change my mind?* "Like I said before, every thought and impulse you have, every image you detect is coming back to us in a nanosecond. That means we'll be seeing the same image at just about the same time as you. As soon as that happens, we'll retrieve it. You'll barely be aware it ever happened."

Catch a Wave

So I'm sitting on the throne waiting for the show to begin, when I get the feeling all isn't right with my world. It's nothing I can see but sounds and voices are creeping into my head. I'm not talking about the usual conversation people have going on most of the day, and night. This isn't my voice asking what I want for supper, or why I made that boneheaded move when I was playing pick-up last week. This is a crowd banging at my cortex, and it means business.

Now believe it or not, I have studied some Zen, and I'm pretty good at losing the mental turmoil. But this is total anarchy, and I can't fend it off, because it's not coming from me. I hear a buzzing. That means HQ is contacting me. "Nick?" Thank God it's Randy. "Your heart rate is going up. I'm assuming things are starting to heat up. Okay, don't sweat it. You haven't adjusted yet, so all the background noise is beating at your door right now. Pretty soon you're going to acclimatize yourself and..."

"You mean the noises will stop?"

"Ah, not exactly, in fact they're going to get more intense, but you'll start to make sense of them. Separate the wheat from the chaff. Compartmentalize things in a rational way. You'll be fine, trust me."

So I just sit there and take the blows. I start "Zenning" out, letting go. All those crazy thoughts we have all day long, all the matter-of-fact ones, even the epiphanies are just that, concepts, thoughts. You can't touch them, or grab them. They're gossamer. The secret of calming the mind is to just let the show pass, like clouds in the sky. Don't label, don't cling, don't judge.

That idea soon gets put to the test. These buggers are pounding at me like a Nebraska hailstorm. Some of them are funny, others startling, frightening and some as mundane as a new recipe for Jalapeno Cornbread. Even in my wildest, sleepless, dark nights of the soul, I've not experienced a circus like this.

I had imagined travelling down this ghostly highway, expanding and shrinking as the streams of information changed. Instead, it feels like everything is moving through me. Makes sense, like the tree falling in the forest. Someone has to observe it to make it real. I just have to stay where I am, on the receiving end of this panoply.

I know I'm not going anywhere, and that relaxes me. The parade slows down. My mind isolates images and sensations. There's a video of a K-pop band. Interesting, although I can't say I'm interested. Here's something about investing. Keep that for future reference.

I can't explain how it all works in words, but whatever they've hooked me into, lets me record, dismiss, put on hold everything that comes at me. I don't have an eidetic memory, but it's always been good. Suddenly I remember things I didn't know. I'm learning to overlook irrelevant data. Like being programmed with a bunch of hashtags.

I'm just an observer, and that's very helpful. Adding a judgment to the proceedings just complicates things. The thing with consciousness, is the most brilliant scientist in the world still can't tell you exactly where it stems from, or what it is. The boss and his cronies have the part of my consciousness that deals with everyday life, the part that keeps my body going. Feelings, like love, hate and fear, right now they're with the guy in the chair in the chamber, but whether they stay there is another matter. I'm kind of fond of that guy in the throne. I'm sure there are some who might disagree.

Everything is flying at me fast and furious. I'm barely aware of them, but I know they're all locked in some kind of vault in my brain. If I stop for a second, I can bring up anything I choose. Hashtag Hubble Telescope. Amazing images of celestial objects not visible to the naked eye. Hashtag 2021, Stanley Cup Playoffs. I play around for a while. More and more clips of life are filling my brain. They say we only use a small portion of our melon anyway, so I'm not worried about overload. I glance at the time. Good Lord, maybe 10 seconds have passed, and I've taken in enough data to fill a shelf full of encyclopedias.

Someone slams on the breaks. Everything stops. Well, not stops exactly, but now it feels like I'm in a planetarium looking up at the domed ceiling. Images are streaming across that dome, but they aren't in me anymore. I am here and they're somewhere else, although I don't know where that is, and I sure as hell don't know what's going on.

Accept the now. I hear the words of Lama Shyota. Well, I can't think of a better plan. I slow down my breath, let my thoughts just flow, and sit back and enjoy the show in the sky.

"Nick?" If I was in my skin, I'd jump right out of it. My heart feels like it wants to go up and join the dance on the ceiling.

I manage a kind of cross between a squeak and a bark, and look up to some imaginary deity. I clear my throat and start again. "Randy, that you?"

"Nick, we've got what we need. We're bringing you out."

Tsunami

My heart and hand are giving each other high fives, when I perceive something around the edges of my field of vision. I don't pay it much attention, but I do roll my eyes around their sockets to get a better look. I'm a little freaked to notice that the walls are starting to close in. Dark shadows consuming the panorama. "Rand, something is up." Silence. "Randy, are you there, something pretty spooky is going on here." As I wait, I try to centre myself. *It's okay Nicky baby, he just said they're bringing you out. Besides that, nothing in here is real.* Well if that's my idea of a pep talk, it was a dud. Panic worms its way into my already flimsy psyche. I'm looking into an approaching wave of blackness, a tsunami of nothingness. Absolute void. Nothing. No time. No space. No existence. I don't even know if I am here at all.

This time when I try to call out, there is nothing there. Silence on both ends. The blackness overwhelms me. I'm like Dorothy inside the tornado. Except, I'm not just a tourist looking at the spinning wall around me. I am part of the storm.

And I'm not alone. As I sit paralyzed, I sense shapes and figures, colours that aren't colours at all, but rather shades of the dark. They are morphing into shapes. I keep reminding myself they can't hurt me. The real me is sitting in a chair in the offices of DOSARMS, unaware of the hell unfolding. *You think you know everything. If you'd listened and done all those exercises, maybe you'd be a little less freaked out right now.* I remember the waves. Nothing here is real. Just crests on the ocean. I settle a bit. But the light show continues. Now there's noise. Every sound ever made is screaming at me. Clouds. Waves. *What if it is real? I mean what the fuck do these guys know. No one's ever been here before. Shit what is that?* There's a huge ocean. Dark and roiling. In the center, total chaos. Ships are spinning towards... *Is that a whirlpool?* A huge vortex is gyrating maybe half a mile from me. The current is slowly pulling me. Drawing me toward that black hole in the center of this netherworld.

I remember reading *A Descent into The Maelstrom* by Edgar Alan Poe. I recall being awe struck by his description. And here I am on the event horizon, about to find out by experience. The thundering sounds increase and as I move to the giant chasm, they rise in tone until they're screaming like banshees. I try to plug my ears, but my hands are welded to my side. In time terror passes, replaced with what I can only call detached observation. I'm a mere punter, watching a horror movie.

The whole scene is like a sci-fi animator's contest. To say it's surreal is understatement. I'm at the edge of the abyss, lightning flashing on the spinning walls. The noise is tearing through my brain. Metal on metal, grinding to the breaking point. I'm still kinda detached, but I know if I go into that hell hole, I'll never come out again as the same guy I was. Then a word strikes me. Surreal, surreal. This isn't real. It never was.

At that moment it's like a hand grabs me. No, not like. I feel it. It grips my wrist. The gravity of the whorl is pulling at me, but like a fish on a line I'm coming out of the water.

High and Dry

There's no epiphany. I know where I am. The visions of where I've been are nipping at my soul. I look down at the floor. No water. I'm dry. I'm back. But then again, I didn't really go anywhere, so where else could I be? I know my consciousness was rescued at the last moment. *By what or who?* It doesn't matter who was in that magic carpet of a chair, it wouldn't be Nick Bannister anymore.

Randy is giving me the same look my mother used to give me when I had the flu. "Dude, are you okay?"

"I... I think so. I'm really here aren't I? What the hell happened?" Randy nods at Dr. Matrix.

The doc is looking at me with a mix of concern, and, *is that admiration?* "Mr. Nick, after we received the information and told you we were pulling you out, there was an unusual power surge. The cause is nothing sinister, simple lightning strike. The power was off for only a split second. During that time, and please remember time is irrelevant in this situation, you were without any input at all. Having just been bombarded over and over with images, sights and sounds, your mind could not cope with that complete void, so your subconscious kicked in immediately and started to manifest the scenes you witnessed."

"You mean none of it was real. I mean, I know it wasn't real, but you're saying none of it came from the net. It was all me?"

"Yes, and had we not been able to reach you in time, you would likely have been lost forever, at least mentally. There was a moment when you had a flash of clarity and realized it was not real. That was the moment we were able to grab you. Doing so when you were wrapped up in the scene could have been disastrous. It's a credit to your skill and acuity that you were able to disconnect with everything for that instant. *Ah doc, you flatter me.* That is the short explanation. I am assuming you are happy without the long one."

"So how…?"

Randy puts his hand on my arm, "The doc here basically reached in and grabbed you. Metaphorically speaking, of course. Was a pretty risky move, big risk for him too, but here you are and that's all that matters. Now you're going to need to go and get some serious testing done. Plan on being away from the booze and TV for a couple of weeks."

All I really heard though was, "The doc reached in and grabbed you." *Changy, dude, I had you pegged all wrong.*

"Nick, did you hear me? You're going to have to go for an evaluation and observation."

"Doc when I get out of there, I guess I owe you a drink." Matrix is nodding and smiling. "You know doc, this could be the beginning of a beautiful friendship."

Now You See Me

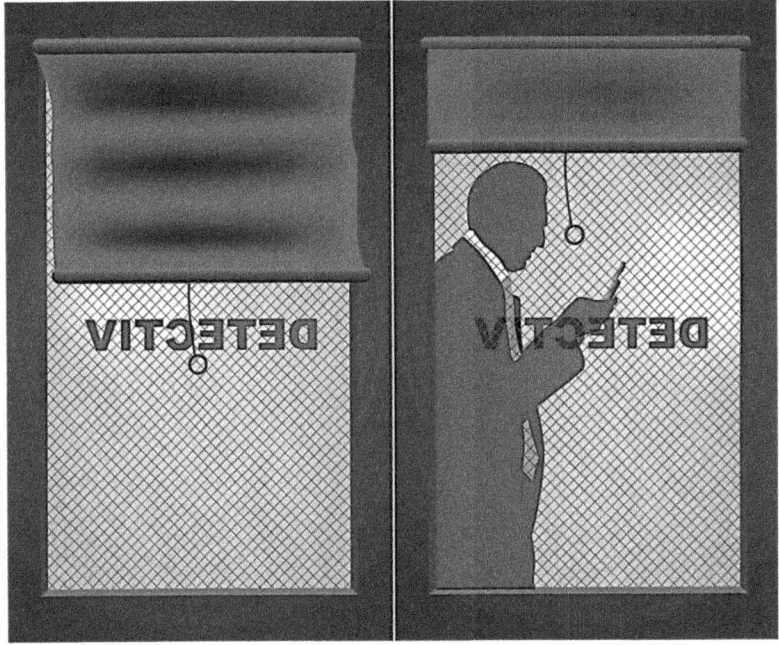

This is the third outing for Nick Bannister and I promise it won't be his last. Nick has shown he is up for any challenge, and can handle any situation which comes in his direction. This time he is able to solve the case and fulfill a *lifelong fantasy*.

Now You See Me

My peanut lands squarely in the middle of the trash bin, exactly 10 feet away. That's optimum. We did the calculations. We, is Dr. Albert Chang and me. He's the tech and math wizard I worked with in my foray into the internet. A story best left for another time. When I met Changy, he grated on me like a bike fall onto concrete. Condescending, pedantic and all of those other annoying habits you would expect from a first-rate science geek. Then came that day he yanked me from an abyss and saved my life. I still don't understand how he got me out, but it pretty much put him out of commission as well.

It wasn't all one way. I taught him a lot too. Like how to lighten up, enjoy life. A sense of humour. Wow, did he need some kind of transplant for that. Also the pleasures of a fine whiskey. So we're hanging, tossing peanuts in the bin, sipping bourbon like two old colonels, when the unspoken question finally comes out of my mouth. "Hey Changy, what'd you think? I reckon I'm ready for some action."

He lifts himself off his chair and tosses a nut. "Tie game. Mr. Nick." He insisted on calling me Mr. Nick when we met and now he does it just to wind me up. "You read my mind. This is wretched, men with our skill and ability sitting around doing nothing." Without another word, I pick up my phone. It doesn't even finish the first ring.

"Wow, that was fast. Randy, Dr. Chang and I have just been talking and...."

"Get down here right away." *And hello to you too.* Changy looks half puzzled, half knowing.

"They need us." I toss him the car keys. I can drive, but during my recovery I got used to being taxied.

I should give you some background before we go on. I'm Nick Bannister and I work at DOSARMS, that's Department of Spatial and Rift Management Systems, translated, weirdness incorporated. We specialize in the kind of stuff you see on those Roswell type shows. Time travel, shifting into alternate realities, all the kind of stuff your mother warned you not to do. I don't have any superpowers. Just a lot of chutzpah and a knack of flying by the seat of my pants. I can go into the fire, put out the flames, and come out without getting burned. I also do some private cases. Integrated Investigator is what's written on my personal business card.

Twenty minutes later, we're in the offices of DOSARMS. Janice leaps up and hugs me like a comfortable pillow. She moves towards Changy, but he kind of pulls back and turns it into a handshake. I said he's come a long way, didn't say he was human yet. "It's great to see you again. You feeling okay now? You on a case?"

"You too. Yes, much. And I dunno yet."

We open the door and go in. Randy doesn't even offer a greeting. "You know how close I was to calling you? Anyway, doesn't matter. You open for business?" We nod slowly. I sense strangeness on the horizon. He shows us a picture. "Know who this is?"

I'm looking at a fuzzy picture of me standing near Janice's empty desk. "Rand, I'm not that gone. So what...?"

"Take a look at Janice's desk. What do you see?" I scan quickly. Her collection of Minion toys border the desk. Box of Hershey's kisses. Lypsyl. Everything she needs to get through a day in the world of crazy. "Come on super kid. One of these things is not like the other." Then I spot it. She's got a Toy Story box calendar on her desk. The date is flipped to November 15th.

"The date. I haven't been in here since August. Dude, what gives?"

"That's not all." He hands me a stack of pictures, featuring yours truly in places I haven't been ever, or not for a long time.

I look over at Chang and he's got that look of blissful inscrutability which comes over his face when he's midway between trying to figure out what's going on, and deciding he knows. That cockiness pissed me off when we met, and I can feel it starting again, so I divert my attention to Randy. "Okay Rand, obviously I'm the idiot in the room, so please, enlighten the dummy. Either I'm sleepwalking or I've got a doppelganger."

"Well, I can't comment on the sleepwalking, but yep, there's someone out there that looks a lot like you and seems intent on moving in here. And the pattern suggests we might have a bit of a problem." Randy says in the same calm tone someone would use to say the candy machine was empty. Geez, I despise them both at this moment. I'm a smart guy. I know how to work my way around cases which would have the FBI filing as a cold case. But sometimes, I'm a tad slow on picking up the clues, and they sure don't hesitate letting me feel bad about it. He hands the photos to Chang.

"Forgive this government lackey for being slow on the update, but what patterns?"

Now I haven't worked with Chang since the internet caper. Since then, we've developed a beautiful friendship. Now friendships can help us forget and forgive idiosyncrasies. But now they're washing over me, like a car spraying slush over the sidewalk. Changy lays the photos on the table and asks me to have a closer look. Geez, it feels like my Grade 11 math teacher trying to explain calculus. I just don't see it. Clearly he has it all sussed out. Now Randy's trying to look sympathetic, but you know what? I don't think he understands any better than me. Finally he speaks. "Okay, maybe it's because I'm in these offices every day...." *Thanks for throwing me a bone.*

He saves face by turning it over to Changy. "Subtleties of lighting, the positioning of certain papers on desks, a few dial settings in the background, lead to one conclusion. These appearances appear to have the same basic source."

Well this kind of opens up the gates for me. In each picture there's a smoky area. Chang looks like he's about to toss me a fish. But I'm catching up. I'm so chuffed about it that I forgive his strutting. Besides, he really doesn't know he's doing it. I conjure up a few scenarios. They run from the simple, that someone is impersonating me to get hold of something in our offices, to the wild; someone or something has stepped through a rift. Occam's razor doesn't usually rule around here, so I go with the improbable.

Randy looks at Changy like a pilgrim who just climbed halfway up the Himalayas to meet the Dalai Lama. "Are you saying those flaws in the pictures are doorways?"

Chang is trying to be patient with his idiot pupils. "I'm not saying anything yet. I'm merely pointing to the areas that seem to display some turbulence. It's hardly likely the camera has a defect, so we need to explore other possibilities. And I suspect we're staring at a vast enigma."

He looks straight at Randy. "I assume there is an urgent need to pursue this?" Randy is nodding like a bobble head.

"All right then. I'm going to need the proper equipment to study these pictures and visit all the places shown. Hopefully in a couple of days we'll be able to discern what we are dealing with."

Well, his study team sure won't involve me, so I relax. "So, where does that leave me?"

Now it's Randy's turn. "That leaves you with a strict regimen of training, diet and concentration for the next few days. I'm not sending you into the ring in your shape. You game?" *Spiffy.*

Running for the hills isn't a viable option. "Let the games begin then."

Changy comes up and gives me a fist bump, which for him, is like a ten Mississippi hug. "I look forward to working together again."

"Yup, I'm sure it's gonna be a bunch of laughs. So, how long?"

Randy's staring at the images on the desk. "Will an hour do you?"

"Come again?" I have an uneasy feeling.

"Go home, get everything you need for say, three or four days, and be back here in an hour. You didn't think we were turning you loose did you?"

"Well it did cross my mind." he doesn't speak, but his face is saying, seriously dude?

He turns his attention to Changy. "All right Doctor Chang, let's sit down and itemize everything you are going to be needing for your...investigation."

Without even turning back. I head out past Janice's desk. "See you in an hour, doll."

Purgatory

Well, they put me up in some pretty nice digs. Nice room, comfortable bed, three squares a day. There's just one caveat. I'm staying at my bosses. I'm unpacking my case when he shadows up the door frame. "Dinner's in half an hour. You need anything?"

How about a move to the Marriott? I just grunt.

"Hey, cheer up. It's only for a few days, and, no offence, but you do have a habit of going a little off the rails without a babysitter, so that leaves you with your Uncle Randy."

My next few days are a tangle of trainers, dieticians, yoga instructors, healing music, curfews, early morning jaunts, physiotherapists, diagnostics and bland meals. All the things I've done a good job of avoiding most of my life. What it doesn't contain is a good whiskey, anything deep fried, a nice cigar and any form of fun. Unless you count Randy watching my pain.

However, as George Harrison sang, "All Things Must Pass", and on the fourth day of my ordeal, Randy interrupts my meditation class to announce that I have 15 minutes to pack up my stuff and meet him in the front hall. Zero to sixty kind of defeats the purpose of sitting in the lotus position, chanting a mantra. I have to admit I do feel pretty good though. Randy's standing at the door jangling the car keys.

Like the first pony out of the barn, I bound down the steps and wait for him to catch up. "I get in and savour a few last minutes of normalcy before we visit Crazytown again.

Randy is as silent as an unopened whiskey bottle. I reckon it won't hurt to put my toe in the water. "So Rand, does this mean we're ready to launch?" The quiet is beginning to unnerve me.

Finally he mumbles, "Too early to say. All I know is they want us."

Okay, won't be the first time they've left me on the beach until they're ready to throw me in the ocean. I stare out the window, wondering what it would be like to live an ordinary life.

We breeze through security without any checks. Janice gives me her best look of sympathy, and before you know it, I'm in my usual chair. Randy's behind his desk, and Changy is there with some Indian looking dude.

"Nick Bannister. This is Veej Patel, head researcher at Caltech Walter Burke Institute For Theoretical Physics." Crap, they've brought out the big guns. Must be some heavy-duty shit going on.

"Goodness gracious, are you trying to scare him off? Just call me VP. I'm just the guy who studies all that weird science fiction shit." He's a big man with a neatly trimmed beard and an expensive suit. I feel like I'm applying for a mortgage. He reaches out, takes my hand in a vice grip and looks me over. "So you're the famous, or is it infamous Nick Bannister. It is an honour to meet you." Now that's what I call an introduction. I like this guy already.

A few moments later, my warm fuzzy feeling is being replaced by something closer to trepidation. I mean Changy is a genius. He handles all the details. I just go in and do clean-up. So what's so perplexing to DOSARMS that they have to call in boy wonder? While I'm marinating in that thought, Randy gives an update.

"Okay Nick, while you've been on your little sabbatical. Dr. Chang here has been looking into the picture conundrum. And so far, the obvious answers don't quite fit."

A smile starts to curl up on Changy's face. He loves a puzzle and from the looks of things, this is going to be a doozy. "Mr. Nick, there are a lot of possibilities. The chance someone is trying to impersonate you to obtain information from DOSARMS. Maybe spatial displacement. Alternate reality colliding with ours. Time warp? Alien reconnaissance? Enemy intervention? And those are the more realistic options."

"Well, that all sounds very thorough doc, but where does that leave us?"

Doctor Patel has been standing like a puppy just waiting for the words, let's go. "The answer is everywhere and nowhere Mr. Bannister."

"Call me Nick please, and...huh?"

"Okay, when Dr. Chang called me, I knew if he was struggling, there was a lot more than meets the eye, no pun intended. Many of the options do have merit, but we're not quite there yet. There could be more than one explanation."

"Kind of like a combo platter?" I remember I didn't eat this morning. "Okay, I'm not always so fast on the uptake, and if this is going to be half the meeting I think it is, someone needs to make a breakfast run. Don't even think of looking at me that way Rand. I've been living like a monk for the past three days." Randy tries to give me a look of disdain, but I know he gets it. He goes into the other room and I see him talking to Janice, and then he comes back in.

Five minutes later, Janice, God love her, appears with a tray of coffee, and a box of redemption. We take time to garnish our coffees. I grab a couple of Boston Creams, and take a chunk out of one of them before it even lands on my napkin. It tastes like an orgasm. Seeing I am amenable to a bit of chit chat, Randy begins.

Changy and Patel are making me nervous hovering near the desk. Finally, Randy motions for them to sit down. "C'mon gentlemen, this isn't a college lecture, relax." They both sit down, as if it's something they've never done before. He looks right at me. "Okay, do you remember when we did the internet thing, we laid out the basics and then left the rest to you. We honestly didn't understand everything that was going on then, and I'll be honest, the same is true now. This is work in progress..."

I venture a feeble, "By work in progress you mean I'm...."

He cuts me off, which is probably a good thing since I don't really think I know how to finish that sentence. "Don't go getting ahead of yourself. We're not sending you into the fire without an extinguisher. But from what our experts are saying, we need to take action in a couple of days. God willing, when we open this book we'll all be on the same page."

Not your most inspiring pep talk, but then again this isn't a football game. "Now if one of you good docs could give us the idiot's version of what we know so far."

Changy and Patel give each other a "You, no you," exchange and after a moment, Changy stands. *Couldn't sit for just five minutes, could you*?

"Mr. Nick, you know by experience there are things science cannot explain. Like consciousness. We experience it every moment, yet no one can say where it comes from and what it is. Your time at DOSARMS has introduced you to different manifestations of consciousness. In the past, we've combined science with technology, and your unique qualities. In each case we've not only avoided disaster, but we've been most successful."

I am totally with him. But for how long?

"Now here's where it starts to get intriguing. Do you believe in ghosts Mr. Nick?"

Well I don't know what I was thinking would be the next thing out of your mouth Changy, but I can tell you for sure, it wasn't that. "If you mean impressions or imprints or energies, the answer is, absolutely. If you mean Casper, the answer is obvious. So let's see if I have this straight. All this tinkering with the universe DOSARMS is doing, is leaving imprints and impressions all over the place. Yes?" *If he acts like I'm a child who just spoke his first word, I swear I'll take the last Boston Cream and throw it at him.*

"Yes, but don't get too comfortable, we've only begun." *Comfort isn't my biggest concern mate.*

"Now forgive me if I'm going back into dumb mode, but all this doesn't sound like that big of a problem. Although, I'm assuming we're here for a reason?"

Now it's Dr. Patel's turn. *Oh good, you aren't going to stand.* "On the surface I realize it may not seem like a big issue. A few lost spirits hovering around, photo bombing our pictures. You can see the same on any episode of Ghost Adventures. The thing is, these appearances are not the problem, they are symptoms. They are telling us that there are some disruptions or cracks in the usual flow of time and space. And cracks can become passages."

"No offence doc, but you're not exactly reassuring me here. Look how long it took to come back from the internet fiasco, and now you want to toss me back into this rabbit hole."

At this point Changy strides over to the table, actually sits, and temples his hands. "Okay, I hope this helps. It's taken almost a week to get to this point. We've eliminated scenarios, one by one. From here, we can plan our course of action. For the next two days, we are going to correlate, organize, discuss and debate and then decide how we proceed. *You mean I am going to proceed and you all sit around here watching me on a screen.* Still I relax a bit. It's normal to have some misgivings, but I do trust these guys completely. I mean one of them has already saved my life.

"So, what do I do while you're planning my life for me?" Randy gives me a knowing smile. "Seriously? I just left boot camp."

He actually looks a bit sympathetic. "Dude, loosen up, all we have to do now is make sure you stay clean, rest, and centre yourself. Not the worst regimen you've dealt with."

"So before we call it a night," I just have to ask. "What is it you're looking for?"

Changy fields this one. "There's still a lot of data to go through. Some I suspect will be right on the surface, and others, a bit deeper. We will be looking for the patterns. Once we find them, I assure you our course of action will be very clear. So please leave it to us, and Mr, Nick, rest and be cool." *I think the word you're looking for is chill.*

The next few days are actually pretty good. Every time I go to put any effort into my life, someone is telling me to sit down, lie down, or maybe go for a walk. But they give me real food, and even a night cap. On the morning of day three, Randy knocks on the door and tells me to meet him at the car.

I'm feeling upbeat when I walk into the office. Janice, God love her, has brought me a present. The smell of hot java pervades the room, and the bag on the table holds promise. The docs are sitting there looking eerily cheerful and relaxed. And Randy looks like the gator who swallowed the tourist.

"Okay kids, you're kinda freaking me out here. You look altogether too happy." I take a swig of ambrosia and pull out a chunk of chocolatey, custardy goodness. "Well?"

It's Randy who starts. "Okay, well the whole crew has examined the photos, CTV footage and logs. Even swabbed the place for anything foreign. And you'll be glad to know that they've come up with a theory. Of course, nothing here is ever a gimme, but we're pretty certain we know what we're up against. Now all that's left to do is throw you in to make sense of it. *Well lucky me.* And not to be all maudlin, but you are the only guy we trust to do this. It isn't always pretty, but you always know what to do when the world stops making sense." *Wow, Rand, don't know what to say. I just go with my instinct and hope when the smoke clears, there's a part of me left.* "So, I'll let the learned professors here tell you where we go from here."

Again they do the silent, "You first, no you," thing. Patel wins. "Our initial hunch was correct. There are energies, trying to make their way into this world. In themselves they aren't an immediate concern. The problem is, it indicates a breach. This is just the beginning, like the first flow of water from a weak dam. If we don't plug it up, then the whole thing is going to burst on us. And we have no idea what the end result will be."

"So, I'm going to be the little Dutch boy? Oh, is that politically incorrect?"

"I don't know about that Mr. Nick." Changy smiles at me. "But you are definitely correct. You are he."

So here's the long and short of it. As usual, I don't necessarily understand the algebra, but I do know the drill. They'll prep me, and then as usual, I'll be flying by the seat of my pants. Not too worried, those pants have done me well over the years.

So my take away from all this is? There's a lot of energy hanging around DOSARMS. A rich, shit load of energy. You did your grade nine science. Energy is not created or destroyed. That means it's still there, only in a different form. Since these entities have no idea of what they are, they're latching on to the one constant, me. The only time I was ever called that, was when my ex-wife called me a constant asshole. Now if you aspire to the metaphysical, you know that spirit, or soul or energy, or whatever handle you want to give it, wants to take form. But the best these little spirits can do is mimic what they know, and hope it'll gain them tickets to our world. And they're likely to show up in all sorts of places and times. Those pictures are just the tip of the iceberg.

So what's the problem with all this? First of all, imagine the panic if a few dozen Nicks start showing up in Times Square, or a football game. Secondly, we don't know how they might affect the world outside of our building. Thirdly, DOSARS is the most covert branch of government, bar none. With all these little bastard Nicks around, we might as well advertise and hold an open house. Maybe serve some Boston cream donuts while we're at it.

By now everyone reckons we've had enough for one day. The world isn't going to collapse overnight, so we agree to call it a night, and meet at 0900 hours.

Randy and I shuffle off to his house, while the docs stick around here to finalize plans. Rand is just as disoriented by all this as me, but there's nothing we need to do right now.

Later I'm pouring our third, or is it fourth libation of the evening, "Dude, what do you think of all this? Does it make sense to you? Can't imagine more than one of me."

Randy offers a toast, "Amen to that." Then he looks serious for a second. "Although I can think of a couple times when a couple more of you might have come in handy."

"I'll take that as a compliment. But seriously, is the science solid?"

"Seriously dude, with those two mega nerds at the helm we're in fine hands. The science is irrefutable. It's what happens after this that gets a bit more dodgy."

I lift the bottle, deciding this will be the last. "Can't be as crazy as the Internet swim anyway."

"I can assure you it won't be as traumatic. But it'll still be a wild ride."

That night I'm having crazy dreams. One is like a scene from Dawn Of The Dead, where I'm shooting at zombies from a window, but they're all me.

Halfway to the office, my mobile rings. It's Janice. "Hey sweetie, I'm running late. You'll have to pick up breakfast yourself."

"Detour," I say to Randy. "Gotta get provisions." I'm starved and hungover, so I swig coffee and nosh on a donut on the way, spilling and dropping crumbs, and looking apologetically at Randy. He's normally a stickler about his car, but in the grand scheme of things, this doesn't, to quote Humphry Bogart, "Amount to a hill of beans."

It doesn't take long to get down to business. Patel takes a sip and walks over to an old fashioned white board. It has a map of the offices, hallways and some of the labs of DOSARMS. On it are drawn a few red X's. "Okay, these are the places where we saw the images on the video surveillance. Now keep in mind some of them are just weak waves, likely not important. But there are some others, which are what I might call hot spots. Places where something is definitely trying to come through."

"Question doc, are all these images of me?"

"The answer is yes. You are the one who's been travelling down the supernatural highway for the past several years. You're the goal." Well, at least that makes sense. If everything else is that straight forward, I'll be more than happy. But we all know the likelihood of that happening,

He takes another sip and then goes to the board again. "These sightings are likely not worth bothering about." He takes a blue marker and puts a big line though half a dozen X's. Well that narrows it down a tad. "But these," and here he takes a Day-Glo orange marker and circles three X's, "these are our rabbit holes. This is where we need to go." He hears my unspoken question. "By go, I mean that we are going to have to find out exactly where they're coming from and then have you do a bit of a follow the leader. We've already narrowed it down as you can see. The others wouldn't survive five minutes out in this world. They're the kind of entities that made a bit of a bump in the night in the haunted house movies, not more than a blip on the radar. All you'll need to do is make some kind of contact, a look is usually enough. They are only a wave, and that wave collapses once there is an observer."

"Like the tree in the forest puzzle. Let's get to the however part."

Changy is raring to go. "Dr. Patel, would you like to start?" Oh my god, you've been working together day and night for the past two weeks, and you still can't call him Veej? God love ya, don't ever change.

"It's clear from all the imaging we've done, there is only one subject that's going to need some serious interaction. That one is an almost completely realized individual. It may have created a past and a persona, cobbled together from observations and impressions. It will be an alternate version of Nick Bannister. How defined it is, will determine how you will have to proceed. A mere glance will not collapse his wave. You will need to go deeply into his world and then do what you do best."

"And that is?"

This is Randy's time. "Why we call you when we're knee deep in mystery. Why we sing, Who You Gonna Call?" *Oh please don't sing it dude.* "To be serious, we honestly don't know much about this being. You'll have to catch up to speed pretty quickly and use the old Bannister magic."

"Okay, it's as clear as it ever is. When do we start?" I'm playing a little game in my head now to guess who's going to speak first. Changy tugs on his tie. That's a tell.

He doesn't let me down. "Tomorrow. we're going to send you into one of the more insubstantial...what should I call it...? appearances? It'll give us a chance to see what kind of materiality it has, and for you, to try out your wings on a fairly simple target."

At that, it seems we're done for the day. Agree to meet at ten hundred hours. Still tickles me that they use military time. Don't even think the military knows we exist.

Aside from staying out of trouble and trying to get some rest, there's nothing really to prepare for, so I look forward to an evening of moderate consumption and bad television.

I'm not worried about tomorrow at all. Whatever I'm going to deal with is small potatoes and I'm kind of looking forward to meeting a ghost face to face.

Randy knocks on my door about 8:00. I'm thinking this is a pretty civilized time to rise. We're out the door at 9. Janice sends me a text. "Auntie Janice has everything ready." God I love that woman.

Between a sip and a nibble, Veej starts, "As we said yesterday, this is going to be a breeze. We set you up, introduce you to our little ghostly spirit. You say hello, take a little tour of the facilities and come back out."

"That's it? You could get Janice to do that."

"But Janice doesn't have to be prepared for the big dive coming later. We just want you to get used to things. Pick up on anything you think is important and let us know. You won't be in there long. Whatever kind of energy this is, is probably not substantial enough to notice you."

"Will it have any human traits at all?"

"At best it has a bit of a stimulus response thing going on. Think of this as an art gallery, you're there to observe, but whatever you do, don't touch."

You know many people have told me that in my life?

Nothing much has changed in the "Rift". It's where the techies do all their hocus pocus stuff. Last time I was here, it was to go for a ride down the information highway. And that was the one and only time I planned to do that. This is more straightforward. They just have to spin me back to the last point where the spook appeared, let me explore the scenery, do a bit of basic reconnaissance, and then come back and make my report. Sounds pretty elemental, but then again nothing is ever as it seems around here.

Now I can tell you pretty much everything about DOSARMS, except how they do what they do. Just like the guy who pushes the button at NASA doesn't know the inner workings of a rocket. He just does what he's best at. Anyway, this stuff is so classified that if I did know, they'd have to send me in with a suicide pill every time. Ignorance is definitely bliss.

Not to disappoint you, but there is no time machine, no TARDIS, just a simple, well it looks a bit like an easy chair. I don't even get strapped in. There are a lot of monitors. They have to keep checking my vitals. After all, virtually skimming across time and space can be stressful. Also, they check out the environmental conditions, energy levels.

As I ease into the feeling of lifting out of my body and floating around, I'm aware that my surroundings are starting to change. I'm not really seeing, so much as sensing the shift. Before I know it. I'm standing in front of one of the doorways to the lab. It all looks very familiar except for the hazy shadow filling the entrance. Maybe filling is the wrong word, it's like a mist. I watch more intently. It has a shape. Humanoid? But even though I know its goal is to mimic me, I don't really see it. I reach my arm out as I would in a dark room. I know, don't touch Nick. I know there's nothing solid there, but instinct is pretty strong. My hand passes right through it. I'm a bit more buoyed now. I snap a couple of pictures and keep walking. Well, here's a new experience, I'm walking through someone. Actually I'm walking through me. I feel a temperature drop, and there's a feeling of being cushioned, hard to explain, like being in a padded freight elevator. The sounds of the lab are dull and distant. Then I pass out the other end. I'm a bit further down the hall, looking back at the murky presence. It's shifting form. Swirling. Whatever it is has definitely been affected by my appearance. I walk a bit further down this nondescript corridor, expecting to see, I don't know what. There's nothing. Just the walls and now clear sounds of the forced air, the hum of machinery. I turn around. The shape is fading. Satisfied this is as good as it gets, I walk back toward the door. I stop briefly, and take in everything, sights, sounds, smell, even the feel of the air. I settle into my senses. Is my heart rate steady, is there any nervousness, giddiness? I look behind and take another photo. Like the haze over the lake when the sun comes out, it dissipates until the hall is clear. Comfortable I've done my duty, I pass through, and go out the door. Now I feel myself returning to my body. I'm in the chair, relaxed. Three familiar faces are standing around looking more anxious than they really need to be.

As debriefings go, it isn't much. I give them the details, and the pictures I took. But really there isn't much to say. When they go through the video, they'll likely come up with stuff I either overlooked or just sloughed off as nothing. My vitals were pretty much steady for the whole thing, and in the end we call it a day. I feel like I could go in and take my chances with the second door, but protocol demands 48 hours.

The next couple of days are pretty quiet. I'm finally allowed to go home on the promise to be on my best behaviour. I pick up a six pack and a pizza on the way home. I agreed to be a good boy, not monk hood.

The Return of George HW

Before I know it, I'm sitting in the chair waiting for the next installment of my trip into freaky. I've been advised this could be a bit more intense, as they pretty much know the subject has more substance, maybe even a degree of sentience. That also means it might be more unpredictable and I'll need to have my wits sharpened and be ready to respond.

Well, to be honest, the first excursion was a giant snooze, so I'm sure ready for a bit more excitement.

The picture they show me is more tangible. I can't clearly see the face, but it sure looks like me. It's also making some kind of gesture, perhaps reaching its arms out. Not much else to go on. I'll find out soon enough.

The first time I did a time skip was like a giant roller coaster. Now the whole thing is pretty routine. No worse than going on the teacups.

After waiting the obligatory five minutes, my alter ego gets itself out of the chair and walks down a long corridor towards the cafeteria. Yup, nerds need to eat too. Blocking the door is a figure, and the closer I get, I can clearly see it's my double. Far from being imposing though, he's wearing a suit and a red tie. Shit, George W. Bush. It's clear that this entity somehow picked up on my experience back at the White House and has come dressed for the occasion.

It's also clear he's totally lost. He doesn't move as I get closer. I can make out the facial features, but it looks like a mannequin who's just come to life and hasn't figured out how to move its face. Some small ticks and twitches appear as I get closer. *Come on buddy, you can figure it out.* I help him out. *Here's how you do surprise.* By god, a moment later I watch as his mouth starts to open and forms an "O". *That's it, Nick 2.0. Now watch my hands.* I lift them up in a "who are you?" type gesture. He's pretty quick to follow. Maybe I should call him Pinocchio.

I decide to try something else. "Hey, I'm Nick, who are you?" Well, you might as well try to teach geometry to a mushroom. I feel bad for the dude.

He looks so perplexed, I think he might dissolve on the spot. But at least he's getting the expressions down. I try another gesture, *let's go for a little walk down the hall.* It takes a minute, but then he slowly starts moving in the direction I point.

As I do, the walls are slowly shifting and changing. It's not defined yet, but there's a transformation. Like someone spilled paint all over, and it's slowly flowing and moving. Pinocchio still looks confused, he's watching what's going on, with...is that a look of interest? My boy learns fast. We both stop and observe. Silence. It doesn't take long before I see it.

This is the office in White House, where I almost got myself caught all those years back. The whole left side is becoming three dimensional. There's a big mahogany desk. A flag. Paintings are forming on the right wall. Suddenly he is looking worried. That's fear on his face. Fear of what? I take his hand. It's solid and it's warm. I hold it and lead him into what is now an actual room. He balks. I try my words again.

"It's okay. It's all right." Again, those questioning eyes. He's trying to process the whole thing. That's ironic considering he's creating it. They are his memories. No, memories isn't the right word. Imprints? I need to take him deeper. I get a notion and take him over to the desk, put his hand on a couple of things. A paperweight. The old-fashioned blotter. He explores them with his eyes and then with his hands. Recognition is fueling fear. He squeezes my hand. His eyes are pleading, *let's go please.* Instinct tells me to hold on a moment more. Something is about to break. I watch him. Is he trembling? Just a bit longer. His hands are clammy, Shaking. Something is coming. He wrests his hand away and runs out the door. I turn after him. The room is losing form. I chase him down the hall. The walls are melting. He is wraithlike. And then, he's gone. And I'm standing in a plain old hall at DOSARMS. Wave collapsed. Pinocchio is gone. Funny, I feel sorry for him. Wonder if he felt anything? Could he feel at all? I know one thing now. This is going to get very interesting.

I calmly enter the main lab, and it morphs into whatever you might call the magic show that is DOSARMS. My nerdy home boys are looking pretty pleased with themselves.

Randy hands me a bottle of water. I find myself chugging. Had no idea I was that thirsty. "Well, looks like you aced that one. We've already done the readings, the energy level isn't registering anymore."

"Poor guy, kind of felt bad for him or it. Reminds of when the Wicked Witch of the West melted in The Wizard Of Oz. No matter what she's done, you feel terrible as you watch her turn into a pool of goop." The other two are giving me puzzled looks. Maybe they don't know what I'm talking about, or they do and just think I'm nuts. "Okay, now I have to ask, what gave that second Nick, more substance? I felt a human connection. Like it was evolving."

Changy helps me out, "Well there are a lot of things at play. Most importantly, it had much higher energy. Once that manifested, it fed off the surroundings. It become more realized, solid. And then of course, it started to feed off you."

"Like a kind of vampire?"

"Nothing that sinister, but yes. Your energy was available and it needed more. It wasn't a conscious decision. It didn't decide to suck your life force, but as you know, nature abhors a vacuum."

I'm catching a vibe here. "Okay Changy, is this a lesson or a warning?"

"You are hitting the proverbial nail on the head my friend. Yes, indications are that our next subject has a substantial amount of force already built up. With that will come a strong push to become more actualized. As you are available and very close, that makes you an energy tree, ripe for the picking."

He's got my attention, that's for sure. "So, you're telling me our next little ghost is going to be a lot more...complex, and I'm going to have to be ready for anything."

His eyes say "Bingo", although his mouth would never say that.

"Okay," I'm happy to hear Randy's voice. "I think that's enough for today. We need to do this quick. So tomorrow we spend the day getting you prepped and Friday morning we go in. Well, you go in, we'll be with you in spirit. Pun intended." He gives me a wink.

"I'm touched dude, but right now I'm starved. Dissolving ghosts works up a fierce hunger."

Randy springs for brunch and we go our separate ways.

The evening is pretty quiet, and I head to bed early. Ghostbusting is tiring. I sleep well and wake up refreshed and ready to go to school.

After a quick breakfast we make our way down to the "Rift". There are a couple of other guys in white coats milling around. I've seen them around, but wouldn't know them by name. Randy introduces them as Berndt and Norbert. *Of course you are.* They get straight to it. "Okay we're here to give you an idea of what you might be up against tomorrow. Now, before you get worried, *What me worry?* there's a distinct possibility this entity will actually be docile and not try to use your energy. If it is actualized enough it could see you as some kind of partner in whatever it has in mind. But if it hasn't yet reached that state, it will do anything to get there. We're pretty sure you don't need any help with either scenario, but a few tips won't hurt." I'm fine with that.

A couple of hours later, Berndt, or Norbert, wind it up with, "Any questions?"

"You know what guys? I don't think I do. You've done a great job." I give them both a hearty handshake, and I realize I actually mean it.

Randy makes his way into the room. He looks a bit surprised. "Done already?" He looks at the techies, "Thanks guys. Okay, tomorrow morning, 0800 hours. Class dismissed."

We're in Randy's car, heading to his place. "So?" I forget he wasn't there for the briefing.

"Well, it was a lot of information, but mostly what I expected. It's gonna be harder because this spook is fairly well developed. It's had more time to start to form a real self, personality, story, history. It's likely created some kind of reality, with other characters, scenarios. Most of it collected from all the shit hovering around here. I'm going to have to pull down a whole world here. Going to have to go into that world and play for a while. Without doing that, there's no way to collapse the wave and get rid of this dude. I assume it's a dude. I asked them what would happen if we fail. They said, it's not like Godzilla, it ain't gonna start destroying New York. But its energy could interfere with everything we do here. That could make the world a lot more dangerous place.

They explained why these things are there in the first place. We've been messing around in their playground, and they've noticed. And I'm the star of this show. So they're playing copy-cat. Only this one's smarter, has a lot of input from all my past adventures, and it's own ideas about the world. I've got to expect anything and everything."

He's staring straight ahead for a few seconds like he's thinking what he should say.

"Well dude, I'm glad we've got the right man for the job."

Here's Looking at You Kid

I'm sipping my coffee at 7:00 AM. I pick at a donut, but I'm not really hungry. Can't really say I'm nervous. I've been through worse, but as always, the idea of travelling into the wild reaches or space and time is not conducive to savouring a meal.

Berndt pokes his head in the door, and I know it's time. I give Janice a smile on the way by, and she gives me a thumbs up, combined with a little pucker. What an angel, always knows what to say and when to say it, and when to just be quiet and give her silent support.

Changy and Patel are in the Rift room, where my favourite Lazy Boy awaits.

"Anything you want to ask?" Randy is standing behind the glass, with a half-smile.

"No I'm good, let's just do this?" *geez, did I just say that? such a cliché.* They leave me, and I hear the countdown, and pass into Neverland.

As I slowly feel my senses again, I begin to wiggle my fingers and move my feet to make sure they're ready to follow the rest of me. Everything seems to be in working order, so I slowly get up and look around. I move towards the corridor in front of me. As I inch down the hall, the lighting changes. It's getting darker. The passage is narrower, and the walls are like an old office building. Wherever my ghost is, he ain't here. I continue down until I find a set of stairs. With nowhere else to go, I start to climb. I get to a landing and see a door. It's got a frosted glass panel and below it, in black lettering, is the name; Rick Bannister P.I.

Okay, looks like this guy has latched onto my persona. Well, he could do worse, I suppose. For once, I don't know the rules, so I do the polite thing and knock. A woman answers from the other side. "Come in," says a familiar voice. I walk in and check out the room. Plain grey walls. Couple of certificates placed at eye level. An old coat rack with a grey fedora perched at the top, like the star on a Christmas tree. Couple of office chairs and a small table with a few magazines. I scan quickly, Ladies Home Journal, Hot Rod and on the second shelf, discreetly pushed to the back, an issue of Playboy. Those are pretty eclectic picks.

Then my eyes move to the desk by the window. Oh my god, it's Janice. I say her name out loud. She gives me a puzzled look and says, "No one with that name here mister. I'm Eunice, Mr. Bannister's secretary." I introduce myself and without batting an eye, she says, "Have a seat Mr. Bannister, Mr. Bannister is expecting you."

Well I was promised weird, and it's already living up to expectations. She presses the intercom, "Mr. Bannister, Mr. Bannister is here." *Am I the only one to see the irony here?* Well my mind is now conjuring up an image of this dude. I don't have to think for long. This man is definitely my doppelganger. But in disguise. He sports a perfectly pressed pin striped double-breasted suit, plain tie and black shoes. For someone who isn't real, this guy's pretty well turned out.

He walks up to me all confident like, and offers his hand. I reciprocate. Good grip, solid. As real as it gets. "Come on in, Mr. Bannister. Eunice doll, please hold my calls."

I'm flying by the seat of my pants now. My favourite airline. So I let him lead. He offers me a cigarette. I don't smoke anymore, but I've learned to be sociable without coughing up a lung, so I accept. He lights us both and begins. "Mr. Bannister..." I break in,

"Please call me Nick."

"Nick, the reason I called you is because I think you can help out on a case I just got started on. I understand you've done some similar jobs, and before I go up a bunch of blind alleys, it would help to know which ones I can write right off before I start." He opens his desk and pulls out a bottle of Jack Daniels and two glasses. He doesn't ask, just pours. We both take a pull and then he continues.

I start with the obvious, "How did you find me?"

He reaches for his glass, "You're in my rolodex. Someone must have given it to me after a case. For some reason, your name just came into my head this morning. Looked it up and you were still there, thank god."

There's a knock on the door. Eunice comes in. Now she has my attention. What a doll. Curves in all the right places. She's wearing a low-cut black stand up collar blouse, a black and white striped pencil skirt, long dirty blond hair, parted a couple of inches to the left side. Just the right amount of lipstick. I'm thinking, Lauren Bacall. Why not, her boss is a Bogart Bannister. In a voice like red velvet, she just says a simple, "This just came for you Mr. Bannister." She puts a simple manila envelope on the desk. He doesn't even have to ask. "Short guy, slim, curly hair, dark suit, bow tie."

Peter Lorre. My god this guy has created a Hammett-Chandler paradise here. I know what they said about him collecting impressions to create himself and his world, but why this black and white gumshoe playground? Holy shit! I hadn't even noticed. It's all happening in black and white. I'm in a noir detective movie here.

I'm waiting for him to open the envelope, but it just sits there on the desk while he continues. "There's a package I need picking up."

"I ain't no soldier." It hits me how I'm talking and thinking like a real gumshoe. Is it me or is it him doing it?

"I wasn't saying that. I know you better than that. *Funny, I thought we just met.* I'm getting a lot of conflicting information and I need your expertise to help work me through it."

"What's in the package that's so valuable?"

"Let's just say it's a rare sculpture. And it's worth a lot of dough. *Of course it is.* "So let's see the intel?"

"Intel?"

"Sorry, local term. Information. Dope." There's some 21st century left in me.

He pours another shot. "Well it's not that simple. We've got to go there in person. The leads should be in that envelope the short man delivered a few minutes ago. Now he's a soldier, not bright enough to handle a major job. Sharp dresser though."

"So where are we going boss?" I have a notion.

"First we head down to Chinatown. Little restaurant on Grant? You like Chinese? Then down to the Ferry Docks to see a man about a package."

I see my chance. Now I'd heard that if time travel was open to everyone, the mobile wouldn't work, but the techies at DOSARMS have managed. So I take it out and show him.

I remind myself this isn't real, but it feels pretty damn solid. The fact is, it's all a compilation, a greatest hits of the internet if you will. Something in him has fixated on this noir fairy tale, but all that other stuff is still floating around him. So I go for it.

"What street did you say? Grant?" He nods. I pull out the phone. Go into google maps, stick the map screen in front of his face, and wait for the reaction. Not quite what I expect. Of course he's surprised, but no more than if I produced a bouquet of flowers from my sleeve. Fact is, somewhere inside, he knows this already. He just isn't conscious of it.

"That's a pretty nifty device. Like Dick Tracy's wristwatch." I expand the view and he shows me the route. I'm seeing cracks in his wall.

Twenty minutes later we're travelling down Grant into the heart of China-town. We park on a side street, and walk a couple of blocks. I have to stop myself from gawking. I'm in Chinatown, San Francisco and it's 1950. I've done a lot of crazy things and seen a lot of sights, but this is one for the books. The sights, the sounds, the smells. It's a foreign world. In my time, I'm sure it's crawling with tourists. But today it's the world of the Chinese immigrant, doing their best to make something in a new land. Either that or carrying on a business that may have been in the family for a couple of generations. I don't hear any English. This is the real McCoy. Rick's looking at me, maybe a bit puzzled, but like everything else, this just runs off his back.

"Here we are. Doesn't look like much, but they do a damned good Chow Mein." I look up at the flickering sign, *"Far East Chop Suey."* He opens the door and motions me in.

The place is full. Full meaning maybe 25 people. Many of them are in suits. Office guys from the nearby streets, having lunch. We sit at the only available table.

The waitress is a pretty Asian girl in a flowered dress. A little over done for the place. "Oh hi Mister Rick, you want see boss?" That's a nice smile. "He in back."

"Thanks doll. Hope you don't mind Nick. Get us a chicken chow mein, and beef with vegetables." Then he gets up. "Gimme ten minutes."

"You want me to come?" I already know the answer.

"Nah, business owners here are not too big on cops. Took me a long time to convince him I wasn't one of them. You being there might shut him up, and I need his mug to be open." *Wow dude, you sure got the banter down.*

A minute later the waitress brings a red patterned teapot and two small cups. I pour one for me and sit there sipping and taking in this once in a life-time experience.

About 15 minutes later, he's back. Our waitress puts our chow mein and beef on the table. I realize I haven't eaten since breakfast. Of course, in real time I don't know how long it's been, but enough to make me want to dig in. I nod in approval. I use chopsticks, he opts for a fork. Have to remind myself he's just an imaginary baby in grown up clothes. The look on his face is inscrutable. Not sure if that's because he's trying to be covert, or simply because he is still trying out his facial expressions. Anyway, he doesn't say anything, and I don't press him. I don't want to pry, so we eat in silence. He pays. I slide an extra two dollars on the table for the girl, forgetting that's like a half day's pay.

It's raining lightly. Geez, San Francisco can be chilly in the winter. A couple of blocks in, he hands me a folded piece of paper. *Golden Star, August 23rd, 4pm, Taipei, Pier 23, First Officer Chang*. God, this is such a cliché. I nod and hand it back to him. Fifteen minutes later, we pull up near the docks. The rain has ended and been replaced by thick fog. I can barely make out the outlines of the old hulks in the harbour. The sound of seagulls, ship bells, fog horns and shouting sailors make a kind of audio tapestry. I breathe in the salt air, and despite the possible danger ahead, I'm enjoying this. If things get tense I'll know what I have to do.

We get out and start along the Embarcadero. I've got to get this thing started. So I quickly google some up-to-date pictures of the area. "Hey Rick. Check out what this looks like in the 21st century?" Again, there's that half indifferent, half puzzled look. But he takes the phone and looks at the screen. I show him how to slide the pictures, and he follows without any hesitation. I decide to go all in. "Hey it's only 3. Let me show you some more." As we sit on a bench, I start searching my brains out. I show him images of things I've never seen myself. Well at least, I don't remember them. But deep inside, they're in my subconscious from my trip into the web. And I know they're triggering something in him too. I mix in a few videos. Rock concerts, sports games, idiots showing off on YouTube. Now I've got him hooked. He asks to see videos of cars, planes and rockets. I take a chance and snap a couple of pictures. He doesn't react until I show him the results.

Then he offers a single word, "Film?" I give him a quick phone photo 101. He asks a few more questions and asks me if he can take a picture. I flash a smile and then hand him the phone. He's pretty quick on the update and proudly shows me his work.

It's ten to four. We walk about 100 feet and turn onto the dock. After about 5 minutes, this sailor appears out of the fog. Soon, I can make out a brown parcel in his hand. "You Mr. Bannister?" I almost say yes. I'm looking around carefully. Something doesn't feel right. And my friend, well he's all dressed up for the part, but he sure doesn't know the ins and outs of his trade. For all I know this is his first case. The sailor dude is about to hand the package, when I catch some movement on the deck. I'm the only one that sees it. This other guy's got a gun, and this ain't no Glock. It looks like an AK-47. On top of that, he ain't dressed like a sailor, 1950 or otherwise. Worlds are colliding. He's in military fatigues, the kind the wacko dudes who are waiting for Armageddon wear. And I can tell this sucker means business.

"Rick, get down." He looks up at the guy on the deck. I can tell he sees the gun, but he doesn't know what the hell it is or what to do. Anachronism can mess up the mind. Now there's terror in his eyes. But also complete confusion. I see the guy's got him in his cross hairs. I hear the release and grab him by the hand and pull him down to the ground. The last thing I see is the fog lifting, the ship and dock are fading into a swirl of mist.

And I hear Randy's voice. "For God's sake Nick, let go of his arm."

Too late. What's left of him has a hold on me. Suddenly, we're in the Rift. I look at the floor and there's Rick, looking like he's just been born. I look at him closely. He's not fading, I can't see through him. He's solid. He's real.

Aside from my heart pacing like a racehorse, I'm okay. Actually more than okay. I've had a good time. No wonder Rick picked this noir detective fantasy. Guess it's always been one of mine too. He tries to get up, and Norbert or is it Berndt, helps him over to a chair. "What the hell was that?"

I'm getting my bearings too. Realize the whole crew is there. Randy is just coming in the door. "Nick, you okay?" He does a double take when he sees Rick. "Is that...?" That's as far as he gets. When Rick stands and extends his hand, I think Randy is going to run out of the room.

"Rick Bannister at your service. I guess you're the head honcho here." Randy moves his head slowly up and down and Rick continues. "Before you explain, let me see if I've got this straight." He sounds just like Bogey. "For whatever reason, you guys have been casing me for the past while. You sent in Nick here on this caper. Now here's where I go out on a real limb. Obviously, I've gone through some kind of time travel here. It became clear when Nick started showing me all those weird gadgets from the future. When we got to the docks to make the deal, time started unravelling. That mug on the ship. That space gun he was packing. Just before he shot me, my friend Nick here pushed me down and grabbed my arm. Now, here I am in Tomorrowland. And I owe Nick my life."

Our collective jaws are on the Rift floor. This guy has it all sussed out. Whatever happened in transit turned our ersatz Bogey into a bona fide dick. Then again, that energy was already out there. He just found a way to reel it in. We silently agree there's no point in filling him in on the rest of the story.

We take a walk into Randy's office. Janice is putting out coffee. There's a big bag sitting on the table. Rick does a bit of a double take when he sees her, but then seems to comprehend. I give her a hug. "Nice to be back in Kansas." She gives me that knowing look she always gives. If only she wasn't married.

Rick takes a sip of Joe and gives a smile of approval. I offer him a Boston cream. He examines it while Patel begins. "Well this is going to take a lot of analyzing and review.
It's going to keep us busy for a long time to come. But from what I see Mr. Bannister," we both look up and smile, "you just might be here to stay."

I hand my phone to Randy. "Almost forgot, here's my holiday pix."

Rick's finished scrutinizing his donut and finally takes a bite. It takes a moment and then he breaks into a big grin. "I hope so. I think I like Tomorrowland already." *That's my boy. Think we're gonna get along just fine.*

THIS STORY SOUNDS VAGUELY FAMILIAR

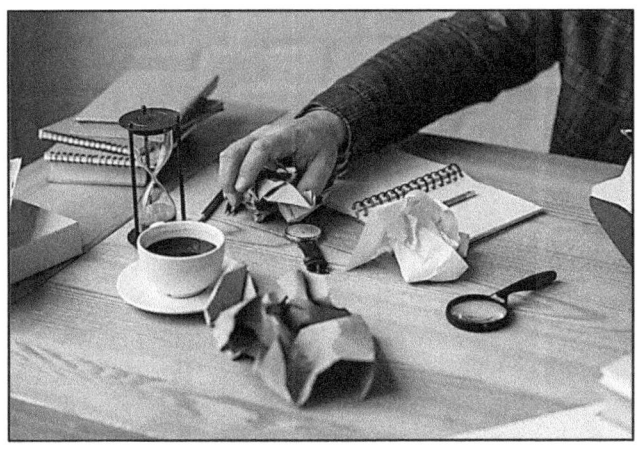

This was my first published story. The idea of a writer creating someone's reality is not new. It was portrayed brilliantly in the movie "Stranger Than Fiction". My penchant for noir seeped into the story line and the result was this very short portrayal of a man caught up in someone else's fantasy.

This Story Sounds Vaguely Familiar

Agent Harry Flash felt the beads of perspiration on his forehead. He continued into the darkened room, gun poised, eyes swiveling 360 degrees, and ears trained like a Bloodhound. Outside he heard the sounds of back-up wailing in the distance. A light breeze wafted through the open window. Whoever had been here had left. He hesitated for a moment, waiting for his keen instincts to guide him to his next move. It wasn't long in coming. He caught the brief twinkle from the device in the far corner of the room and jumped a split second before the explosion ripped the building to shreds. He fell from the second-floor window and blacked out.

Harry slowly came to his senses. He remembered falling from something, but now he was aware of a different sense of motion. Realizing he was in a moving vehicle, he drew himself off the back floor and looked out the window. Lights flew by in the night. Rain lashed against the glass. The car was speeding down the highway, and for some reason he was a passenger. The sound of a siren drew his attention to the back window. They were being chased. The driver of the car shifted gears and they speeded up. Now he recognized the landscape even in the dark. They were on the Coastal highway North of Carmel. The next few miles were nothing but hairpin turns and sheer precipices. This was not going to end well. No car could make these turns safely at this speed. As they neared the next bend, Harry noticed the glow of approaching headlights. It was far too late, the driver tried to swerve. He wasn't going to stay on the road. In a flash they were airborne. For one instant they stood outside of time before starting their plunge into the ocean. The last thing Harry saw was the lights of the other car.

As Harry regained consciousness, the events of the past few moments surfaced. He'd been in a car which had fallen straight into the Pacific. Surely nobody could have survived that wreck. And he clearly wasn't in that car now. Rather, he had the sensation of being elevated. He opened an eye and gripped the rail in terror. How the hell had he ended up on the ledge of this building, on the wrong side of the fence? Harry had never been fond of heights, but this filled him with dread.

And now another man burst through the door and onto the ledge. He started clubbing Harry's hands with his gun handle. Harry realized in horror that he intended to shove him over. As hard as he tried, gravity was his enemy. His hands came loose. For a moment he was suspended in space. The lights of the city were strangely beautiful. Harry was not conscious for the rest of the fall.

Now this wasn't possible, Harry thought as he regained awareness. He'd been pushed to his certain death and come close to drowning in the ocean. There had been a fall from some kind of building. Yet here he was. And this was no improvement. He became sickly aware of the sound of rushing air. When Harry looked to his left he could see a man slumped in the chair beside him, a bullet cleanly through his chest. Incredulous, he saw the man was the pilot of the plane he was in. Worse yet, the ground was suddenly rising to meet him as the plane sped dizzily out of control. He desperately grabbed at the controls, but his fate was no longer in his hands. The aircraft burst into flames as it hit the ground.

Rick Gardner sighed. This wasn't working for him. It wouldn't work for his publisher either. Harry Flash was better than this. The story line was tacky and predictable. He eyed his latest page, crumpled it into a ball and tossed it into the wastepaper bin. Gardner took out a fresh piece of paper, stuffed it into his typewriter and once again, began to write.

With a sigh, Harry began to pick himself out of the burning hulk which lay on the tarmac and surveyed the wreckage.

THIS STORY SOUNDS VAGUELY FAMILIAR

AND I SAW THAT IT WAS GOOD

I love the writing process, except when I loathe it. Coming up with a good storyline and then turning it into something that works on all levels, can be frustrating. But it's all worth it when you have that Eureka moment and scramble for pen and paper, to scrawl down that precious thought before it slips away into nothingness. I seem to get my best inspirations at the gym and then I just have to keep that idea in my brain until I can write it down. These kinds of moments led me to contemplate some of the circumstances which may lead to that same epiphany.

And I Saw That It Was Good

I bring her into the world in the late evening, when the streetlight sketches a slanted crucifix onto the far side of the living room wall. The air in the room is as still as midsummer dawn over the lake. Outside, misty apparitions climb their way upward. Shades of Hammett or Chandler. She materializes under the lamp post. She feels a bit like Lauren Bacall. Sleek waves rolling from under her perfectly slanted, dark beret. Is she wearing a checkered jacket over that black blouse? And heels. She must have stilettos, audible from the sidewalk, as she moves from that miniature moon that relaxes the darkness.

Now where's she headed? A rendezvous with a secret lover? The cheerless baritone of a foghorn drowns the air with its unrequited call. Oops, maybe a little overdone. She turns towards the docks. Maybe a few hours of heaven spent in some seedy hotel on the waterfront. The whistles of some drunken sailors spray off her like rain from a slicker. Wait, what if she passes by the hotel with its neon electric buzz, and makes her way onto those squalid planks, rank with dew, mist and sea water.

Then there's the music, coming up from a basement club, somewhere unseen. Billie Holiday, perhaps *The Man I Love*. What about some Charlie Parker? Whichever it is, it hangs in the air, merges with the fog, and seeps into the soul, until you can't tell one from the other.

She can just as easily have come to life today at the diner, where the stench of Chanel Number 5 mugs my senses as I pass by on my way to the gents. Do women actually like that? She carries her grey suit like a second thought. Not the stuff of romance and intrigue. But still, that scent takes me somewhere else.

She's plunked herself down at a table in the Automat in New York City. A thick white coffee cup sits cooling in front of her. Her lipsticked cigarette sends jet grey whorls which fade as they rise. The sound of conversation, punctuated by the knock of cutlery on plates and constant clicking of the coin dispensers, is part of the mania that is lunch on Sixth Avenue.

What about him? You know the story about God ripping that rib out of Adam, and making it grow into a dame he called Eve? In this world it's the reverse. The guy in this story comes from the doll in the Automat. Or is it the one down by the docks? Anyhow, it's the ladies who come first, have to. Maybe it's that perfume, gave him life, or my lady of the harbour's wiggle. Either way, it starts with his Bogey style Fedora. Then the suit. Well, you don't actually see the suit, because it's under that classic trench coat, all wide lapels and high waist band. Stick a half- smoked Chesterfield in his mouth and voila. I've his got image down, but still have to fill in the man underneath.

I take a drag of my own, sip on my twelve-year-old bourbon, close my eyes and think. Believe me, that's not always the best thing to do. What's the deal with all these folks? Everyone has some kind of motivation, something that drives them to the most heroic or blatantly stupid acts life has to offer. Usually the latter. Especially in the kind of story these guys and dolls are trying to write. It works this way. The writer creates his crew, and if they're just right for the job, they tell him the script and he just jots it down. Damn it, I've lost my vision of them and now they're all fading into the fog outside my front room window. It's hard work being an inventor. No wonder God got bored with us all and left us to wallow. Seems creation isn't an act, it's a lifetime's work. Once you're in, you're all in. Leave it for a moment and it all goes to Hell.

I close my eyes and leave my collaborators in limbo. We'll pick it up tomorrow where we left off. Good news keeps 'til noon they say. Wait a second, I got something.

My princess of the automat has left the cafeteria and started off down 6th Avenue. The ersatz Phillip Marlow is following in the shadows. They end up at the same place, but damned if I remember where. I sit up, grab pen and paper, and scribble a few notes, impressions. Maybe it'll come in the morning.

I wake, still on the couch, and wonder what my images do when I stop writing or dreaming them? Is there a kind of fiction purgatory where all the half-baked story lines and unassembled characters hang out until their benefactor restores solidity to their existence? A kind of Flying Dutchman of literature? Who am I kidding? We're talking noir fiction, hardly up there with Hemmingway or Faulkner. Doubt it's even Runyan. Still, I've brought the troops to the surface, I need to haul them in before they sink away forever.

This thought of abandoning them frightens me back to the keyboard. I collect all my bits of paper and glue-less sticky notes and try to cobble together a clear image of my crew.

Everything becomes a cradle for my story line. The way I sip my coffee. Faceless voices coming through the open window. Even the way the silence sneaks up on me when I've forgotten it was there. I'm working too hard. Any story writer knows that'll make you crazy. I only have to open my files and turn to the dozens of forsaken tales to know that.

I need to put it all aside, go do something normal, try not to think, do no more than be ready when inspiration comes. That's the key. Ideas are floating all around, you just have to recognize one when it comes in for a landing.

So I do something mundane. I take a walk downtown. After a while, I stop looking for things and just start enjoying the ride. Other ordinary people are doing their everyday things and it soothes my brain.

Until I turn onto Cedar Street and see the cover in the window of Eric's used books. There's this sexy dame wearing some kind of exotic two piece. She's with a guy who looks a bit like Clark Gable, dressed in evening clothes. They're in a marketplace, somewhere Middle East looking. A guy is sitting on a carpet, haggling with them. He looks Arabian or something. In the background, all kinds of nefarious deeds are going on. Suddenly I've got it. The doll down by the docks. The harbor and the fog horns. The dodgy looking bloke following the woman coming from the Automat. They all fall into place. Today, I've got my writer's mojo. This idea doesn't just float down, it pummels me like a piece of space rock. I get who they are and where they're going. I turn around and almost bump into the young couple beside me. I tip my hat and throw a sorry while I gallop home. In a couple of hours my limbo living ghosts will be back on dry land and ready to tell me the rest of their story.

WRITER'S BLOCK

We constantly hear the expression, "You can't see the forest for the trees." Although I'm sure most people don't really know what that means exactly. But in this case, I'm pretty sure it has to do with the fact our hero is so busy looking for inspiration, he is missing all the glorious openings unfolding around him. As a writer, I can attest that nothing ever comes from trying, it comes from opening to what's already there.

Writer's Block

Thursday Morning, 11 AM

Arthur Danks stepped out of his yellow Peugeot at number 15 Mulberry Lane, East Croydon, oblivious to the piddling rain drops falling on his "Greetings from Bournemouth" baseball cap. You see Arthur's mind was located elsewhere. As he opened the front door of his ordinary, tidy, semi- detached; the grey of the afternoon, and his mood danced a perfect two step.

"Is that you Arthur? Back so soon? You've only been gone five minutes. Thought you were gone for the week." Busy scanning his four-day backlog of the Financial Times, he neither heard his wife Ethel, nor the slamming of the kitchen door.

Three Hours Earlier

Okay, Arthur Danks. You've slept on it. You gave it your best shot, but Bournemouth just isn't the kind of town to stimulate the flow of brain sap. Nothing but holidayers and day trippers traipsing up and down the pier, leaving trails of ice cream and sweetie wrappers. Best go home and plan your next move. That's what father always said. "Have a plan Arthur," he said. It may be stalemate now. But tomorrow is another day.

Sufficiently rationalized, he neatly folded his clothes, organized them in his charcoal carry on, and headed downstairs to check out.

"Leaving so soon, Mr. Danks? We expected your company a while longer." The pretty young clerk gave her best, *I'm a struggling student who could use any small stipend you can afford*, look; and handed him his bill. Not big on hints, Arthur tendered the exact sum in cash, struggled to make the ends of his mouth curl upwards, and left.

The Previous Afternoon, Wednesday

Had Arthur not been glued to an article entitled *NEST Trustees, Selecting The Best Funds*, in the latest issue of Accountancy Magazine, recently purchased from the chemist on Beacon Road, he would have noticed the spectacle of a lifetime unfolding on the waterfront.

Two hours earlier, a baby Bottlenose Whale had somehow run aground on Bournemouth Beach, close to an ice lolly stand belonging to Mr. Gordon Pinkney, who had immediately dialed 999. The ensuing dramatic and heart-warming rescue would appear in newspapers throughout the UK. Plus a dozen YouTube videos, which would make social media junkies feel all warm and fuzzy for about ten minutes.

Arthur finished the article, moved on to a piece about surviving the Brexit effect, and looked for somewhere to have his supper.

He ate a green salad and poached salmon. Dodgy tummy acting up again, no sense taking chances. Following a small sherry at the Hotel Bar, he headed upstairs, promising himself the question peering around the corner of his mind would be answered by morning.

Thirty Hours Earlier, Tuesday, Late Afternoon

It was a fine day for a bank robbery. Arthur Danks had noted in his weather diary earlier:

> *Fine morning. Light southerly breeze of 10 KPH. Temperature 22 degrees. Partly sunny skies, no immediate threat of rain.*

At approximately 5pm on this glorious July afternoon, three armed bandits relieved The Lloyd's Bank on Old Christchurch Road, of a few bags of superfluous cash. The heist took place a comfortable stroll from where Arthur Danks sat, writing his weather journal and sipping Earl Grey Tea. It was a ripping affair. Gunfire and sirens skewered the air, and police cars were heard as far away as the beach.

Arthur Danks missed all this festivity, and was currently walking what he called his "Writer's Circuit", a large block mapped out the day of his arrival. He reckoned hiking this trek each day could provide ample material to inspire him in writing his upcoming novel, "Murder in Bournemouth" (working title only).

The title for this book had come to him a week earlier. He had no idea what the storyline would be. However, this notion had somehow garrotted the sensible part of his brain and left him with no choice but to follow the whim. Something Arthur Danks wasn't used to doing. He'd taken a fortnight's leave and booked a week at the Beacon Hotel. Just 24 pounds per night, which any associate accountant worth his calculator knew was a good deal. So with something as close to excitement as Arthur had ever mustered, he had said goodbye to his family and toddled off to Bournemouth to change his life.

The problem was, Arthur Danks wasn't the sort to be creating literature. He was more at home with forms and neat columns of numbers, which he executed admirably at Whipple, Beardsworth and Griggs, where he'd been an associate accountant for seventeen years.

"Good evening, Mr. Danks." Arthur looked up from his mobile in time to catch the toadying smile of the evening desk clerk, a middle-aged lady sporting a coif which appeared to have been dropped onto her head by the Tardis, on its latest trip from 1975. "Quite the to do this afternoon wasn't it? All them sirens and such. Never seen the likes of that around quiet old Bournemouth. Then again, this day and age, you never know. Do you?"

Arthur had no idea what this woman was talking about, nor had he a desire to know. You see our hero was many things which begin with the letter "C", such as cautious, consistent, conservative and circumspect. The word curious was not among them.

He tried something approaching a smile, permitted the word "yes" to dribble from his mouth, and headed to the bar for a small sherry.

Monday Evening, Arthur Dank's Second Night in Bournemouth

Arthur finished mapping out his "Writer's Circuit" and put on his Mac, as it looked like rain. He noted this concern in his weather diary before leaving to test his route.

As he turned onto the promenade, he noted a large group of people watching flashing lights over the Channel. Nevertheless, he had already decided to take in a revival of "Witness for the Prosecution" at the local cinema, so he turned the other way.

Twelve Hours Later, Tuesday Morning

Arthur polished his cutlery and dug into his full English Breakfast in the hotel restaurant. He picked up the Guardian and turned to the financial page. Having by-passed the front page, he missed the report of the daily UFO sightings all along the Dorset Coast, including actual pictures, plus analysis from scientific experts. He did however, catch the latest stock quotes and noted the continued surge of the pound, now the Brexit fiasco had calmed. Before setting off for his writer's circuit, he pulled his weather journal out of his brown satchel and began to write:

> *Rather dull this morning, a few drops of rain, but forecast is promising better things this afternoon. Wore my mac just in case. Better safe than sorry I always say.*

Three Days Later, Thursday Morning

"Hang on a minute, just putting something in the oven for tea." Ethel called out.

"Damndest thing, just couldn't get inspired. Guess it was writer's block." Arthur made his way to the kitchen.

One Minute Earlier

Had they been looking, the neighbours would have seen a rumpled, middle-aged man wearing a white shirt, brown tie and hat, holding his trousers under his arm, as he sprinted down the garden path of number 15 Mulberry Lane and out through the wooden gate into the laneway.

EDWIN AND THE WORDSMITH

This started as a children's story. In the end it seems it was neither a children's story, nor a grown-up person story. Rather it was a story about a child and a very special adult and their one common love, the written word. If it also reads like a fairy tale then so be it. It is one of my favourites, and I had immense fun writing it. The ideas flowed down from somewhere, and I just typed them in and dressed them up a bit, like the hero of the story.

Edwin and the Wordsmith

Edwin hadn't meant to drift off. He was just trying to find a place as far away from his math lesson as possible. Short of dropping out the window, the wall was the best he could manage. Crikey, how long could anyone go on about equations, fractions, and those other *tions* he didn't give a toss about? Ah, but Mr. Sneath was not a man to rush. Each speck of his insight was dispensed in the same, steady drone as the one before. Often repeated for emphasis. Edwin was amazed how the other students managed to keep upright, without the aid of some supporting structure.

Old man Sneath often tried to catch him off guard. "Mr. Watkins, will you be joining us sometime this afternoon?"

Edwin would then prise himself upright long enough to mumble, "Sorry sir, I didn't quite...." Satisfied he'd made his point, the insufferable pillock then resumed his recital of all things numerical. After a while, Mr. Sneath realized the pointlessness of this exercise and waved the white flag at Edwin's woolgathering.

Did he never stop? Edwin pictured a giant sausage machine, where great ideas were fed in one side and spewed out the other, in an endless blood pudding of pointless words. For Edwin was a writer at heart. When the spoken language was woven into wonderful tales and grand realms, such as those in Treasure Island and Kidnapped, it was a wondrous gift. But most folk tossed words around as if they hadn't a clue what they were for. People rarely said anything worth listening to. The tongue was meant to convey noble ideas, far reaches of the imagination the pinnacle of mankind's ingenuity, not the meaningless drivel that slavered from most people's mouths.

Edwin drifted deeper, far away from his teacher's dull droning discourse; removed from classmates better able than he to feign interest. *A sailing ship, shearing the waves of sun speckled waters off the coast of Jamaica.* That's where Edwin wanted to be. If he could find just the right words.

It was at that precise moment that Edwin saw him, stooped over a canvas, paint brush in hand. His easel was perched on the sand, at the edge of a vast sea. One moment he seemed very old, the next, almost childlike. As he ran his paint brush over the canvas, words flew in all directions. Like gossamer, they rose into the air and then dissolved. Meanwhile, on the canvas, something wondrous was happening. A white, yellow-sailed catamaran had unfurled, encased in brilliant blue. All around, words drifted. Not Sneathy dull ones, but living words like *azure, spraying, foaming*. As each evaporated, an image emerged on the canvas.

Finally, the strange man turned around and looked Edwin squarely in the eyes. "Well don't just stand there gawking boy, pick one up." Edwin studied the long table covered in paints and brushes. Every colour he'd ever dreamed was there. He picked up a long, white brush and pointed it towards the canvas. "It won't paint itself son. Put yourself into it." Edwin nudged the canvas with the bristle and ambled it across a small section. The man erupted into laughter. "And what, is that? You look like you're poking at a snake. Strokes, lashes, that's what you need boy. You'll be lucky to paint a *the* or an *it* with a nudge like that." Gathering a little more courage, Edwin swirled the brush across the canvas. The sails begin to move. The words *unfurl, ruffle* and *ripple* spun into the air and vanished. "That's more like it boy. Now you're letting it paint you." A loud buzzing sound cut through the air and the landscape faded.

"Hey Watkins, wake up. Time to play school." Jim Frape smirked down at him. "Man, I wish I could do that. That's some gift you've got."

Edwin offered a sheepish "Yeah."

When he got home, he brought out his pad and started to write. *The sleek catamaran glided through the waves off the coast of Jamaica, a stiff wind on its heels.* His pen hovered over the next blank spot on the page. It remained so. He tried to recall the words he'd painted in his dream. Edwin rooted through his memory bank. He asked questions. *Where are they going? Who's on the boat?* All for naught. Edwin closed his eyes, as it seemed the best thing to do.

"You're thinking too much boy. You'll never write anything that way." The old man brandished his brush like a conductor's baton. Words scattered in all directions.

"It's rubbish. I want to write, but I can't think." Edwin flicked at a couple of words which had settled on his shoulder.

"You think you can create with just your brain? If you want to write instructions for making custard, rely on your brain. If you hope to write something of worth, learn when to turn it off."

"I can't use my mind to write?" Edwin bristled.

"Not what I meant at all. Words are all around you. First you have to tune them in. After that you need a little help."

"From you?" The old man tossed the brush to Edwin.

"From us all." He gestured for Edwin to move the brush. "When the picture in your head is so strong you're right there in it, you call up a wordsmith. Every brilliant story had the help of a wordsmith. Alice In Wonderland, Treasure Island and Peter Pan were written by some very clever people, but they still needed direction. A wordsmith helps sort out that gigantic word soup in your head. Then you can turn it into something delicious; a story that makes children laugh and cry. Compels them to check under their beds at night; takes them to faraway castles and kingdoms in their dreams. Without us, your soup wouldn't have much flavour."

Edwin toyed with the end of the brush. A single word, dropped onto the floor. *Open.*

The old man put the word onto his palm. It fluttered like a butterfly.

"Remember that day in old man Sneath's class. What were you really doing?"

"Imagining, but I do that all the time." The *open* butterfly lighted on Edwin's nose.

"Not just imagining, you jumped right in. That's when I came in. All those times you spent pulling words out of your brain that ended up as bland and dull as Granny's pot roast, the key was right in front of your nose." He plucked the quivering word from Edwin's face and launched it upward. "Now, go back to your writing. Only this time, open. Let the words rain down on you. Then pick up your pen and don't stop until it's dry."

Edwin noticed another word at his feet and bent down to pick it up. It unfurled in his hand. *Surrender.* To what? The question was still on his tongue when he found himself alone again. On his desk were the two words. *Open. Surrender.*

For the next few days Edwin wrote all his thoughts on bits of paper and tossed them into a bowl. *My word soup*, he grinned.

A few days later, Edwin sat picking through his word soup. Some of them were lovely, others repelled him. *Is this all part of my thinking?*

"Now you're getting it." The old man sat at the end of his bed.

"What do you mean?" Edwin hadn't remembered drifting off.

"You're opening to writing. Many writers think they need a label. I'm a romance novelist, a mystery writer. There's a world of ideas floating about. That bowl has it all. Humour, horror, fantasy. Pick anything and see where it takes you. If it's not your cup of tea, wave it goodbye and move on. Let me show you something."

Edwin followed his pointing finger into a large field teeming with strange animals milling about or grazing. Some chased each other and jumped over hedges and rocks. As he looked closely, he saw they weren't normal animals. They were words, living words, romping like lambs on a spring day. A few approached the fence, reaching for Edwin. Each spoke a silent, *Choose me*.

"Go ahead, pick one." Edwin inched closer "Don't think about it boy, just pick it up." The word creature *Golden* nuzzled his fingers. Now he didn't hesitate. He cradled the animal in his arms and walked back to the wordsmith. As he stroked it, images came flying out from its fleece. *Sunsets, white sails, crystal water*. Edwin saw them all.

Edwin awoke with his head on the desk. He read what he'd written. Something wonderful then happened. He was at the helm of a sleek schooner, white sails slicing a cobalt sky. The words flowed through and around him, taking him deeper and deeper into enchantment. This was no fable. It was more real than the world which lay just outside the borders of each page. He would have loved to stay forever, but like all stories, there was an end. He put his manuscript down and grinned. A small butterfly flew in through the open window. It opened its wings to reveal a word, a wonderful word: *Remember*.

When Edwin grew up, he did become a writer; one of books that children begged their parents to tell them at bedtime. Stories read under covers with a torch, when their readers are supposed to be asleep. They were tales that became the seeds of dreams, which dwell in the wonderful worlds which live only under closed eyelids.

Edwin always visited those places before he sent others on the journey. Sometimes they were wondrous and joyful, other times dark, and laden with menace. He missed seeing the wordsmith, but he knew his old friend was always at his canvas, helping turn words into life. On the few occasions when Edwin found himself struggling to put his ideas onto paper, he opened the little wooden box on his desk and pulled out the three sacred words which had changed everything. *Open, surrender, remember.*

UNTIL WE SLEEP

This is one of my darker offerings. Maybe the idea came from one of those shows where they take young offenders into prison to scare them straight. The idea provided a playground for some pretty horrific scenes mixed with a bit of old-fashioned fun. It's still one of my favourites.

Until We Sleep

"If I should die before I wake, I pray my soul the Lord to take."
Children's Hymn

November 15th 2048

My name is Father Robert Simmons. I have been the chaplain at Correctional Innovations Research Facility for the past twenty years. I met Gary Wyatt for the first time in his holding cell. The spectre of his impending "Treatment" had prompted him to call for me before they sent him into "The Big Dream." This is his story, word for word.

They were crawling on my legs. Sticky, evil-smelling demons. Hairy steps shuffling up my shins. I couldn't scream, my throat was sealed. My body was like an anchor. Somewhere deep down, I knew it was a dream, but at that moment those demons were real. With all my will, I forced myself awake. Only my eyes could move. As I turned towards the far wall, dozens of the black bastards inched their way towards the bedroom floor. I had two choices. Lie there and pray, or jump up before the first one had a chance to chow down.

You know Father, long as I remember I was terrified of spiders. Even a daddy long legs would send me out of the room, slamming the door shut behind me. You can't imagine what this was like. My God, I don't know where they were coming from, but I was their mark. My heart felt like it would burst. I wanted to scream but I knew that would send them into a frenzy. Maybe that'd be better. Scream and have done with it.

No, I had to act. I heaved the covers off and dashed for the door, squashing their nasty, crusty bodies.

My scream woke me. Sweat blinded me, and my heart bumped like a road drill.

Legs were glued to the mattress. But thank God, it was over. Give it a minute and maybe I'd be okay. But I wouldn't be would I? This nightmare had repeated itself for days and as soon as I fell asleep, they came again.

I managed the bathroom. God, the lines on my face. How could someone age so much in so little time? Much more of this and it wouldn't take spiders to finish me off.

Figured a drink might help. I flicked on the kitchen light and opened the cupboard. So help me, they must have heard me downtown. A huge, orange monster threw itself at my face.

This pink-faced, porky guy in a grey prison suit stood over me, handed me some water, and untied my straps. He says, "Okay Mr. Wyatt, that's it. You can go and get your stuff and get discharged."

It took me a moment. "Are you sure this is it?" I gasped. Geez my heart, was it ever going to come back into my body?

"Absolutely," he said. Then he told me he didn't think I'd be troubled by the night terrors again.

I tried to smile and told him, "Not if I can help it."

He told me it was my hands now. Then piggy man was gone.

I'm with you there, I thought. I'd rather spend the rest of my life rotting in a putrid jail than five minutes of that hell again. Five minutes. How many horrors can you experience in that time? Why a whole day in a dream is just a flash in real time.

Jeez, what a bloody ingenious idea! Paying your debt to society in a few minutes instead of bein' in the slammer for years at taxpayers' expense. And it worked. Not many people reoffended. Who in their right mind would ever do anything to get put back under? My take from the National heist sure wasn't worth that.

So I picked up my stuff and got the hell out. It was strange, but when I stepped out into that morning sun, felt the breeze, I felt better. All those nightmares seemed to be moving away from me. I'd had bad dreams before that shook me for days.

Howie was parked by the curb. I got in the car. Good old Howie. Could always count on him.

His mouth was trying to connect with his brain to find the right words. "Bad, was it?"

I told him, at the time, I'd never been so scared in my life. I was sure I was a goner. But suddenly it was all foggy, like I didn't know what I was scared about.

Howie pulled out onto the motorway and told me it was the same for him when he was in. They knew he had vertigo, so they programmed him to be perched on cliff tops, straddling swing bridges and balancing on girders, five hundred feet up. Like me, he thought his heart was going to jump out of his chest, but now it was so unreal.

The next thing out of his mouth came right out of left field. "You know Gary, I swore I'd never get into another scheme, but you know I think I could chance it one more time, if the stakes were high enough." I couldn't believe what I was hearing.

I lit a smoke and looked at him. "Dude, I'm just out the door and I get the feeling you're cooking up something already" For God's sake, I didn't even have my land legs back.

But I did know better than to try to stop Howie when he was on a roll. He goes on to tell me it's the biggest break we ever got and how he's been saving it just for me. He says if we pull this off we can go straight. Now he was kind of pleading, "Just come with me and hear out the plan. Nobody's going to put a gun to your head." But I had this awful feeling, I might have to do that to someone else.

We parked down near the docks by this old shack that looked like something out of an old gangster Holo. Two shifty looking guys were sittin' behind an old wooden table, with a bottle in front of them. The whole scene was a bloody cliché.

So Howie does the introductions. "Gary, this is Bones and Spike." *Of course, what else would they be called?* He explains how I just woke up from the Big Dream so to go easy and explain the scheme. He reminds them I'm the best safe hacker in the business.

Then this Spike, or maybe it was Bones, pushed a shot glass in front of me and filled it with something brown. It sure wasn't single malt. He explained the operation.

There was nothing to say. I was crazy for even being here. Don't I ever learn? If we got caught, there's no telling what they'd do. But what choice did I have? No job. Couple hundred bucks stashed away, wouldn't last two days. No family, no prospects. I drank up and held out my glass. Crazy bastard; I was in.

We didn't talk until we got to Howie's, when he says, "Listen, I know this isn't sitting easy with you, but relax, it's a sure thing." He tells me those guys have pulled a dozen heists, without getting caught. Got nice respectable homes in the suburbs, complete with families. He reassures me, when it's all over we just take our cash, disappear and start living. I think I grunted, once.

On the day of the operation, everything went like clockwork, that is except for the one worker who was late finishing his shift. Stupid idiot. What was he doing there? Heard he had a wife and kids, but there he was, washing the bank floor with his blood. Before we could figure out what had happened, cops were pouring in from every door and there was no way out. Now that felt like a dream. You know I almost expected to be woken up, told to get my things and go home.

So three days later, we were standing in the dock waiting for the verdict. Our lawyer was trying to prove that the death had been an accident, a bad set of circumstances. The jury didn't buy it though. Zero tolerance and all. Guilty of second-degree murder for both of us. I still don't know whose bullet hit the guard. Doesn't matter much, does it? Those other two jerks, Bones and Spike had waited in the car with the engine running. They only got nicked for armed robbery.

Well, that's it then, isn't it? Now Howie and I get to spend the night in "The Cradle". Don't you love their cute names they have for their torture chambers? Anyway, it's given me time for the paranoia to sink in. Can you imagine what it's like Father? I mean nobody ever got caught twice before, let alone for murder. God only knows what they got cooked up for us this time.

You know they have a personality profile of every prisoner in their main database? Fears people didn't even know they had, are there. Even you have them Father. All those Psychologists and Dream Specialists sit around figuring out what scares us most, and they come up with a program to shock us straight.

Howie there's been lying in the corner all night, head on his knees. I asked him what he thought they'd do. He didn't answer. You know it must have been easier in the old days. Think I could handle knowing I was going to be in for 20 years. Maybe some time off for good behaviour. But this. Who knows, maybe we'll never be sane again.

I dunno, after that I guess I dozed off a bit, because the next thing I knew the door opened and you came in. Thanks for listening father.

Epilogue

The official transcript stated Gary Wyatt and Howard Scott entered the Vision Implanter together at 8:00 AM July14th 2043. The program would have them both boarding an elevator on the 123rd floor of the New Empire State Building in New York, where they had just successfully applied for jobs in sales at a new Holo production firm. As the elevator started its descent, a malfunction in the gears would cause the car to accelerate at an exponential rate until it disintegrated on impact. The report would also note that a malfunction caused the program to repeat three times before shutting down.

"Well let's see how they fared," whispered prison guard Shawn Jenkins, as he opened the door to the dream chamber.

His colleague, Bonnie Parks, shivered as she entered the room and walked over to the two convicts. Both men lay motionless on their gurneys. "You know I always thought it was an old wives' tale that when you die in your sleep...." She stopped when she saw the shock in their eyes. "Guess they never knew what hit them." For the records, she checked their vitals. When she shook her head, Jenkins pulled a cover over both of them.

"No, I suppose not. I thought these programs were safe proofed against killing them. Maybe they had heart conditions." Jenkins started to wheel one of the men out of the door to the autopsy room for the final examination.

THE DOOR

Inspiration is everywhere. You just need to have your eyes and ears wide open. This one came from a simple walk with the dog. As we entered the park, I saw the house at the corner had a wooden door on the lawn. Just a plain old fashioned, green wooden door. I briefly pondered the reason for its presence, but when I took a closer look, I saw a lot more. What if there was something under that door? What if a bunch of kids in the neighbourhood found it and started some rumours? How about they decide to lift it up? When I got home, I wrote them all on sticky notes to be sure I didn't forget one. A couple of the members of my writer's group said it sounded like an episode of Goosebumps. I suppose it did, and I'll take that as a compliment. Everyone loves a spooky kid's story.

The Door

Alex Baines pushed at the doors. He banged, he screamed. Straining every muscle, he thrust his shoulders against the wet planks. The foul chittering of those filthy black creatures grew louder as they came closer. His frantic legs groped for some footing. One of the beasts nipped at him, just as his foot found a groove in the earth, enough to let him force one side upwards. He launched a mighty kick down at the unseen beast and pulled himself through the opening, onto the grass. Alex lay panting like a thirsty dog. Relief flooded through him as he took in the familiar surroundings. The white clapboard house with its worn out, khaki trellis, overgrown with wild roses, the huge green hedge which surrounded the garden, all seemed like a castle to him. He studied the door lying beside him.

He'd been lucky. Others had not been so. At least that's the way the stories around town went. They say the Nelson twins had gone in there and never come back. Alex hadn't known the Nelson twins. They'd gone missing almost twenty years ago, in 1956. Police concluded it was a kidnapping, but Alex and his friends knew better. They'd gone through that cursed gateway and not been able to find their way back.

Alex lay watching the sky. He felt exhilarated. He'd learned that word in history class last week. His teacher told him Winston Churchill once said it was exhilarating to get shot at. Alex wasn't too sure about that. He did know that whatever exhilarating exactly meant, this must be it. He'd gone through the gate, into the breach, another word he'd learned in school, and unlike the Nelson boys, he was alive to tell about it. Exhilarating. He turned the word over in his head and said it out loud a couple of times.

The town clock struck six. Jeepers, supper time. Mom would have his hide. Third time late this week. He picked himself up and headed home.

He never talked about the adventure to his family. They'd never believe him, because big folk knew kids made up crazy stuff all the time. Besides, if they thought even the smallest bit of it was for real; they'd forbid him from going there again.

But his friends. That was another matter. Every kid in town worthy of the name kid, had a door story, most of them made up.

Betsy Stubbs and her gang had been the first to see it. Least in modern times. Seems up 'til last Hallowe'en, no one had noticed any door. Maybe it'd always been there. Must have, cos the Nelson boys found it all those years ago. Guess they paid for being curious. Funny that no one had seen it before Betsy and her group. Seems the adults weren't able to see it, period. That's because grownups have no imagination. Every kid knows that.

Anyway, this was the way it happened. As Alice Kearney tells it, it'd been about 9 o'clock on Hallowe'en night. All the good candy had been picked over and most houses had blown out their pumpkins and shut down for the night. Betsy and her gang were heading home along Elm Street when Alice called out. "Hey there's a door here on this front lawn!"

"Yeah sure, and there's a balcony here in the hedge!" shouted Ted Sawyer.

"No really, come and look; number 27." With a few grunts and complaints, the tired group shuffled ahead to where Alice stood. Sure enough, right in the middle of the lawn, was a green door. Rather, doors. They lay side by side and met in an arch at the top. One side had a big brass knob and the other, an old knocker with a kind of wolf face. They agreed it was more of a gate than a door.

"It's nifty," Alice reached down and touched it, like she was trying to see if it was really there. "What's it doing here?"

"Maybe the Keene's are going to have a new front door put in," volunteered Ted.

"Don't be stupid," Betsy looked at Ted as if he'd suggested it was an alien spaceship. "How would they put that big old door up on their front steps. Besides, who'd want that ugly thing on their house."

"Reckon we should open it?" Charlie, who usually didn't say much was twiddling with the brass handle.

"Whaddya mean open it?" Betsy gave it a lame kick with one foot. "It's on the ground, what do you expect to find?"

"S'pose it can't do any harm," said Alice, "There's just lawn underneath."

Alice looked at the others. "You guys keep a look out. I'm going to try to pull it up." She grabbed onto the big handle with both hands and pulled. To everyone's surprise it flew wide open.

"Holy cow," bawled Ted, "Will you look at that." Everyone moved closer and stared down into a dark hole. After a minute Alice and Betsy slammed the door shut.

There was a lot of door talk in the town that summer. Some kids said the door, or gate as it came to be called, was an entrance to the centre of the earth. Others said it was an old cave that got buried under the ground and the gate was the only way to keep in a horrible monster. Jennie
Vandermere said it was the entrance to Hell, and that some angel had cursed it to keep the devil from coming out and destroying the world.

Nobody really knew for sure, but they made a vow that nobody would open that gate again.

Except Alex. You see Alex was a different kind of kid. Everyone knew it. He always liked creepy things like spiders and snakes. He loved graveyards and had the biggest collection of horror comics in town. Someone said he had a real shrunken head hanging in his bedroom.

After hearing about the Stubbs gang's adventure, Alex decided to check it out. That was the afternoon he found the wild creatures. Although he was scared at first, the thrill of it all made him want to go back. You see, Alex was more excited about going into the cave than he was scared of what was in there. He was also smart enough to never be caught.

Anyway, Alex went to the library and found some books with spells and magic words to protect himself. The next time he saw the creatures, he said those words and made the magic signs he'd learned and guess what? They didn't hurt him.

Pretty soon those creatures were treating him like he was their king or something. They
showed him an enchanted room full of treasure. But when he couldn't help bragging about what he'd seen, the other kids decided to get a kind of posse together to find out what really was under the gate. That made Alex mad, because he figured it was his cave.

So he made a plan. When he found out where the other kids were going to meet, he asked if he could join. He told them how there were beasts down there and he'd learned how to handle them. The kids weren't sure they really believed all his stories, but they reckoned it'd be a whole lot safer to have Alex with them. So they agreed and planned their mission. With that big hedge hiding the front lawn, they figured if they were really careful, they could go in after dark without being seen.

After making excuses to their parents and promising to be home by nine, they met the next night at 7 o'clock sharp, on Alice's lawn. Alex kept them waiting until 7:15, just to show who was in charge. He told them if they did what he said, they'd be safe. When they got to the gateway, Alex recited a couple of spells and then pulled one of the doors open. He told them to go ahead because only he had the right spell to close the entrance without the creatures getting out. As Ted Hughes followed the others down, he saw Alex scramble back up through the opening and pull the cover over.

When the kids didn't come home, their parents combed the neighbourhood. The next day, the Police were out in full force, checking back yards, garages, under porches, anywhere kids could hide. If they had been a bit younger, and had a little more imagination, perhaps they would have seen the door on the Keene's front lawn. Maybe, just maybe, someone would have tried to pry it open and look underneath.

After a few months, everyone knew they would never find the members of the Stubbs gang. Every so often, one of the little kids in town would walk by the Keene house and be surprised to see the big green door laying on the lawn. They also thought they heard bangs and yells coming from underneath. But they never said anything, because adults never believe little kids.

Camp counsellor Alex Baines, known by his newest group of campers as Skip, finished his story about the gateway. He paused and looked at the circle of kids around the fire. For him this was always the best part. The terror in their faces exhilarated him. Alex told them to sit quietly, while he went back to the cabin to get a treat for them.

THE THRILL OF THE HAUNT

I've always loved the old school masters of horror, such as HP Lovecraft and Poe. I admired the atmosphere of dread they constructed before they even delved into the story. I decided to try my hand at this craft, although at the beginning I didn't have much of a story line. But half-way through, the plot began to unravel by itself. I wanted to avoid a clichéd ending. I think I managed to do that.

The Thrill of the Haunt

I had decided to walk from the station up to the old house. It was a decent day for October; warm, almost oppressive. There would be a storm before this day was out. The structure revealed itself as I turned the corner. It was as I had expected; dark, gloomy and imposing. A ghoul's macabre birthday cake, complete with widow's walk. I took a deep breath and walked up onto the modest wooden porch. A faint rumble of thunder echoed. "Ah, a dark and stormy night, perfect."

The simple, iron door knocker felt cold to my touch, despite the sultry air. A couple of taps brought instant results. A tall, stolid woman stood, matted by the door frame. Her dress was severe but neat, and her long hair was tied in a bun, crowned with a black hairnet. She gave me what she might have considered a smile, or perhaps a look of weariness at the intrusion into her routine. I supposed we would now play the who was going to speak first, game. I made the opening move. "Good afternoon, I am Niles Penfold. I believe you were expecting me."

"We were Mr. Penfold. Please come in." Her right hand indicated I should go through the first door into what I assumed was the parlour. It looked like any of those restored Victorian Houses people are so eager to visit when they come to Massachusetts. She added a perfunctory, "Please have a seat," and vanished from the scene. I had barely started scanning the room, when she reappeared with a small tray, containing a silver tea pot, one China cup and a plate with three plain biscuits. I would be having tea alone.

I had done my homework. After many incarnations of the Pierce family inhabiting the house, misfortune and death had caused them to abandon the cursed mansion and use it as a rooming house for some of the most ragged and disreputable characters the small town of Gardner had to offer. But tonight, there would be no boarders. This was by design, not coincidence.

I am an author, not terribly well acclaimed, although I had managed to acquire a situation as a regular contributor in Amazing Stories, specializing in rather clichéd horror tales. My main inspirations were Poe and Hawthorne and I always have attempted to employ their style of prose, while not imitating their work. Before his untimely death, I had the privilege of having several conversations with the all too overlooked H P Lovecraft. I believe his graphic depictions were often too unsettling for the average reader, so my goal was to mesh his horrific images with a softer, more sympathetic story line.

For the past several months I had experienced the dreaded writer's block. My backlog of short stories was the only thing which kept me from falling short of my obligations to Amazing Stories. I had convinced the editor that a recount of a visit to one of the most haunted houses in the country, may prove to be an enticing offering for our readers. He acquiesced and within 48 hours I was on a train to the small town of Gardner, having secured permission to spend a night in the accursed house, and record my experiences.

Miss Grimshaw, returned to take the tray. She had not told me her name, but the lawyer had furnished me with a few details about the old marm. Nobody could remember a time when she had not managed the place. "If there is nothing else, I will be leaving now. I shall return in the morning, Mr. Penfold. Should you require assistance I must advise you, we are not equipped with a telephone." At that, she turned on her heels and walked to the kitchen. A moment later the door closed.

I had called in a favour from a friend in the recording industry and procured a device which would enable me to document events as warranted. My hope for one of the recently developed audio-visual recorders would have to wait for a future investigation.

Once the equipment was at the ready, I poured myself a generous brandy, took out my notepad, and settled into my evening.

I mused. What was I hoping for? Shadow figures emerging from the corners of the room? Severed heads floating through the air? Screams, moans and bumps in the dark? Disembodied steps? Perhaps a good old fashioned smiling skeleton. I truly had no idea, and no inkling of how I would react to any of the above.

I poured another glass and sat there, listening, watching, sensing.

Sleeping? That wasn't in the plan. I'd drifted off for over an hour. God, I hoped I hadn't missed something. I reached into my satchel and brought out the research I had obtained from county court records and sifting through library shelves. I had first made note of events one could consider supernatural or at the least, the preternatural. Then there were the usual accounts of strange noises, visual aberrations, and the ubiquitous cold spots. I am neither skeptic nor believer. I look at the evidence and draw my conclusions without bias. Debunking the reports was not in my agenda.

Many of the depictions were mundane, bordering on cliché, which I attributed to natural phenomena blown out of proportion by an active, on-edge imagination. But there was a class of incidents which bore closer scrutiny. Passersby with no investment in the house whatsoever, described seeing shadow figures on the lawn, apparitions at the windows and hearing unearthly chatter.

Perhaps the oddest and inexplicable accounts came from two journalists who each stayed in the house for one night. Both report having fallen asleep and woken to find themselves completely dislocated. One, a well-respected writer for the Boston Globe, had gone to investigate the stories surrounding the house, in 1935. The following are some of his diary entries found in the house a few weeks later.

> *The first part of the evening was uneventful. Possibly nerves caused me to take note of every creak and bump in the night. None were significant enough to have me leave the comfort of my armchair. A couple of false alarms turned out to be little more than a branch slapping against the window, and the house cat chasing a hapless mouse. I fell into a deep sleep, haunted by strange dreams.*

> *Voices awoke me after daybreak. I rose and pulled back the curtains. What I next saw led me to believe I was still asleep. While much of the scene was recognizable, odd vehicles travelled down the street, and there were buildings I had not seen the night before. A large rumbling sound guided me to look upward, where a large airship, unlike anything from our time, appeared to be descending. Then I noticed several people, dressed in unfamiliar fashion, were on the front steps.*

The following day, he did not report for work, nor the following. No one was willing to investigate the occurrence. The other man had been missing since his visit the previous year.

Until the last entry, this was standard ghostly house fare. One only need read books about *Haunted America* to see dozens of similar scenarios. However, this account from a fellow, respected journalist, jarred me. What was he describing? Did he believe he had somehow passed through a doorway into a different time? One might be inclined to say he was dreaming or hallucinating, but the disappearance of both men, without a trace, was very unsettling. Was it a publicity stunt, perhaps to boost the paper's circulation? My mind ran through all the standard explanations. When these were exhausted, I turned to the inexplicable. These proved to be more intriguing, and perhaps would be fodder for one of the longer works of fiction I had been promising myself I would one day write.

I dozed off again and had the sensation I was leaving my body and travelling through time and space itself. Images flashed through me, too fleeting to identify. I can't say how long I was trapped in the kaleidoscope world, but when I awoke sunlight was streaming through the window. I was conscious, but struck with the realization I had nothing to impart, except for the visions encountered during my slumber, maybe nothing more than phantasmagoric dreams. I considered pouring another brandy but thought better of it.

The sounds of voices, likely from the front porch, alerted me. Miss Grimshaw perhaps? But who was with her? As I inched my way towards the hall, they became clearer, and I realized there were several of them. I didn't want to confront whatever was at the door and about to enter. I quickly slipped into the hall closet, as the door opened.

"Welcome guests to Pierce Mansion. You are the first outside visitors in fifty years, to pass these doors and explore this cursed house. As winners of the Netflix LG B&Binge contest you have the dubious pleasure of spending the night in one of America's most haunted buildings. This manor has been featured in *Ghost Adventurers* and *Haunted America* and will soon be available to the public for tours. Please have a seat in the parlour." A female voice went on to describe to the guests the sordid details of the house, of which I was already all too familiar. But what manner of talk was this? Where was I?

Physically, I knew I was still in Pierce Mansion, but that was where reality ended. In all other aspects, I was somewhere else.

Eventually, their host bid them to go into the hall and then directed them downstairs. The dimming of voices indicated this was my chance. I grabbed my notes and my recorder and made haste for the front door. When I opened the door, I received the shock of my life. There, before me, was only open space, a hole in the fabric of the world. I stood pondering my options. There was nothing to do but go back inside and wait for our guests to leave. It was too late, steps were coming back up. I could only wait and face them. But they paid no heed. It appeared they didn't see me. I counted six of them. One seemed to turn in my direction and stare a moment, but then looked away. I was invisible, and I was trapped.

The paper is still delivered each day. Tossed from the sidewalk by the paper-boy, to avoid his having to approach the damned edifice. The clipping I re-moved from the Worcester Telegram and Gazette a few days ago, sits on the parlour table. It reads as follows: *Unearthly Sounds in America's Most Haunted House: Visitors to the Pierce Mansion continue to report strange oc-currences.*

Several paragraphs follow, which depict various encounters, both plausible and fantastic. We have passed the piece around and voiced our own views about the various accounts.

Every day the three of us meet in the parlour to talk about the events of the day. We share a brandy and cigars by the fire. The guides are kind enough to fill the decanter before it empties, and replace the cigars in the humidor. I'm not clear how this all works. If we are indeed spirits, then why are we able to enjoy the comforts of the living? Either way, we are grateful and I suppose it serves no purpose to question. Even the logs and matches for the fire have been replenished. It's a simple but pleasant enough existence, and my two journalist friends have proved to be amiable enough companions. We repay our hosts by offering typical horror fare experiences for the guests. Rattling chains, things that go bump in the night, scratching, disembodied voices. All dreadfully cliché, but enough to add authenticity to the tour and cause unease in the visitors to our home. Each day we go through the rooms and try to find a way out of Pierce Mansion. I am beginning to suspect none of us is trying as hard as we did at the beginning of this adventure.

NIGHT OF MYSTERY AND IMAGINATION

Edgar Alan Poe and H.P. Lovecraft are considered masters of the American Horror genre. The strength of their writing, aside from telling a whopping good yarn, was in the creation of atmosphere. A constant aura of menace grabs hold of you from the opening line, and tightens its grip until the climax. I hope they would approve of this tale.

Night of Mystery and Imagination

To the best of my recollection, these are the events which occurred on the evening of December 4th, 1847, at the New Theatre in Baltimore. I must admit the entire affair now seems more like a wild dream than reality.

I stood in front of the old stone building. It looked more like a federal prison than a venue for the performing arts. Its gloomy facade was in keeping with tonight's performance. We were promised something not only unusual and unique, but something we would remember for the rest of our lives.

This was the night when Baltimore's famous literary son would be returning home. At least in spirit. Edgar Allan Poe had passed away the previous year after a long undetermined illness. It is most likely the death of the love of his life, his wife, Virginia, drove him to despondency and the eventual alcoholism which led to his final spiral. An icy wind drove sleet into the crowd as we started into the theatre.

A year after his death, an unknown writer by the name of Callum Hamilton, who claimed to have worked for Mr. Poe at the Broadway Journal, proffered a most fantastic story. He claimed to have come into contact with the spirit of EAP. in the months following his demise. He also maintained the late author had spoken to him in a dream, instructing him to share his works by conducting public readings across America. Although Mr. Hamilton was to present these recitals, Poe himself claimed he would be partaking from beyond the grave, channelling his insight and opinion.

Finding a good publicist, Hamilton was soon able to create a huge fanfare around this spectacle, and by the opening night of what was to be a series of single performances in over 30 cities, it had captured the imagination of the higher strata of Baltimore society. Indeed, a queue of those hoping to obtain an unused ticket, had formed outside the box office since early evening. The banner outside boasted:

An Evening of The Fantastic and Mysterious from The Spirit World.
At the Behest and With the Blessing
of The Late Edgar Allan Poe, Mr. Callum Hamilton
Will Perform, Interpret, and Channel Selected Works
from The Master of The Macabre.

It should be noted that although Mr. Poe was largely unheralded in his earlier years, the publication of "The Raven" in January of 1845, had earned a large following and fame.

Being a literary critique employed by the Baltimore Sun, I was quickly ushered to my seat by a young boy who couldn't have been more than twelve, and was able to observe as the rest of Baltimore society slowly filled the hall.

The Theatre Bell chimed. A moment later, the lights dimmed almost to extinction, and the sounds of a storm started to grow. Flashes illuminated the scene. There was little doubt where Mr. Hamilton was about to start the evening.

> Once upon a midnight dreary, while I pondered, weak and weary,
> Over many a quaint and curious volume of forgotten lore—
> While I nodded, nearly napping, suddenly there came a tapping,
> As of someone gently rapping, rapping at my chamber door.[1]

The cavalcade of sound continued. This was an impressive start. Hamilton's voice was both mellifluous and ominous. It rose and fell with the sounds of the tempest, which issued from all directions of the theatre. Something inside of me plunged into despair as he mournfully called the name "Lenore", and then rose in terror at the sound of the Raven's enigmatic, "Nevermore".

I looked around to see the reaction of my fellow passengers on this curious voyage, but the darkness was so intense that it didn't offer so much as a shadow or a silhouette. I began to feel that I was present in that dark, dismal, wind swept room, kept company only by the flighted intruder at my window. Of the next few minutes there is no memory other than the oppressive tapestry woven by Mr. Hamilton.

---

[1] Edgar Allen Poe, "The Raven", *American Review: A Whig Journal* (1845)

And my soul from out that shadow that lies floating on the floor
Shall be lifted—nevermore![2]

A pall hung over the auditorium. Whether the audience was unable to speak, or could not, was hard to determine, but before any reaction could ensue, Hamilton spoke. "Ladies and gentlemen, I thank you for braving the night to come and honour the master of the fantastic and mysterious, Mr. Edgar Allan Poe. As stated before, although I will be reading from his passages, I have it on the authority of the man himself, that he will have a large hand in tonight's proceedings. To quote the ancient Egyptians. "To speak the name of the dead is to have him live again." You may have felt carried far away during the performance of the Raven. During the evening I encourage you to let the feelings sweep you where they may, so that you can experience the depth of genius that was and still is Mr. Poe."

The stage lighting shone precisely onto a small table, covered in a red cloth. On it was a simple portrait of Mr. Poe and a vase containing a single rose. Mr. Hamilton spoke once more, "The house lights have been brought down to the minimum level, to enable you to focus on everything you hear and see, and in that way it will bring you closer to the author himself. I remind you that despite any doubts you may have, Mr. Poe is indeed making his presence felt during these proceedings, so I invite you to let your feelings become part of the adventure.

At that, he moved back to his podium, opened his notes, and began to read.

The thousand injuries of Fortunato I had borne as best I could, but when he ventured upon insult I vowed revenge.[3]

As he uttered the last word, the back of the stage glowed. A red curtain opened, revealing a pile of grey bricks. Whether it was real or a façade I could not tell, for the lighting dimmed once more, so only a ghostly image remained.

Mr. Hamilton continued to relate the tale of horror in which a man named Montresor, seeks revenge on an enemy, by getting him drunk, luring him into his wine cellar and walling him up for eternity. As the story unravels the silhouettes of two men lumbered towards the mound of bricks, one clearly aiding the other. The sounds of trowel on cement uttered from every corner of

[2] Ibid.
[3] Edgar Allen Poe, "The Cask of Amontillado", *Godey's Lady's Book* (1846)

the otherwise silent hall. Muffled moans and groans joined the macabre montage. What a marvellous feat of showmanship this was. The tale came to its startling conclusion as Hamilton screamed the line,

"For the love of God, Montresor!"
"Yes, for the love of God!" Montresor replied.[4]

The two voices, almost in tandem, ripped through me as if propelled by a blade. My heart ached in despair. I wished dearly I could see my fellow patrons, but obsidian shadow engulfed everything except the man at the dais and the misty apparitions behind him. How was it physically possible to create such darkness?

The sounds became muffled, unintelligible. The stage lights came up just enough to reveal that the abominable funeral pyre behind Mr. Hamilton was gone.

Again, the silence was deafening. Again Mr. Hamilton spoke. "I thank you for being part of this momentous occasion. Your participation is making it possible for Mr. Poe to make a triumphant return to the fair city of Baltimore." I pondered this for a while, trying in vain to see anything in that ominous atmosphere, filled with palpable menace. I suspect more than a few of the audience wanted to shout out for him to stop this blasphemy, or to bolt from their seats. As for me, I can only say I was unable, or unwilling to do so.

Our host recited a few of Mr. Poe's more benign works, including the heart wrenching "To one in Paradise." The last lines of which moved the theatre goers to audible tears. I recall feeling relief to hear my fellow patrons were indeed still there.

And all my days are trances,
And all my nightly dreams
Are where thy dark eye glances,
And where thy footstep gleams—
In what ethereal dances,
By what eternal streams.[5]

Mr. Hamilton placed his hands on the rostrum, and then thanked us once more for the energy we were giving to the spirit of Mr. Poe.

---

[4] Ibid.
[5] Edgar Allen Poe, "To One in Paradise", *Godey's Lady's Book* (1834)

He then made an odd request. "For my last passage, I will ask the assistance of a member of the audience. As the sounds evoked by a man suffering at the hands of his accusers are so visceral and integral to the tale, I feel the mood must be conveyed by a second reader. Someone to take us away from the narrative and into the horrific reality of the scene."

For the first time in the evening, I heard a voice from the crowd. Moments later our intrepid volunteer compatriot walked to the stage, whereupon Mr. Hamilton gave him a hearty embrace. The stage abruptly went dark, and we were assailed with the sounds of moans and the chittering of rats.

> I WAS sick—sick unto death with that long agony; and when they at length unbound me, and I was permitted to sit, I felt that my senses were leaving me. The sentence—the dread sentence of death—was the last of distinct accentuation which reached my ears.[6]

Our second man seemed to know exactly where he was to come in. While Mr. Hamilton read the chilling narrative of a man slowly awaiting his impending and inevitable death, the other summoned the sensual terror, the sounds coming from an inescapable tomb.

> For many seconds I hearkened to its reverberations as it dashed against the sides of the chasm in its descent; at length there was a sullen plunge into water, succeeded by loud echoes.[7]

The two men alternated the part of narrator and victim. As the story built to its hideous conclusion, the evocations assaulted our ears with menace and despair. I felt the zephyr from the slicing, swishing blade, as it lowered to almost touch the doomed man's flesh. The whispering of the inquisitors, as they watched the sentence carried out. The rats on the floor, chittering. They all transported us to a place of madness and delirium. The final line came not in a scream of pain or horror, but a barely audible whisper.

> The Inquisition was in the hands of its enemies.[8]

The house lights came on, the stage was empty. No people, no table, no wall, no dais. I looked at my fellow travellers as they slowly stood and headed

---

[6] Edgar Allen Poe, "The Pit and the Pendulum", *The Gift: A Christmas and New Years Present* (1842-43)

[7] Ibid.

[8] Ibid.

to collect their coats and valuables. To the last, every face showed no reaction, except for the same unspoken question in their eyes.

THE BEAST

What is the beast? Is it the shrieking sound coming across the moors on a stormy night? Is it the banging noise coming from the basement in the old dark house? Perhaps the restless big cat prowling the length of its cage. The unknown, never mentioned horror, that waits for the unsuspecting traveller in the deep dark forest. Or is it something even more insidious?

The Beast

With a shout out to Bill Watterson.

I eyed the beast. It hadn't made any attempt to move, and I in turn, remained motionless as I considered my options. There weren't many. The only thing certain was that the hideous monstrosity must die. How this was going to be achieved, was another matter.

It seemed I had been sitting there for ages, although it couldn't have been more than a matter of minutes. Time and space had folded into a giant fist, and clenched themselves around my trembling body. Once, I fancied it had begun to throb. My heart raced as I recalled the horrific climax from *The Tell-Tale Heart.*

With some small degree of satisfaction, I noted the gouge on its wretched side where a moment's bravado had allowed me to get close enough to inflict a wound. It had been a reckless act, but for that moment, I had forgotten my fear and seized the opportunity. Snatching the shiny weapon at my side, I'd raised my arm high in the air and then brought it down into its slimy flesh, only to instantly recoil, sickened by its fetid stench and ghastly wail. I cowered like a wounded animal, unable to muster the courage for another assault on my mortal enemy. All too aware time was running out, I tried to will myself to do something, anything that would put an end to this nightmare. To delay would surely unleash unspeakable consequences. Yet dread and disgust fixed me in their grip.

I have not yet described the thing. In truth, words can do no justice where such an abomination is concerned. Nevertheless, I will say it was the stuff of which madness is made. Here was an evil so vile, only the most intrepid soul could bear to be in its presence, for even the briefest of times, let alone long enough to engage in battle.

Strangely enough, it wasn't the first time I had faced this horror. On our first encounter I can only assume it grew weary of our standoff, for after some time, without fanfare, it withdrew. I had prayed I'd seen the last of it.

What motive drove it to taunt me again, I cannot imagine. This time I knew there could be no simple resolution.

Though it had no eyes I felt it stare into my soul, mocking me, enticing me to come and try to vanquish it for all time. It seemed to be swelling. Was a tentacle unravelling from its bloated green body?

The moment had come. Lack of action meant certain defeat. The tool lay covered in green slime, where I had left it. I reached for it once more and gathering all my nerve, thrust the metal shaft deep into the heart of the demon. *Die beast, die!* I looked at my weapon. A putrid, murky blob hung from its side. The rest of the carcass lay still. I fell back, exhausted with disgust and loathing. The room appeared to spin, and then a distant voice broke the silence. At first it was only meaningless noise, but then I grasped its chilling message.

"Stop messing about Stephen, that spinach won't eat itself."

Hmm, interesting theory mum, let's give it a little while longer and see.

CROSSES TO BEAR

At one point everyone was writing vampire stories. Most of them were either very dark, or extremely romantic. Then I thought, "What about an ordinary dude, who suddenly finds his life spinning off in a direction he could never have imagined?" The story almost wrote itself, and it was great fun. My problem was finding a satisfying ending. The punchline is often considered a cheap way out, but when this one came to me it was a true Eureka moment. I had no choice.

Crosses to Bear

About 2 o'clock in the afternoon Aug Silvestri noticed something very odd about his shadow. He had none. Last night had been a late one. He'd emerged from his front door, aching eyes and head grateful for the clouds which hid the sun. His earlier queasiness gone, the thought of fresh coffee and breakfast pulled him in the direction of Gerrie's Diner.

As the sun made a brief appearance, he'd checked his shadow, or the lack thereof. At this time of day his silhouette should be strolling beside him. Where the hell was it? Like an idiot, he reached down and felt the sidewalk. He turned around several times. Aug took one more look at the sky and entered Gerrie's.

Aug mopped up the last piece of egg with his toast and left the diner. A few dozen wooden posts lay crossed on a nearby lawn, where a fence was being erected. He felt a sudden, irrational panic, a need to cross the street. Aug ran the rest of the way home.

The front door offered relief. Something was very wrong. Maybe it was the after effects from last night, his 30th birthday. What was the last thing he remembered? Chatting up those weird Goth chicks on Richmond Street? Where had they gone after that? Complete blank. Thirty years old. This crazy life had to end. Boy, his parents were spot on when they named him Augustino, patron saint of brewers. What's a nice Catholic boy doing in a state like this?

He smiled at the line, baptized himself in cold water, and almost fell into the sink. When he looked into the mirror, it didn't look back. The only reflection was that of the opposite wall.

His stomach surged into his head. This was no hangover. On a notion, he ran his fingers over his neck and rechecked the mirror. My God, were those two small punctures?

Maybe he'd seen too many movies, but Aug Silvestri, good Catholic son, found himself in front of his laptop Googling *Vampires*. The header announced 47,100,000 results. Maybe he needed to narrow the search down a tad. Under *Vampire Traits* he made a few notes. This was not looking good. He scanned some other pages. On the middle of page thirty-seven was an intriguing title, *Just Bitten? Advice for the newly vampired.* Despite himself, Augustino read on;

JUST BITTEN INC.
Helping those souls who have entered the realm of the undead.
Advice, counselling and a full catalogue of necessities for the neophyte.
Discretion guaranteed.
Becoming a vampire is not a death sentence.

"Very funny," Aug said out loud. There were contact numbers, but no address. He tapped in the number.

"Just Bitten, Count Yorga speaking." There was a short pause and then a great asthmatic laugh. "Sorry, I cannot resist. Jake Palmer here, how might I help you?" Aug told his story, while the other end of the phone made a few encouraging noises. "Sounds like you have had a bite all right. I need to meet you in person and do an assessment. Can you come down to my office?"

"You have an office?"

"Well we tried working from the coffin but it was a little crowded." That great guffaw again. "Can you be here in about an hour? There is no time to lose."

"Can you fix it?" Another pause. Jake Palmer gave Augustino the address and directions, and rang off.

He found the building in a small lane off Queen Street. It looked like a shoe repair or tailors. A bell sang as he entered and a rather large man with a pointy nose emerged from a back room. "Augustino, I presume," He offered his hand. "Come right in, I will not bite." He wheezed through another laugh and slapped his side.

"Mr. Palmer?" Aug ventured.

"You expected maybe Christopher Lee? No, you are too young, maybe a more dashing model like the fellow on Twilight?"

"I don't know what I expected or why I'm here."

"Let me help you," Mr. Palmer offered a chair. "You have had some very odd experiences. You have tried being rational and now you are ready to consider the preposterous. And you are scared enough to consider that this vampire business might just be real."

"I suppose...."

"You do not suppose anything. In fact you do not really believe this is possible. But let me tell you, from my long, long experience, it is. It has happened to you, and hundreds of others. You probably passed a couple on the way over, only you would not have noticed. Contrary to the legends, we do not all look like undertakers with out of style tuxedos. There are a lot of myths out there. Can I see your neck please?"

Mr. Palmer asked some questions while taking notes on a small pad. He examined Aug's neck, eyes and mouth, listened to his heart, felt his pulse and looked at the mark once more.

"Now, please just do as I say. Open the drawer on the desk and look inside."

Aug did as he was told and withdrew in shock. Inside was a large silver crucifix. He slammed it shut. "But I'm a Catholic, I go to Mass every Sunday."

Mr. Palmer didn't speak, but instead motioned to another drawer. Aug's shaking hands dragged it open. He quickly shut it again. "Garlic? You mean it's true? My God, I'm Sicilian! I suppose you're going to tell me I'm going to turn into a bat every night."

"Well now you are just being ridiculous. That idea went out with the idea of sleeping in coffins. Now don't get hysterical. Being undead is not that bad. Granted there are inconveniences, but it has its advantages. You are going to live a long, long time. And with all the hype these days, being undead is very popular with the ladies. You would not believe how many women are looking for an eligible young vampire."

Aug could only shrug. He looked at the titles on the shelf near the desk. They read like the self-help section at Indigo. He picked up a copy of *I May Be Undead, But I'm Okay.*

"That is one of our most popular books," Mr. Palmer took the book and read from the table of contents. *You may be undead but you can still live. How not to bite the hands that feed you? You have not been bitten, you have been chosen.* Really positive stuff, you should read this." He handed the book back.

"You sell these?" Aug thumbed a few pages.

"Look, just think of it like having the flu bug, some people are only carriers and pass it around. They live nearly normal lives. Others have a few symptoms, and of course you have your full blown, pasty faced, only come out at night vampires. Not many though. Most of us grow into our condition and move on. Most likely that will be you."

"For the next week, I want you to keep a journal. Write down anything unusual. You will come here again, show me and we will see what we are looking at."

"But what happens when I start getting the urge to bite my mother's neck?"

"Myths. Fairy tales. You have choices. Just write it all down and I will see you in one week. Oh, and Mr. Silvestri, try to get some sleep." He rasped out one final laugh and smacked his thighs.

Great, thought Aug, *a stand-up vampire*. He was happy to see the sun setting. There were no plans for tonight. He was between girlfriends, and now, given the circumstances, he didn't dare risk an intimate encounter.

Aug picked up some beer and pizza and went home. He revisited yesterday's site and drew up a checklist. As he bit the end off the first slice, he noted it tasted the same as always. Aug swallowed and to his delight everything went down normally. He read; *Most undead can eat normal food, but cannot derive any nutritional benefit from such,* "I'll consider that an okay," he said out loud, as he checked it off on the list of symptoms he'd drawn up.

So, this was going to be hit or miss, no rules. That had an upside, but it could also be embarrassing if he decided to take a chunk out of the next Jehovah's witness who arrived at the house. And the food. Well pizza was no problem, but for God's sake he was Sicilian, what happened the next time he went for the family dinner?

He spent the rest of the evening building his checklist. What was he going to do about his friends? Could he keep seeing them? Was there a vampire support group? Did they all hang out together? As he settled into this new mind space, he started to become more upbeat.

"I guess it's not the end of the world," he muttered to his keyboard. He finished the last of the beer and headed off to bed. The night was filled with disturbing dreams which he had trouble separating from reality, whatever that was.

Aug woke up and pushed off the covers. "You know what? I'm gonna make the best of this thing and take it one step at a time." His alarm buzzed. Aug glanced at his phone. Sunday, 8:30 AM. "Oh my God, I have to take Nona to mass!"

DANCING ON THE GRAVE

It's hard to say how this came about, but I'm pretty sure it has to do with my love of words. The right word can change the direction of a story, even when it isn't planned. The first word in this story became the cornerstone of this tale. It's actually a love story, but a pretty sordid one at that, and my only one that comes close to having a sex scene.

Dancing on the Grave

Juxtaposition. Marcie smiled. That's the word Mr. Folkard had used. It means opposites, used together to highlight their difference. Big literary technique. Lots of the best writers used it.

Funny thing to be thinking of. But there it was. Jack thrust hard. She knew he was getting close. Her ass was cold, pressed against the marble slab. But Jack's body, pressed against her, was hot and sweaty. Yup, that was juxtaposition. Wonder if she could talk about it in class on Monday. Geez you are one crazy chick, she thought. No surprise people avoid you, whisper about you. Jack was there. She let out the obligatory moan, cried out to a deity she wasn't sure she believed in, said Jack's name a few times, and then sighed, as he collapsed on top of her.

Not that she didn't enjoy making love to Jack. It's just this was kind of weird. I mean, weird was what they did. But fucking on a tombstone? That was pretty blasphemous. Another of Mr.F's contributions to her verbal lexicon. And *lexicon.* She turned the word over, *blasphemous, blasphemous, blasphemous.* Each time she emphasized a different syllable. Jack's breathing was starting to slow down, and she could feel him growing soft inside her.

"You okay babe?" he offered.

Marcie winced as he pulled out. "Yeah, guess so."

"What's the matter, you seem a bit distracted?"

"Dude, have you forgotten the last 12 hours? We're not only fornicating on a grave slab, but there's a fucking body lying five feet away from us, and we're responsible."

"I thought you said it would be exciting to do it here?" Jack was standing now. He slipped his T-shirt on and zipped up.

"Yeah well that carcass staring up at us, kinda weirds me out." Marcie, now dressed, was looking for her left shoe in the damp grass.

"Hey, we said no cold feet."

"Yeah, well my ass is cold and my feet are fucking numb. What the hell were we thinking of? We got away with it once, but lightning doesn't usually strike twice." This is what it had come to. Months of planning and scheming and shitting themselves that they were going to be found out. But they hadn't been.

They weren't just the school freaks; they were probably the smartest students in that school full of doorknobs. Hmm, wasn't saying much, Marcie supposed. Still, this had been the perfect crime up to now. Not that they considered it a crime. Those two jerks had it coming. They'd made Marcie and Jack's lives a living hell for the past two years. Maybe others too. If anything, it was karma. Karma, that's what it was.

Westhaven was a pretty small Midwestern town, with a pretty small mentality. Westhaven High was home to about 600 students, ninety percent of them mindless narcissists. God, Marcie loved words. Sometimes she went to the online Thesaurus, just to find other ways of saying what she wanted to say. She taught Jack to use them. Those dopes at school probably thought they were speaking in tongues.

Jack and Marcie were imports from the city, where there was more to life than prom queens and cornhusker parades. They'd made an instant connection, and right away incurred the wrath of the student body at Westhaven. They were the only Goths in the school, in fact in town. Maybe the whole stupid county. They talked different, looked and dressed different. They were freaks. The more they were picked on, the closer they got. That made it worse, now they were a freak couple.

They had a lot in common. Style, music, movies, and a mega fascination with the macabre. Soon they were plotting fantasies of blowing away all those rubes in school. Of course, they'd never do it, but mind revenge felt good. Then Frank Stewart crossed the line. He started putting up some nasty posts. Most of it, fake. But it did the trick, added to the vilification. Frank's friend, Jamie Peters had joined the action, and pretty soon they had a "Goth Geeks" post.

Jamie got ahold of some compromising pictures and soon they were up for the world to see. That's when fantasy turned to scheming. Those jerks were going to pay.

However savvy Jamie was at social media, he couldn't hold a candle to Marcie and Jack. When you are an outcast, you have a lot of time to get good at other things. With some fancy dancing they'd lured Jamie out to the Forester Farm, long abandoned. All they meant to do was scare the shit out of him. But Jamie had fallen and cracked his head. They'd panicked and left him there. After some investigation, it was ruled a tragic accident. No one could figure out what he was doing at the old Forrester place. There really weren't any solid leads to pursue, until they checked out his laptop. Seems he'd been having a bit of a fling with some girl called Loni, which was supposed to end up in a romantic encounter at the barn. But the mystery girl could not be traced, and all leads led to dead ends. The case went cold.

The crazy thing was, after it died down, Frankie took to the keys again and started pumping out more vitriol, trying to connect Jamie's death to Jack and Marcie. The police had questioned them, but they'd concocted a good alibi and Frankie was warned to cease and desist.

But Frankie was not the brightest bulb on the tree, and while he toned it down a bit publicly, he continued to harass and stalk them privately. Jack and Marci decided if the police weren't able to do their jobs, they would take care of things themselves. They spent a few evenings inventing ways in which they might end Frankie's reign of terror. It was all hypothetical at first. Another of Marcie's favourite words. But before long, they both realized this was going to happen.

It didn't exactly rank up there with *The Black Dahlia*, but it was quick, clever and easy. They covered all their tracks, had a full proof alibi. And the excitement of dumping the body right next to Jamie produced a strange sexual energy, hence sex on the grave slab. *Anticlimactic.* Maybe that was the wrong word. She thought about what they had done, and reconsidered. Yup, that was the right word. Anticlimactic in several ways. And now, despite the high they had felt, they knew they would spend the next few days with their hearts in their throats, every time there was a knock at the door. Keeping their heads down when they passed a police cruiser. Could they really pull this off? Marcie wanted to jump into the pickup with Jack and just drive, disappear into the night and never see Westhaven again. As long as they were together, it wouldn't matter where.

It would be several hours before anyone came into the cemetery. By that time, there would be no sign of the two fugitives. It might take days before someone came across the body, or maybe a few hours. Either way, there was nothing to link them to this. Their messages to Jamie and Frankie had been carefully eliminated. They'd never publicly threatened either of the two guys. Nothing. It was going to be okay. Besides, they'd done the world a favour, purged the net of two more useless trolls.

A flash of thunder lit the sky. A gust of wind blew dust in Marcie's face and she felt the first big drops on her face. It soon became a torrent. First rain in months. The next flash revealed water was starting to run into the dried cracks in the dirt road, leading up to Jamie's tombstone. "Marcie! Babe, what are you doing? Get in the truck, it's pouring." Another flash exposed Frankie's lifeless feet, sticking out from behind the stone. *Pathetic fallacy.* Geez, if Mr. Folkard could only be here, he'd be so impressed. Well, sort of. The storm, the rain, the corpse lying next to his buddy's tomb. He could use it the next time he taught literary devices. "Marcie, for God's sake, get in." She snapped out of it and walked towards the revving pick-up. "What were you doing?"

"Oh just savouring the moment, babe." Jack put his hand on her knee.

"We're gonna be fine now. No little twerpy trolls to make our lives miserable." He started to back up slowly in the fresh mud. As he did, Marcie peered into the headlights.

"Jack, the rain, the mud. We're leaving tire tracks!"

SMOKING BULLETS

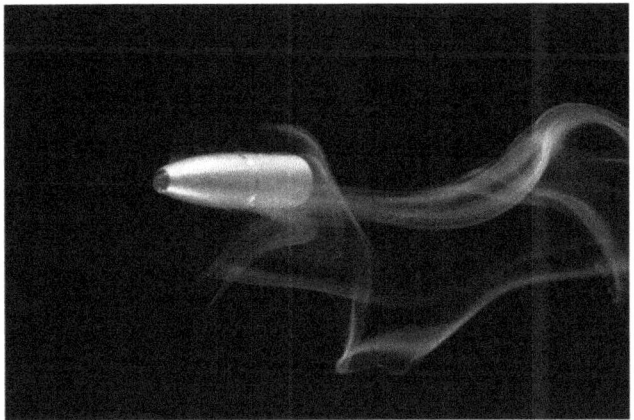

I don't often wade into controversy. Then came the events in Sandy Hook, followed by other school shootings such as Parkland, and Virginia Tech. The most mind-numbing thing to me was that it changed nothing. The gun lobby has so much sway and power over the government, that even those who champion change are handcuffed. Once the screams and protests fade, so does the outrage. And we spin our wheels and watch, again, until the next one.

Smoking Bullets

Bradley Stewart loved Jesus. He loved it when Jesus began speaking to him again.

Brad was a good kid before his dad came back from the army. Things were never right after that. Sam Stewart started drinking and took to abusing Brad's mom. Then he started on Bradley. One day Chief Warren came to the door. Bradley never saw his dad again.

Soon Brad began to act out. He hurt some animals, stole stuff, and hit his mom. Nobody wanted to be too hard on him, but after he said voices told him to do bad things, appointments were made.

A special doctor up in Lincoln told him how those voices weren't real. Used words like chemical imbalance and paranoia. He explained how his dad's behaviour had triggered something in him and awakened these conditions. But there was still hope. Brad went onto meds.

Life got better. He graduated from high school, landed a job at the fertilizer factory and things were calmer at home. The voices didn't speak any more. Brad hoped to find a girlfriend, start a family. Still, he knew he was different.

Then he forgot his pills for a few days. That's when the voice he loved spoke to him again. He didn't go back onto his tablets. After that, things got clear. Jesus told him who was bad. Showed him who needed saving. How to save himself. So when he walked through the open playground door of Madeleine Albright Elementary School, he was on a mission from God, one of salvation.

Bradley scanned the classroom. Saw the danger. No time left. He raised the gun. Save as many as he could. Then he heard screams. Others were coming. He prayed for those he had to abandon. Bradley Stewart then took himself into deliverance.

Mitch Church stood outside Madeleine Albright, ready to dissect the echoes of Bradley Stewart's shattered psyche. The Omaha Detective stomped out his cigarette and glowered at the throng snapping pictures from behind the yellow tape. He turned to Hank Warren, Chief of Police in Elk City. "Christ, where do they come from? I bet half the parents don't know yet."

Warren guided him past the main office into a primary class. His stomach turned over as he looked at the small, innocent frames, lying on the carpet.

At the modern, single story police station, just off Main Street, Church watched blank faces as they shuffled around trying to feel useful. Warren closed his office door and gestured toward the street. "I've gotta tell them something," He poured coffee. "It's a small town, I owe them that."

"Call a press conference once all the parents are notified." Church absently looked at the wall plaques of former Elk City Police Chiefs. "So, let's start with the boy."

"Local kid with a history of mental issues. Lives with his mother. She works at the diner. On her way now. Nobody saw him come into the school. Gun's gone to forensics. I reckon he could have fired twenty more rounds before reloading. We're checking nearby gun shops."

Church nodded. "How many are there?" Church watched as a shaking, middle aged woman was escorted past the front desk.

"Just one in town, Baker's Hunt Shack. Record's clean as Monday's wash. Rick Baker's a stickler. He'd sure never have sold to Brad. Musta got it online. Easy enough. Three, four hundred. Cash."

A nervous looking young officer tapped at the door. "Chief Warren. Ella Stewart is here."

"Alex, there's an officer here to see you." Alex Bayless was on his way back from afternoon break at Elk City Fertilizer. His mind went into overdrive. *Dylan, Madison? Had something happened at school? God, maybe Jenn had an accident.* He edged into the office.

Alex had attended Madeleine Albright and met his wife Jenn, in high school. They were married a few years later. Dylan, their first, would be ten at Christmas, and Madison, eight next month.

Alex's two passions were his family and hunting. As a kid, his dad would take him up to Wisconsin to bag some deer. A few of the guys still went hunting each fall. They were decent guys and aside from Sam Stewart, there hadn't been a violent act in town as long as Alex could remember. He had two guns, both locked safely away from the kids.

Many nights at the Legion, conversation turned to how they had to fight gun regulations, or soon they'd be defending themselves with slingshots and hunting with rocks. Alex had gone to one NRA meeting near Louisville, but Jenn snuffed out any notion he had of joining.

The officer's words floated about him like dandelion fluff. *Shooting, Albright. Dylan.*

"Jenn, has anyone reached her yet?" Alex muttered to no one in particular.

From the diary of Madison Bayless:

September 3rd 2012

I can't wait til tomorow. I have Miss Clarence this year and shes the nicist in the school. Mom bot me new shoes and a yellow dres for the first day. Did I already say I cant wait?

Over the following days, Alex and Jenn lived on automatic. People came and went, dropping off condolences and offers of help. Plans were made. Questions were asked. *Why would God let this happen? How did that maniac get into the school?*

Now they had Madison to worry about. Their outgoing, upbeat daughter had barely spoken since the shooting. She hid in her room, where meals came back, untouched. Doc Taylor said to let it run its course. So they walked on glass, for fear she might go completely to bits.

Messages retrieved from Bradley Stewart's Twitter account:

@ApocalypseIsHere

Open your eyes. The Devil is everywhere. We must save ourselves before he takes us.

Posted August 28th 2012.

@ApocalypseIsHere

It's getting closer. He wants us to move. Listen to His voice.

Posted September 2nd 2012.

From the diary of Madison Bayless

September 8th 2012

Why would anyone shoot my brother and my frends. What if somone tries to kill the rest of us. Why did God do this? Im never going to see my brother again and Im never going back to school

On a bright, crisp Sunday morning, people gathered at St. Francis's to say goodbye to Dylan and five of his classmates. As Alex drifted through the rituals, he noticed the first flashes of anger when he saw his friends. He mistook it for grief.

Alex wasn't ready to return to work, but couldn't afford the time off. Jenn stayed home to be with Madison, who wouldn't be walking through the doors of Madeleine Albright for a while.

The days couldn't go fast enough. Alex had no interest in talking with his co-workers. Found no solace in their sympathetic, bumbling efforts to make conversation. All that mattered was his family. That and warding off the demons that visited nightly.

One morning, Madison padded down the stairs, dressed for school. Jenn almost cried in relief. But as Madison rallied, Alex started slipping into darkness. He spent most of his time hanging out in the barn, barely speaking to either of them. Jenn could only watch and pray.

Now guilt hijacked his thoughts. His only boy murdered by a crazy kid who'd gotten his hands on a deadly weapon, hawked by someone who only cared about making a few bucks. Alex thought about his own guns, the hunting trips. Somehow, he felt they all had a hand in this. Conflict ate at him. Alex couldn't change the past, that he knew, but he knew had to do something.

From the diary of Madison Bayliss

October 12th 2012

I went back to school. It was kind of weerd. Everyone was realy nice to me but I know its becawse of Dylan. Everyone is realy sad. Me too. I wish daddy was okay. I hardly ever see him and he doesnt play with me. Mom cries a lot when dads away. I wish we were happy again. I wish Dylan was here.

Retrieved from the laptop of Bradley Stewart by Omaha Police Department:

From: angelofgod@hotmail.com

To: therighthandofgod@gmail.com

Matthew 19:14 Suffer little children, and forbid them not to come unto me: for of such is the kingdom of heaven.

Twitter feed from Bradley Stewart Sept 6th:

@ApocalypseIsHere

There is no more time. Tomorrow the Angel of God will suffer the children to come unto him. Wait for his messenger and be glad for they will have come home. He gives thanks to his faithful servant.

Further investigation found no owner for angelofgod.

A couple of weeks later there was a community barbecue. Kind of a memorial to the children, a message of hope. As they drove up to the park, Alex saw his buddies around the barbecue pit. Next thing he knew, firm hands pumped his, another passed him a beer. Voices said how good it was to see him again. Vague invitations were offered.

The afternoon drew on and the drink flowed. The caution that had started the affair was abandoned. Alex fell into the old rhythm of hanging with the boys. But when Tom started to talk politics, things went south. His tongue unleashed from its cage by a mixture of beer and bourbon, Tom started talking about how the Democrats were ruining America. The rant began with Obamacare, then welfare. When it turned to gun control, the damage was done. Tom's wife tried to stifle him, but he kept on, oblivious to the looks of even his closest friends.

At home, Alex didn't remember much, but his bloodied knuckles told the tale. "For Christ's sake, we've been hanging out since we were kids. Some friends, they're a bunch of assholes." Jenn put cream on his scraped fingers and led him upstairs to sleep it off.

From the diary of Madison Bayless:

October 12th 2012

I hate this. Dad got into a fight with Melissas dad today. They hit each other and yelled bad things. Our moms took us all home. Its like everyones gone crazy. I keep praying to Jesus that things can be the way they were. I don't want to go to school tomorrow.

Alex dreamed he was in a jungle. From a green jeep three hooded figures fired into the trees. Alex walked into the swaying bushes. There, in a clearing, was a mound of crimson, mangled animal corpses. To one side, a gigantic bear carcass was split wide. The fetid odour stung his eyes and nose. Inside the decaying pulp, he made out the terrified faces of his family. Pleading hands reached out. Someone handed him a gun, "They're still alive Alex, finish them off."

Dark visions met him each night. Alex pumped himself full of coffee. Exercised late. Anything to avoid sleep. He couldn't concentrate at work. The slightest provocation flew him into a rage. He hated this town and everyone in it.

Jenn finally convinced Alex to see Doctor Henley. "Doc, I'm losing it; I've been ignoring my family when they need me the most. I'm terrified to fall asleep. I can't stand to be around my old friends. I know it's wrong, but I blame them for what happened. And myself. Why didn't we see it? They were my buddies, now I want them to feel my pain."

Doctor Henley edged his chair closer, "Alex, depression is natural, but you're beyond that. You need help now. You're going to see a specialist in Omaha, tomorrow if I can arrange it."

A tipping point is that moment which moves you one way or another. Alex's tipping point proudly covered the front window of Baker's Hunt Shack. NRA president Wayne LaPierre stood resolutely in front of an emblem of the American Eagle. Underneath him, the words: *There has never been a more important time to join.* A smaller notice implored: *Stand up for your rights. Concerned citizens of Elk City. November 20th, 7 pm. at the Community Centre.*

That night he fell into a deep sleep. He dreamed Dylan was crying out from upstairs. Alex sat on the porch listening. The voice pleaded. A scream and blast followed. Alex sat there, running his finger over the rim of his beer bottle.

The next day, he'd shaken off the disturbing images and drove home feeling good about his appointment. Dr. Hoffman assured him people come back from breakdowns and take control again. But serious decisions needed to be made. His lifestyle and heart were playing tug of war. He told Alex to come up with a plan. Something he could change right away.

As Alex pulled onto Highway 91, he came face to face with the ghost from Baker's store window, this time billboard size. *Time to make some decisions,* he heard Dr. Hoffman saying.

When Jenn came home, he told her about his session, said he was going for a walk. Think a bit, make a plan. Jenn allowed herself a flicker of hope.

A light frost coated the lawn, as Alex walked to the barn in the half light. He came out carrying the slate-coloured case he'd always carefully hidden. Then he turned onto Cedar Street and headed for the Community Centre.

The phone rang at 12:30 in the morning. Detective Mitchell Church crept into the hall to avoid waking his wife. Fifteen minutes later, he turned the ignition key. A light dusting of snow grains peppered his windshield as he pulled onto the Interstate, towards Elk City.

THE WRONG SIDE OF THE TRACKS

The next few stories deal with one of my favourite topics, the afterlife, or maybe more precisely, what happens when we pass through this bit of existence. Many religions have their own ideas about what happens when we die, and they pass this on as Gospel Truth, if you'll excuse the blatant pun. The fact is, unless you have died, spent a few months there filming some videos for YouTube, maybe taking a few notes and hanging with the locals, nobody really knows. That leaves the possibilities wide open. So for fun, let's look at a few of them.

The Wrong Side of the Tracks

You ever have that feeling like something big is gonna happen? Well, I had it for the last couple of days. Some pretty bizarre stuff has been going on.

Anyway, first things first. I guess it was Wednesday it all started to get weird. I come out of the liquor store with a couple of bottles and I notice these two old ladies gawking at me all kind of sad. Like they found out I had something fatal that I didn't know about. So they look at me, then at the bag I'm carrying. Then they whisper some stuff I can't hear, but I know they're talkin' about me. I figure it out that they don't approve of alcohol. They look at me real upset again, shake their heads and cross the street and then they're gone. I think to myself, *You could use a couple yourselves.* That's the first one.

Number two comes the next day. I'm coming home after work. Decide I'll pick up a lottery ticket at the corner shop. As I'm leaving, I see near the counter, they've got this newspaper stand set up and I think, *oh that's new.* Then I take a better look and I see it's all full of those religious magazines, you know like *Awake* and the *Watchtower*. All those, Jesus is coming, better put the kettle on, kind of things. I reckon maybe the owner suddenly got religious. That's okay by me, it's his choice.

Now this morning I go in to get a coffee and the stand is still there, only now there's a big sign above it in red day glow, says, "Last Chance, Jesus Is Coming." I dunno but I'm thinking maybe it's time to move.

So Sam comes over about 7 o'clock that evening. Figured we'd just hang and watch some TV until we find something better to do. You see both of our girlfriends dumped us in the same week. Long story. Of course, now I suppose it doesn't matter much anyhow. Well we're kinda half watching what's on and half moaning to each other about what bitches our exes are, when the program suddenly gets interrupted. This news guy looks all serious and worried and says there've been reports of unidentified lights and objects in the sky all over the world, and that NASA is checking it out right now and there'll be more details later. Well Sam and me look at each other and say "cool", almost at the same time. I flip on the radio to see what's going on there. Well, I can't believe what I'm hearing. Instead of their usual, there's all these religious songs playing. Feels like it's Christmas morning or something.

Well, it doesn't take long before all Hell breaks loose outside. There's sirens wailing and horns honking. The news is showing all these scenes of people out in the streets, looking at the sky and then screaming and running. It's nuts. Just like one of those alien invader movies.

So, naturally I go to the window to check it out. "Holy shit," I say to Sam. "Get over here quick, you gotta see this."

Well, Sam gets up and comes over beside me. His jaw looks like it's gonna land on his chest. He says, "Son of a bitch, those Holy rolling bastards were right."

Right there coming out of the sky, right over Main Street there's this train. It's movin' real slow and you can hear people singing all happy like. They're singing "Glory, Glory Hallelujah." I recognize it from the old Elvis record my parents had. And there on the sign at the front of the train, in big letters it says, "This Train's Bound for Glory". And right behind it, there's another. This one's got a band playing and people all shouting, "Praise the Lord" and "Amen" and all that other religious stuff I heard in church when I was a kid. Then the trains land right beside the First Baptist Church and a bunch of people get in. Now there's tons of others pushing and shoving, trying to get on I guess. But when they get near the doors, these big dudes push them away. The doors slam shut and then they take off again. We both say almost at the same time, "Son of a bitch, the Bible thumpers were right."

A moment later the phone rings. I pick up and it's Mike and he's asking if we want to do something. I say, "Dude, what are you talking about, don't you know what's going on?" He says no, he just woke up. So quick as I can, I fill him in. He tells me to wait while he looks outside. When he gets back, he's real quiet for a minute and then he hollers, "Jesus Christ!"

I find that kinda fitting considering what's just happened, so I say, "Yeah, maybe he's the conductor." One thing I know for sure is we ain't invited, so we might as well make the best of it. God knows, my folks have been warning me all my life.

He doesn't laugh, in fact he doesn't say anything for a long time, but then finally he sighs and says, "Well, I guess we're not going anywhere. So, poker at my place in an hour?"

THE WRONG SIDE OF THE TRACKS

I take some time to consider the offer, "Sounds good, we'll make a beer run."

TWEETING THE END OF THE WORLD

Perhaps the ending of civilization may become a social media event.

Tweeting the End of the World

"The Internet is just the world passing around notes in a classroom." Jon Stewart

Social media was sleeping, wrapped in a tidy, sallow container on the Ikea desk by the window. Disinterested, it had no preference who operated it, and took no responsibility for the deeds of those who acted on its messages. Yet its words held the power to make or destroy lives, corporations or even nations. Never in the history of humankind did something so seemingly benign have so much potential.

The mirror which split fantasm from reality shattered. Emily sat shaking. The dream again. Three nights in a row. Her consciousness tried to clutch at the threads that fled from her by the moment. Like other nights, she was left alone in the dark, holding on to only a sense of loss and urgency.

The one thing she knew was that in that other world, life had ended. Something catastrophic had happened, but now, sitting on the other side of the glass, she was still here, alive and aware. As she probed her memory for flashes of recall, she realized the details weren't important. She had gone through the end of times and come out the other side.

Too troubled to sleep, she turned on the light and ambled to the kitchen. A small point of light from the study begged her to detour. She logged on, brought up her Twitter account and tapped in the line, "Had the same dream three nights in a row now. Something awful is about to happen." There was nothing to add. As if this small act had unloaded a burden, Emily closed her eyes and fell into a deep, dreamless slumber.

The sun coaxed her awake. Her neck was stiff, and her mouth felt like the bottom of a bird cage. She pulled herself up, slipped into the bathroom and checked the mirror. The woman looking back said, "You're too old for this foolishness, they're just dreams."

Still, she was compelled to check her messages before the rest of the day could be turned loose. Just two. Emily scanned them. "Yeah, like I care what you had for breakfast. Hello, what's this? Yikes! You too?"

She read it aloud. "Three dreams like that the past month. Scary. So real." Emily shifted to her Facebook account and posted, "Having apocalyptic nightmares. Really creeping me out. Any thoughts?"

Emily realized she wasn't feeling well. She dialed up work and messaged that she had the flu and wouldn't be in. *Just need some time to pull myself together. Jeez, I hate this. Afraid to sleep. Useless during the day. Maybe I need to see somebody, some kind of dreamologist.*

She cobbled together some breakfast, fed the cat and forced herself to walk to the corner shop. When she got back, the computer was silently screaming for attention. Facebook had a dozen messages. Nearly all of them told of similar dreams. Some in detail. No suggestions. She switched off and sprawled out on the couch.

In her dream she was hunkered down in some dingy basement. It was pitch dark and she smelled and felt the fear around her. Anticipation filled the blackness. Someone started a countdown. Five, four, three, two.... Following the count of one, their bunker shattered. The last thing she remembered was blinding light and the sickening sound of destruction and death. Then emptiness.

She nursed a cup of black coffee while her mind ran marathons. What was going on? These were no ordinary night terrors. This was a premonition. Was she responsible for warning the world, alerting them that everything may be on the verge of collapse? Sober thoughts intervened. *Don't be ridiculous. It's stress, too many deadlines at work. Deadlines. Maybe a shrink would see something in that. What if it's more?*

Emily's head was pounding. These damn headaches. Well no wonder, she wasn't sleeping, forgetting to eat most of the time. She needed to see someone, before she went completely off the rails. She glanced over at the screen. Nothing new, thank God.

It's estimated that there are over 3 billion email accounts world-wide.
Include the over 1.2 billion on Twitter and Facebook and you have a

web of information blanketing humanity. People spend hours each day sending and receiving messages. Some of these are part of their livelihood, others, simple correspondence. Then there is the gossip, the insults, the haters, speculation, and idle banter. The latter group have the farthest reach and the potential to change lives.

The screen went dark. Emily pondered the number of people who had commented on her dream, the number of people with similar experiences. Not given to superstition and hysteria, she had to concede something was demanding she take notice. Danger was out there and it was waving a red flag. She took a couple of tablets to ease the banging in her head, and called her doctor.

A cancellation had her into the office that afternoon. After some consultation her doctor had cautioned her to have some time off, take the meds he gave her and above all, leave the computer off for a couple of weeks. He would make an appointment for a scan, just to be on the safe side. The throbbing convinced her to follow his advice.

Meanwhile, without any assistance from Emily, doomsday messages started to ricochet through electronic space. Survivalists and doomsayers took up the cause. Aided by some dodgy interpretations of the scriptures, a theology professor from Oral Roberts University conjured up a date. Whatever this cataclysmic event was to be, it would occur during the summer, July 17th at 3:00 pm EST, to be precise. Some trips down Google alley highlighted similar predictions for that day.

In an isolated region of New Mexico, a bizarre sect called The New Apostles of The Chosen Light adopted this as their personal second coming and through the Net urged the world to get themselves saved before the inevitable conflagration. Other groups, each more loopy than the last, endorsed and propagated the claims.

The media carnival followed. Recognizing a great hook when they saw it, Fox News aired a short documentary about the prophecy and its faithful. Through unsettling, but wildly inaccurate Wikipedia searches, more data was fabricated to validate the claims.

The naïve, gullible public became kindle for the fires of hysteria. As the heralded date approached, usually sensible individuals began to stock and hoard supplies. Another spin-off group of the Apostles, called the Disciples of Joyous Armageddon climbed to the top of Paradise Butte in Arizona, where they intended to greet the end of the world with the appropriate rapture.

On July 17th, over half of the workforce in North America remained home, or gathered in church. To the delight of news networks all over the globe, this provided a full day's coverage. Life insurance commercials littered the programming, most people not catching the irony. Those who declared the whole affair to be a load of rubbish, found themselves scanning the sky at the appointed hour.

Emily Harris had kept her promise to the doctor and avoided all news and Internet contact for two weeks. Withdrawing to her parents' seaside cottage in Cape Anne, Massachusetts, her headaches persisted, but she slept dream free. Emily's personal world ended on July 16th, when she passed away peacefully in her sleep, from an undiagnosed brain aneurysm.

The next evening, the survivalists climbed out of their bunkers. The Disciples and Apostles acknowledged they may have miscalculated, and retired to study the gospel and rework their computations. CNN scooped a story about a philandering senator. By 5 o'clock, the end of the world was old news.

RE-INTARNATION

What if we could choose the next step in our journey. Our hero in this story finds out that it's not a choice to be made in haste.

Re-intarnation

It was a Friday night in the Bardo. Yeah we have days of the week. How else are we going to keep track of things, and fill in our logs and such? A few of us guides were hanging around waiting for the next arrival. It usually doesn't take too long. I mean at the rate of 107 per minute, (those are the stats), there's a lot of traffic. But we do sometimes have some down time. Some people don't need a whole lot of direction, they kind of have it all sussed out before they get here. Others, my gosh, don't believe people get suddenly enlightened when they die. A lot get stupider.

Think about it, in our line of work there's a lot to explain. Just imagine all the crazy ideas people have about death, or after death. They come in here with the oddest notions. Endless paradise, virgins all around for martyrs. People believe all manner of things and when they get in here, they're actually waiting for it to happen. The first thing we need to do is straighten them out, bring them back down to Earth, metaphorically speaking. Get all those ideas out of their head, so they can start to figure out where to go from here.

I was just hanging around catching up on the log books, when the arrival chute opens and out pours the white light. That's one indulgence we make for people. They've heard about white light all their lives so this kind of makes them feel at ease. It's the least we can do, after all, they've just died for crying out loud. Well, this middle aged guy appears and has the usual mix of reactions. First he has to realize he's dead. Then he's got to figure out where he is. That can be the scariest bit. It's a lot for a guy who's just had his brains knocked in by a street car. That incidentally is what had happened to this poor sucker.

I come up to him slowly. The guy is freaked out enough already. He's looking down at his body and it's not a pretty sight. I try to cheer him up. "Don't worry about that, we'll get you a new one soon enough."

After all this time it still makes me smile when they use *the* line. "Am I in heaven? Hell?"

I give him the standard answer. "There's no such thing. You're in the waiting area."

"Purgatory?" he kind of lets the word drop off his tongue, like a bad peanut.

"We don't use that word around here. Has such a negative connotation. All that burning and cleansing. What's that all about? Ever heard of the Bardo?" I say it slowly, like you would to a child.

"Of course I have," he sounds a bit indignant. "So the Buddhists were right?"

"Not necessarily, but if you want we can go with it. Best not to get hung up on semantics." It's so hard to explain this stuff to someone off the street. Now, he's looking the place up and down. Like he's checking to see if it measures up to his expectations. Then he asks me what happens next.

I love the face they make when I say, "What would you like?"

He doesn't disappoint. "You mean I have a choice.?"

"Of course. You had choices to make all your life. Why should it be any different here?" At this point he's looking kind of hopeful, kind of confused. Like a dog looks when you start packing a suitcase.

"What kind of choices do I have?" This isn't easy stuff to grasp after all, so I throw him a bone or two.

"Listen, let's back up a bit. Might make things easier. Do you know who you are? Do you remember your life?" Some do you know, although it's happier for everyone if they don't. He tries to shake his head. Not easy in his condition. So I give him a quick rundown. "Your name was Matthew Pearce. You had a successful real estate business in Montreal. Nice wife, good marriage, nothing passionate, but solid. Couple of good kids, almost grown up now. You were only forty-five. Then you decided to leap in front of a bus while you were texting. Dumb way to go, but pretty common these days." It's clear he doesn't remember, but he nods as best he can.

"Yikes, that's embarrassing. Always was afraid I'd end up in a nursing home, kids not even bothering to see me. Drooling into my oatmeal. So what's this about choices?"

"Okay kid," I start in. "First of all, this isn't a restaurant. I'm not handing out any menus here. But let's start with all the things you already know."

"You mean about the afterlife?"

Oh boy, he used the "A" word. "Here's another thing. There's no such thing. You were there and now you're here, but you're still alive. Ergo, no afterlife. Just life, only different." Now I see a bit of a light go on, so I continue. "It's kind of like getting re-married, or starting a new career. Now tell me what you think you know about your so-called afterlife."

"I never bought that silly Heaven idea, sitting around playing harps and eating grapes all day." I tell him that's a good start. "Then there's Hell. Don't like that notion a bit. Never made sense, some dude with a pointy tail torturing a bunch of losers for all eternity. Reincarnation isn't such a bad idea, but I always kind of liked my life. What if I end up as a jerk in the next one? Besides, I heard them talk about millions of lives. Wouldn't you just get sick and tired?"

At this point I can't resist. "Or there's complete annihilation." That always gets a good response. I give him a wink. "Anyway look, I've got another arrival in ten minutes, what's it gonna be?"

"Do I get some kind of choice if I go for another round?" He's looking really hopeful.

"I told you, choice is the name of the game." I lead him over to the closet. I love their faces when they see the outfits.

"You kidding me," his eyes are as big as manholes. "A costume?"

"Take a closer look. It's a model, prototype if you wish. Shows you what you'll be like at thirty, you'll fill in the rest as you go along." Then he sees the paper attached to each one. Before he can ask, I tell him. "It's a list of must happens."

"Must...?

"Yeah, you people who believe in free will are sort of right, but those pre-destination ones aren't so far off. You get to make all those choices you love so dearly, but some things are gonna happen no matter what. This one," I point out a pretty well shaped blond. "She'll marry a lawyer. Have two kids and save someone from drowning when she's seventeen. The rest, well there's your choices you talked about. This guy here", South Asian, nice complexion. "Married when he's nineteen, works in a bank for thirty- nine years. Oh, maybe not for you, says here he has seven root canals when he's in his fifties."

"That's it? Just a couple of little conditions and the rest is wide open."

"Not so little. You heard of the butterfly effect. Think of it as quality control." "How long do I have to pick?" Now he's rifling the rack like he's at a sale at Macy's.

"Forty nine days is the max, but you don't want to stick around that long. This isn't Club Med you know. Besides some folks are in and out of here like a change room at the Gap. Then just when you think you've found the perfect fit, bam, some barber in the Bronx has a heart attack, comes in here, sees he has the chance to be a movie star, and you're back to the rack."

Well, he's standing there all confused and hesitant. Like Baskin Robbins, too many options. He then gets some kind of brain storm and he asks if he has to decide. He says something about taking potluck. Says it would be better not to know ahead of time. Just go into it. After all, he says, he won't remember anyway. I'm nodding my head when he says, "What's this door here? It's got no label. A mystery door? Think this is for me."

Well, he's half way through before I can get the words out. "That's not for you I say, that's the replay option, it's only for...." Too late, he's gone.

Matthew Pearce had a pretty good life. He became a successful real estate agent, had a stable, if not passionate marriage, and a couple of kids. He was walking to lunch, thinking about how decent his life was and how the future looked pretty bright. Distracted by his thoughts, and texting his next client about a meeting, he stepped off the curb without looking; right into the front end of a tram bus going full tilt. He never felt a thing.

When he woke up a familiar face was smiling down at him. "Welcome back, I've been expecting you."

HOUSE OF CARDS

What would it be like if some of the greatest minds the world has ever known could get together for a while. What would they talk about? Maybe they'd just hang together, have a beer and shoot the breeze? How about a good game of poker? That's the one. I'll let them take it from here.

House of Cards

"You create your own universe as you go along." ~Winston Leonard Spencer Churchill

The time and place are the after world. Jesus, Buddha, and Albert Einstein are enjoying a friendly game of poker.

"I fold." The Buddha placed his cards on the table. Two pairs, Kings and 10's.

"Read it and weep, Buddha boy," Jesus laid his hand down, with a compassionate smile. "Full house. Seems like this is my night."

"Don't be so sure of yourself." Albert Einstein had been lost in thought, but then stared across the table. "I've run the odds and your luck, my dear Messiah is just about spent."

"No matter," Jesus started shuffling. "We do have all the time in the world."

Jean Paul Sartre entered the room and flopped down next to Einstein. "Remember, only the one who isn't dealing, has time."

And so, these great souls spent their Friday nights sitting around this table, playing some cards, trading their most famous quotes, and debating the possibilities of creation. They also waited to see if God would emerge from his office, perhaps sit with the group, and validate their theories. Some of the players had been waiting over 2000 years.

Whatever you may have thought about the afterlife, Heaven or whatever you want to call what happens after you carelessly step in front of a tram, or forget to take your meds; time moves on. Keeping time is a man-made invention, but eternity is a long stretch. If folks are going to keep their appointments and be punctual, they need to have some system of tracking the hours. Mind you, since folks have all of infinity, they aren't hung up about it.

"You know, we've been waiting since we got here, and not a word from the boss." Albert dealt the cards. "I mean, look at you dear Messiah, two thousand years and not so much as a how do you do from Dad. And that *Be Back Later* sign on the door; wearing a little thin don't you think?"

"Everything in time," Jesus said, "Consider the lilies and all that, you know the world wasn't created in a day." He winked and picked up three cards.

"There's no one there and there never was," Sartre mumbled into his hand.

"You don't think, therefore he isn't?" Buddha placed two cards down. "I'll take two."

"Well, there are two possibilities. He's either there or he isn't. As long as that door stays closed, it's both." Nobody had noticed Erwin Schrodinger pull up his chair.

For those unfamiliar, Irwin Schrodinger is one of the fathers of quantum theory, famous for his hypothetical experiment called Schrodinger's cat, which involves a make-believe feline that is either dead or it isn't or both.

Schrodinger motioned for some cards, "And if he isn't there, then logically, we can't be here."

"He's there," said Jesus.

"You've been giving us this God tale forever. All I've seen is a closed door and bad cards. Both proof there is no God. I'm out," Sartre dropped his hand.

"But how do you explain all the new folk that keep coming from each day? You know I'm a bit peckish." A plate of sandwiches arrived in front of Einstein.

Although people may not need to eat in the afterlife, it was an enjoyable experience on Earth. So why give it up just because you've slipped across some kind of chasm in the cosmos? Food works a bit like the simulators in Star Trek. Possibly the basis for Jesus' famous quote. "Ask and ye shall receive."

"That's because the universe has always been there. Those people aren't new, they're just getting recycled." Buddha looked up, "You forgot the veggie."

"If it's always been here, then what's the old guy doing with his time?" Schrodinger's hand hovered over the plate. "So many possibilities."

Einstein took a bite, "When we got here, we were all so cock sure of ourselves, preaching this, theorizing that, and now nothing fits. Last draw."

"Fold," Jesus put his cards down. "You have to have faith. Remember the mustard seed, Field of Dreams. It's a test, Pop's big on tests. I, of all people, should know that."

"Well, I'm no longer in the mood." Einstein ferreted around the plate. "Any mustard?"

Wheezing, Abdus Sallam plunked himself at the table and produced a sheet of white parchment. "We're in big trouble. The boys in physics have finally done it."

"Now what?" JPS found these know-it-all physicists exasperating.

"The Grand Unification Theory. Decades of searching and theorizing. Look at this." Sallam looked pale as he handed the parchment to Einstein. "According to all this, the universe as we know it, cannot possibly exist. Look at the evidence Albert."

To put it simply, the Grand Unification Theory or GUT, is an attempt to take all the theories of creation and existence and wrap them into a neat little package which explains the meaning of everything. Down on Earth it hasn't panned out too well, either in theory or in reality.

"Good God man!" Einstein leapt off the chair and began to pace the room. "This is irrefutable; existence just doesn't work."

"Hold on everyone, I mean we know the world out there exists; we've all been there." But even Jesus looked a little rattled.

"That was before, this changes everything." Einstein circled the table for the third time. "It's all retroactive. Show them Abdus."

Abdus swept up the cards. With a series of nifty maneuvers and parlour tricks, he shuffled them around, erecting structures and taking them apart again. He employed Aces, Kings and Queens to explain string theory, Jacks and tens to describe the Higgs particle. Lower cards were relativity. After a half hour the cards were in complete disarray. "You see, none of the pieces fit, creation can never have happened."

"Look, let's not get crazy, we'll hand the paper to the boss and see what he says." Buddha grabbed the parchment from Einstein and slipped it under the door.

"Good luck with that," Sartre said in frustration.

Moments later a booming voice behind the door uttered a single word, "Oops!"

The same night near Ahnapee, Wisconsin

Lars Anderson was just drifting off, when he heard the racket outside. Nights at the Anderson cattle farm were usually pretty quiet. When the din failed to subside, his groggy mind conjured up all manner of terrible scenarios. A massive crash catapulted him out of bed. As he sprinted down the stairs, he determined the clamber and clatter was coming right from his barns. He inched the door open, and feeling a little more daring, stepped onto the porch. Everything seemed to be intact. He looked upward, scanning for lightning. There, in the darkness, stars were blinking in and out. Great jagged seams split the Heaven's, out to the horizon. Like a house of cards, the sky was starting to collapse.

WAITING FOR A CALL

I often think of my characters as being real, living people. It almost feels like they are taking on their own identity and are creating their story. But what happens, if for some reason they don't get any more input from their writer? What if their creator aborts the story for any number of reasons? Is there a kind of purgatory where they hang out, waiting for someone to rekindle their character?

Waiting for a Call

Private Investigator Guy Crane had stumbled onto a dozen scenes like this since leaving the department to go solo, five years ago. This was likely a money drop gone wrong. The delivery boy lay face down, oozing scarlet onto the pavement. Fresh, still warm enough that wisps of steam rose into the icy, January night. The killer couldn't have gone far. He scanned the length of the small laneway, which at this point ran between Roxanne's Bar and Grill, and Chang's Chinese Grocery. The air reeked of rancid cooking oil and rotting cabbage. But something else smelled real bad to Crane. Although this wasn't his case, he'd been trailing the same guy he figured had wasted this poor sap. Now, like it or not, he was in knee deep.

Crane reached into the man's coat pocket. Nothing but a deck of Luckies and a beat up silver lighter. Maybe an engraving? He looked it over. Nothing. "Yeah, losers like you don't have no one cares about you enough to even give you a lighter, much less have it cut. Let's see if your wallet is still there. Bingo." Out of John Doe's back pocket stuck a worn, black, leather pocket book. He opened it up, found eight one-dollar bills, and a business card for Roxanne's, with the word "Molly" written in crimson lipstick. "Okay Molly, now what do you know about this?" He pocketed the card just as the squad car pulled up.

"Well, Guy Crane, why ain't I surprised to see you around here? You musta been a bloodhound in another life." Officer Paddy O'Sullivan of 63rd precinct in Brooklyn, walked up to the crime scene, pawed his feet on the wet gravel and unceremoniously rolled the body over with his left boot.

"I'm on another case, which I'm not at liberty to disclose to anyone, especially you. All I can tell you is I was taking the shortcut through the alley when I came across this."

"Isn't that a funny coincidence? You didn't hear any gun shot?" O'Sullivan was studying the still spreading pool of blood.

"I think if the genius detective from the 63rd was to look a little closer, he might see this poor stiff was stabbed, not shot."

Ignoring the knock, the tall Irishman stood up straight and pointed a bony finger in the P.I.'s face. "Listen Guy, I know we've had our differences, but if you have any wire on this guy, I need to know it now. There's some dirty stuff going on round here, and it's only gonna get worse if I can't stop it. I got no leads and nothing to go on."

"Sure Pat. Here, for old time's sake." He handed the cop the old wallet, still containing the eight sweaty bills. "That's all there was. Oh, and this." As he walked away, he turned and tossed the package of Lucky Strike cigarettes to O'Sullivan. "If I find out anything more, I'll call."

Crane walked up the laneway and turned into the space between two buildings, on to Flatbush Avenue. Taking a quick look to see he wasn't being tailed, he headed to Roxanne's. He slid the business card from his pocket and scanned it. "Well, let's see if we can find Molly."

The scowling bouncer looked a bit like the end of a freight train. When he saw Guy, he gave him a nod, and what might pass to some as a smile.

"Evening Big Frank, looking good tonight. Hey, listen buddy, you know anyone called Molly, comes in here?"

"Check the back room, you know the 'back room' I mean." Frank turned away to frisk a guy who looked like he might be carrying heat.

So John Doe had dropped in to have a bit of pleasure before doing business. Maybe he ticked off one of Molly's friends.

Guy Crane took one last look at the street and walked into the blend of cigarette smoke, soft jazz and conversation. As he continued in, the scene faded until it was no longer the Roxanne's he knew. He was stunned to find himself in what looked like a train station. What shocked him more, was the sight of Detective Paddy O'Sullivan sitting in a black wooden chair, reading the New York Times.

Jackey

Jackey Price tried to make sense of things. A moment ago he was standing at the door to his girlfriend's apartment. She'd opened the door, but this sure wasn't her place. Marble floors and high arches made him feel very small. A few people shuffled about to the concession stand, or the large wicket in the centre of the massive room. Some sat in chairs reading papers. A few played with phones, while new arrivals stood in stunned silence.

Questions ricocheted across his mind. Where the hell was he? How'd he get here? What happened to Wanda's apartment? He needed to think back. He knew he'd been bleeding. His leg burned. How? Oh shit, he'd been shot. Still frames started to unravel. A cash loan store and his friend Jamar. Oh god, they'd tried to rob the Cash 'n Go on Grand River. It'd all gone south. Stupid cashier had decided to play fucking hero and hauled out a gun. They'd run for it, but one bullet had Jackey's name. Funny, he didn't remember feeling a whole lot of pain when it happened. Just shock. Like he couldn't believe he'd been fucking shot. He'd lived 21 years in one of the most dangerous areas in Detroit and never once crossed paths with a gun. That couldn't be said for most of his friends.

Jonathan Woodrow Price, aka Jackey, was born and grew up in Brightmoor, one of Detroit's infamous abandoned communities. These once ordinary working class suburbs had gone bad when the economy turned. The search for jobs had led to an exodus to more favourable areas and earned the place the nickname, "Blightmoor". Then the crime had started. That was enough to convince those able to leave the decaying burg behind. But Jackey, his mother and five siblings didn't have that option, so he'd grown up with violence and crime being part of everyday life.

Still, he'd kept pretty clean. He didn't want to end up like his dad, who'd been in and out of jail up to the time he'd left altogether, when Jackey was thirteen. Being the oldest, he became a stand-in dad to his three brothers and one sister and that left little time for him to get into much trouble. After his mom's penchant for heroin had earned her a one way ticket to hell, Jackey's life was consumed with his family's survival.

Blessed with above average intelligence and filled with determination to make a better life for his siblings, Jackey had breezed through High School. He mostly ignored all the turmoil around him and stuck to studying, basketball and caring for his "kids".

He had dreamed of becoming a social worker and was looking into his community college options when "it" happened. His grandma, the closest he'd ever had to a proper mother, had fallen ill. Early onset of Alzheimer's. Widowed for many years, "Umi" was clearly unable to cope in her home and Jackey had done the only thing possible, brought her to live with them.

Things rapidly went downhill and when she started leaving cigarette butts burning in ashtrays, and burners on the stove lit, Jackey knew he couldn't risk his family's safety, and explored his options. All of them involved money he did not have.

In desperation, following b'ball at the community centre one cold February night, Jackey had met up with Jamar and told him he was ready. Jamar and he had been fast friends since grammar school. Only Jamar had gotten into some shady dealings. Two bit stuff like petty theft and running errands for one of the many crack houses in the neighbourhood. Jackey didn't approve and had kept his distance from it all, but a friend was a friend and he'd stuck by Jamar. Jamar respected his old buddy too much to pressure him to join in, but it was understood there was always a standing invitation if need be. Well, tonight, the need was never greater.

Jamar told Jackey about the cash store scheme. Said it was a done deal. Another guy named Kenroy would be waiting in the car. It'd all be over in ten minutes.

Now, as Jackey looked at the red patch on his jeans, it all came back. Except, this isn't where it ended. He was supposed to be in Wanda's apartment, getting cleaned and patched up until they could figure out the next move. She should be giving him royal shit for getting involved in such a stupid scheme.

Instead, here he was, in this kind of waiting room, with all manner of strange people around. They were all dressed differently, like some giant Hallowe'en party. He was checking out the scene when a voice from the loudspeaker called out. "Mr. Price? Is there a mister Price here?"

Rebecca

Rebecca awoke in a cold sweat. As her dream world relinquished its grasp, she did as she had for the past two weeks. She slipped out of bed and went downstairs. There, she put on a warm coat, and grabbed a lantern from the kitchen on her way out the door. The thick November frost was a shimmering, silver carpet under the full moon. She tread softly so as not to wake the dogs.

Ten minutes later, she stood at the door of Brentmoor Manor. The old house had been vacant these past three years, and dark tales lived in and about the walls of the ancient structure. Rebecca knew the stories of murder and an icy suicide in the cold waters of the River Avon.

Rebecca Turner-Davies, an only child, had lived all of her thirty-seven years in the same cottage. Following the tragic death of her parents in a carriage misfortune, she had stayed on in the family home. She was a strong woman, not given to the wild speculations of the locals. But she knew what she had heard, and these nightly visions strengthened her conviction that something was dreadfully wrong at Brentmoor Manor. A child was in danger. Yet the visits to the old house had yielded nothing but a severe chill and ensuing cough.

The grey brass felt cold as she turned the front door knob. As always, she felt a shiver as she stepped into the cavernous hallway. The silence clung to her. Rebecca immediately headed up the steps to the nursery.

She stopped half way up the lavish wooden staircase to consider her situation. Was she being foolish? The murder had taken place three years ago. The coroner's reports were still housed in the county records. What did she hope to accomplish by digging up the ghosts of the past. But they weren't staying in the past, were they? Every night she re-visited the ghastly event, waking to the cries of the infant, so brutally murdered by its nanny. There followed the sobs of the tormented woman, as she walked to her death in the icy waters.

The chill clung to her as she resumed her climb. Her footsteps vanished into the clammy darkness and it felt like she was part of the old house, as it dreamed. Now footsteps echoed across the wooden floor. The Nanny was going into the baby's room. Rebecca gasped as the door closed. Her feet were glued to the stair. Then came the sound she dreaded most. A child whimpered, trying to call out, only to be stifled by something covering her tiny mouth. The plaintive cry stabbed into Rebecca's soul. She covered her ears as she reached the landing.

Rebecca realized she had not lighted her lamp. The hall fell silent. She fumbled for a match and struck it against the stone wall, just as the nursery door opened. The flare illuminated something down the corridor. Something she wished she had never seen. Rebecca dashed to the nursery and shone her lamp on the room. Dear God, she had done this so many times, but prayed this time might be different. Her heart beat like horses' hooves at the gallop. Rebecca inched further into the room.

Bard-o

"Jonathan Price. Paging Jonathan Price. Would Mr. Price please come to the Central Information Booth?"

Jackey looked around to track where the voice came from. The pandemonium all around was going to make it tough to locate the booth. He tried to make his way to the centre of the huge hall, using the vast, arched ceiling as his marker.

"Steady on boy." A cultured British voice launched in his direction. Jackey looked around in time to avoid a panoply of royalty moving not three feet in front of him. White horses pranced past, hitched to a red and gold carriage, driven by a gentleman in full riding gear. Inside were the figures of a man and woman garbed in regal attire. Jackey didn't know if they were a King and Queen, but he was pretty sure they were a hell of a lot more important than he was. Instinctively, he tipped his hat in the general direction of the procession, which parted the crowd as it meandered away.

"Holy shit," he said aloud, as a couple of giraffes bent down to nibble at his hoodie.

"Mr. Price, Jonathan Price?" He stepped around what looked like Roman Gladiators. Unlike the ones he'd seen in the movies, these two seemed to be completely without purpose. They stood a few feet apart, weapons half poised, as if they didn't know what to do next. They eyed each other briefly and ambled into the pulsing throng. Nobody seemed to know where they were going. It reminded him of *The Walking Dead*.

"Paging Mr. Price. Please come to the Central Information Booth." It was now more a plea than an invitation.

"That's what I'm fucking trying to do." A few sets of eyes glared at him, making him realize he was talking out loud again. He lowered his voice. "You move through all of this shit, and try to get to somewhere, when you don't even know where somewhere is."

"Move towards the monster Mr. Price. We are right there."

"Monster? Is this some kinda joke?" Jackey looked up. "Holy shit." There, not 25 feet in front of him was this kind of King Kong ape creature. It was about 30 feet tall and steel blue, its gangly arms limp at its side. It looked as if it needed a book of instructions. If a 30 foot monkey could be called dejected, this one definitely was.

"Behind the creature, Mr. Price."

Jackey snapped out of his reverie and moved past the massive body. He smiled to think he'd only been here ten minutes and yet something as crazy as circling a giant monkey hardly phased him.

As he rounded the ape's bend, flashing orange Day-Glo letters proudly announced "Bard-O. Central Information Booth". Jackey stepped through a large revolving door. The next room was a lot more unremarkable than the one he'd just left. Six empty chairs lined one of the plain, yellow walls. At the far end was a single wicket, the kind you buy your tickets from at a baseball game. On the wall was a notice which read, "Serving #5". A small slip of paper had somehow found its way into Jackey's hand. He was not surprised it read #5.

He made his way up to the metal grill and found himself in front of a red-headed woman, with a face like an over-inflated pink beach ball. She smiled. "Mr. Price, we've been expecting you. Please go to the side door."

Jackey made his way round and walked in. A large mahogany desk displayed the sign, *Manager's Office*. A small, middle-age, balding man in a three-piece suit, stood to shake his hand. "Ah Mr. Price, so nice to finally meet you. Leo Pulsifer. Please sit down. Of course you want to know what is going on. Why are you here? What's going to happen? Well don't worry I am here to answer all your questions." Jackey's mouth opened and closed again.

"First off, you are here, because I regret to tell you your author passed away suddenly last night on page fifty-seven. A ripping good page it was too. You'd just been shot and were headed to your girlfriend's."

"My what? Who? Where?" the words came out like puffs of smoke. "What are you talking about?"

"Perhaps it might be more helpful to show you." Mr. Pulsifer pushed a manila folder across the desk. Jackey opened it. Inside was a stack of neatly hand-typed pages. "Mr. Blade went for the classics. A 1945 Underwood typewriter."

"Who the hell is...?"

"Mr. Blade. Daytona Blade. Rather pretentious pen name, if you ask me. He's the author. The author of your story." He looked at Jackey's baffled expression. "Read the manuscript, Mr. Price."

Jackey silently read, looking up once. "How the hell do you know all that stuff about me.?"

"I didn't know anything. Mr. Blade knew it. He had it in his head, wrote it down and voila, Jackey Price came into the world. Mr. Price I know it sounds fantastic, but you are the creation of an author. Your whole life has been his doing."

"Are you on crack, dude? I know my life, I'm the one who lived it, not him."

"There you are correct, Yes, you have lived that life, but it's only because he created it all."

"That's ridiculous. No, I'm just a regular guy, trying to make it in the world. This is bullshit man."

"Go back into the main hall and look around, and tell me what is bullshit, as you say. Now, more important is what to do with you. You are here because Mr. Blade created you, you might say. But Mr. Daytona Blade is no more so...?"

"Woah, I don't like where this is going. You mean I'm gonna stop existing because that asshole decided to croak in the middle of page fifty-five?"

"Fifty-seven, and no, you don't have to cease to exist. There's an alternative you may find quite... interesting." Leo Pulsifer opened the cabinet behind him and pulled out some folders.

Jackey stared as Mr. Pulsifer placed them in front of him. He wasn't sure what each contained, and was in no hurry to find out. He ran his fingers over the first folder and started twisting the corner. Leo Pulsifer watched on, his face showing amusement and empathy.

"What...?"

"Dear boy, don't look so dismayed. They will not jump up and bite you. These are manuscripts, but more important, they are opportunities. You have a choice of six possible outcomes to your, situation, and let's face it, when you left your former life, the prospects for a happy ending were grim at best. All you need to do is pick one."

A great din erupted outside the office. They both looked at the monitor in time to see a rowdy bunch of yobs in football gear entering the waiting room. Hoisting bottles of ale and smacking each other about the head, they moved their way into the crowd.

"Oh dear, I was afraid of this. Ronnie Potts is on the drink again."

Although Jackey knew better, he asked "Ronnie Potts?"

"Oh, nobody you'd know son. Ex third-rate footballer turned author. Couldn't make it in the big leagues, or the minors come to think of it. Decided he could make a living writing soap operas about the lives of footballers in the F.A. Wasn't terribly good at that either. Took to drink. His characters keep showing up at our door, every time he goes on a bender.

"All those people. Are they like me? Stuck in limbo?"

"No, no, no…. not at all. They were never developed as characters, so they don't really have a separate life. They come as part of the set. Like a colony of ants. No intelligence or persona. Something like real football hooligans, come to think of it. Still they are a problem. Didn't have a clue what they were doing in their story and still don't. You'll have to excuse me as I go and sort them, before they get into trouble. In the meantime, please read the stories, Mr. Price. They've been picked to suit your… circumstances. I'm sure you'll find at least one of them tempting."

Mr. Pulsifer bowed slightly and left the room. "All right you lot. Free beer. This way please."

Just before returning to the envelopes, Jackey noticed a rather severe looking woman of about 40, dressed in what he recognized as Victorian attire, moving aimlessly through the unruly mob. He watched with some concern, wondering what was about to happen.

Rebecca Turner-Davies was more irritated, than shocked at the turn of events. She studied the room. Never in her 37 years had she seen such an eclectic collection of people. Now, she was dismayed to find her memory fading. Just as she'd been so close to solving a mystery, she had been whisked away into this folly. What was it she had been searching for? She was dismayed to find her memories abandoning her by the moment. She repeated her name over and over, for fear of losing all sense of identity and purpose.

A hand tapped her shoulder. Who had the audacity to commit such an intimate act in public? "Miss Turner-Davies? I am so sorry for the intrusion, but it is important you come with me."

She turned to see a striking young man wearing some fashion of business attire. "Unhand me young man, or I shall call for a constable. Why should I come with you?"

"Sorry Madame, but did you have somewhere else you needed to go?"

Fear crept into Rebecca as she saw the chaos around her and realized she had no clue where she was or where she was going.

"Please come with me Miss Turner-Davies. Hale Finn at your service. I am here to help you."

When Jackey saw a handsome blond man leading the woman through the crowd, he relaxed and decided to get down to business. His unsteady hands opened the first folder. It held maybe fifty pages. "That's not much of a book." He picked up the first page and began to read.

Antwan Lewis hunkered down in the alley behind the 7-11 in Gramercy Park, California. He heard the sounds of squad cars speeding by on Arlington. "Stupid." he whispered into the air. Somehow he'd become separated from his fellow gang members and now it was just a matter of time before he got picked up by the cops, or worse, got wasted. Antwan glanced at the tattoo which proudly identified him as a member of the Rollins 100 street gang, one of the most notorious in LA.

Jackey closed the book and laughed. "For chrissakes, you gotta be kidding me. How fuckin' stereotyped can you get. Besides, the writing sucks, and I don't see no happy ending coming up here."

He heard Mr. Pullsifer's voice, but didn't see him. "Okay Mr.Price, perhaps that's not for you, but the computer picked it based on your profile. Keep reading. I'm sure you'll find something. Forgive me, as I am still tied up, but I will endeavour to be with you as soon as possible."

Jackey checked the monitor again, and saw Mr. Pulsifer leading the rowdy horde towards a large pair of French doors. Jackey made a rude gesture at the screen and pulled out the next folder. He looked at the first few lines. "Oh for fuck's sakes this has to be a joke."

Kali Akintola had been born in the village of Kumassi on what the British had named the Gold Coast of Western Africa. He had lived twenty-four dry seasons. The rumours of men arriving on the coast in tall ships had started to stir the peaceful life of his tribe. Men with white skin were only a few suns away. They were carrying terrible weapons which they had already used to subdue and kidnap the males of other villages.

Jackey shouted at the monitor. "Okay Leo, you asshole, the joke's over. Who wrote this shit, the fucking KKK?" He paused for a moment, while he considered the advisability of calling the man who currently held complete control over the rest of his life, an asshole. "Look, forget about where I came from. Find me something, anything that wasn't picked for me. I'll be a carny in a travelling fair in Nebraska if you want, but spare me from your fucking profiling."

As he was shouting into the monitor, he saw Leo Pullsifer walking with a younger blonde man. At a short distance behind was the woman he had seen a little earlier. They were coming towards the manager's office.

"Please be seated Miss Turner-Davis." Leo Pullsifer pulled out a chair, while she gave him an icy glare. As if only noticing Jackey for the first time, she fixed her eyes on him and gave him a look as if he had a hump and a horn. "Miss Turner-Davis, allow me to introduce you to Mr. Jonathan Price. Mr. Price is from America. He also happens to be in a similar circumstance to yours."

Raising herself as high as her seated position would allow, she replied, "I very much doubt that."

Jackey resisted the urge to reply with any of the caustic comments his mind was busy shouting at him. Instead he tipped his hand to his head, like he'd seen in the cowboy movies he'd loved as a child. "Ma'am."

"I'll try to make this as brief as possible. As we have explained to Mr. Price, you have been forsaken by the author who created you. Therefore, it remains our job to find a place for you to continue your life. That can only happen in another book, as another character."

She's pretty good at making that face, thought Jackey, looking at Rebecca's dour expression.

"Now before you object and say that I am mad, please recall what you have just witnessed. I am sure what I am suggesting to you is no less plausible. The fact is, this is the way things are, and we need to do something about it, and as soon as possible. Now if you will just be patient for a moment, we are waiting for the third to arrive."

Jackey and Rebecca both uttered a puzzled "Third?" in unison. Jackey smiled, while Rebecca looked as if she had just bitten into a very sour peach.

"I thought that might get your attention. There is something I have not cited thus far. You see, you were all penned by the same author." Raised eyebrows and dropped jaws were all the two could manage.

"Hard to believe, I know, but you Miss Turner-Davis, a heroine in a Victorian gothic novel and you Mr. Price, a hard luck kid in a tale, which if it had been allowed to reach its conclusion, would have eventually led to redemption; both come from the mind of a second-rate spinner of yarns from Boise, Idaho. This would-be Ernest Hemmingway has also scripted narratives involving knights in middle age France, Emperors in third century Japan, migrant workers in the Depression, an aging baseball pitcher in Omaha, who gets a second chance at a career, and a dog named Diesel. Mr. Daytona Blade, as Mr. Price is aware, passed away suddenly last night. He was a bit of a "jack of all trades, master of none, type author who hadn't found his niche, and so, moved from genre to genre. At the time of his passing, he had three novels on the go. Ms. Turner-Davis and Mr. Price, you represent two of them. This situation is so...unique, we have made it top priority.

The door burst open and a rather rumpled looking man in a brown suit strode into the room. "Where's Molly? I'm lookin' for Molly."

"Ah Mister Crane," Leo Pullsifer offered his hand, "Do come in, we've been expecting you."

The three of them eyed each other and then turned to Leo Pulsifer. Guy Crane looked at Rebecca. "Molly? Is that you?"

Jackey burst out laughing, "Dude, does she look like a Molly?"

Rebecca looked as if she couldn't decide who she should stare ice picks at first. In the end it was Leo Pulsifer. "Mr. Puliser, you are responsible for this bother. What do you propose to do about it?"

For the first time Pulsifer looked a bit ruffled. "Ms. Turner-Davis, I am neither responsible for the unfortunate demise of Mr. Daytona Blade, nor for this "bother" as you say. It is, however, my job to sort it out, and sort it out I shall."

Guy Crane had finally found some words, about three to be precise. "Would someone please...."

"Ah Mr. Crane, of course. Dreadfully sorry, you have no idea what is transpiring here do you?" The private detective swivelled his head a few degrees to either side.

"Well then, let's begin at the beginning." Over the next few minutes the Bard-O manager explained the situation with all the patience of a teacher explaining calculus to a not overly bright high school student. Jackey and Rebecca were content to inhabit the same glacier until it was over.

"Okay, I see, I guess." Crane marinated in the idea for a while and then mumbled. "So, what next?"

"There are a few options. We can bide our time until we find a story suitable for you to be inserted into. Meanwhile, you are free to remain here. I must warn you though, the longer you are without an author's input, the more you will begin to lose your integrity, your substance. You may have already noticed some of yourself, slipping away.

Alternatively, we can put you back right away into a perhaps less appropriate setting, Ms. Turner-Davis, there's an opening right now as a Nanny in Southern Georgia in the 1850's." Pulsifer winked playfully at Jackey.

Rebecca jumped when the phone rang. Leo Pulsifer picked up, said a couple of "I see's" and a "Thank you" to whoever had called and put the phone back in the old fashioned black rotary dial cradle.

"Well it seems as if fortune smiles on us today. As it happens, a rather old, discarded manuscript has turned up in a memorabilia shop in New York City. From what I see it provides the ultimate solution to this dilemma, and I think it will also ensure that your lives will continue to be filled with adventure and excitement."

"Hold on there," Jackey raised his hand for effect. "If this story's only half done, that means the characters are still hanging around in limbo. Maybe they're here in this crowd right now?"

"Very astute observation Mr. Price, but you need have no fear of that. This half completed work is over 40 years old. It's highly unlikely those involved could have retained their identities for that long. No, I think this is just "what the doctor ordered", if you'll pardon the cliché. All right, best to get started right away before someone burns the draft or uses it as a litter tray for the family cat. Here's what we need to do."

Epilogue

Eoin Garson had found the job his twelve year old self could have only dreamed about. Now thirty-two, after years of slogging in the trenches as a free-lance writer and graphic designer, one of the honchos at DC comics, who seemed to have more faith than sense, had seen a piece of Eoin's work and asked him to come out to Burbank for a job offer.

His personality and quick wit had carried him through two ensuing cross examinations and now he sat peering over downtown Burbank, sipping his coffee from a large, blue Batman mug. So far it was a big letdown. His first two weeks had seen him editing copy and doing the occasional bit of graphic artwork.

A knock at the door pulled him out of his reverie. "Mr. Garson. What are you doing right now? Well drop it, I have something for you." Hank Benson was Eoin's boss, at least in this part of the building. "Look, this old manuscript turned up in some comic shop on West Riverside. They reckon it's gotta be at least 40 years old. Author, some guy by the name of Buck Cannon, yeah I know, but this was back in the 70's. He was trying to make a name for himself by creating a new set of super heroes. Never finished it though. Turns out he was run down by a trolley in LA. Anyway, it's kinda promising. It's about three superheroes, two guys and a woman, all got special abilities and talents. Well, all the preamble is there and the background, but he never got to his first episode. Well buddy, this is where you come in. I like what I've seen of your stuff and I gotta feeling you might be the one to bring this corpse back to life. And hey, I don't need to tell you what a boost this'll be for your career if you do good. Buddy, you could be the next Stan Lee."

Eoin took the manuscript from Hank and just sat smiling, staring at the old pencilled drawings. "Yes sir, Mr. Benson, thank you sir. Thank you. I won't let you down."

He went to the coffee maker, gave Batman a refill and started going over the faded panels. An hour later something clicked in his head. He picked up an old fashioned black and white graphite pencil and started his first drawing.

Re-boot

As they approached Police Headquarters, the new recruits stood briefly to take in the massive bronze statue of the "The Flash", Central City's most famous son. The icon dominated the yellow marble courtyard. No one broke the silence which was already cementing their partnership.

A recent crime wave had given the department more than they, or even the Flash could handle.

The force could not cope with the number of felonies spreading through the underworld, and the Chief decided to bring in reinforcements, but not ordinary detectives, operatives with unique skills geared to quench this spree of corruption. These three promised to be the solution to Central City's woes.

Becky Blaze looked up and saluted her hero. She turned and said to her two partners, "Okay guys, our whole lives have been leading up to this moment. Let's go." They started up the large marble steps, towards the imposing doors.

DETOURS

I think I stirred up some ghosts on my last trip to New York City. The town exudes drama, heartbreak, laughter, redemption. You name it. You just have to stick your hook in the water, wait for the nibble and then reel it in. Had I been there a month, I suspect I could have filled this book with the stories that were floating around. I'm grateful these two story lines literally smacked me on the head. I jotted them onto my laptop, and eagerly waited to get home to fill in the details.

Detours

The Bronx

Twilight in Spanish Harlem and the steamy air jams to the rhythm of car stereos and Latino street talk. I relish the energy, a passion long gone AWOL from middle class Toronto. A quick fill up and I start the crawl down the Hudson into Lower Manhattan.

Scanning the radio for a station not compromised by the forest of concrete walls, I settle for Q104, classic rock. Between the DJ's Bronx bur and the periodic assault of sandstorm static, I'm aware of the upcoming Springsteen concert in New Jersey. An excited woman has just scored two tickets for being the somethingth caller. She hangs up and the jock intros Jersey Girl.

Perfect choice Mister DJ. I sing along with The Boss. Well, they don't call him that anymore, but to whoever knew him when he was called The Boss, that's who he'll always be. The song takes me back to life in small town anywhere. Fast cars, good pals, working hard all week to afford a night to let loose with your best girl. Hoping one day to build a good life for you and your own. Yup, that was the real American dream.

I roll down the window, huff a slug of sticky late August, and start raising the ghosts of someone's summer past.

Danny Marino finished up on the neon orange, Dodge Charger Daytona. He took a last, longing look and hung the keys on the hook in the office at Nick Carbone's auto shop, Bronx. Two years of playing grease monkey had earned him a decent wage and title of head mechanic, not counting Nick. He whistled something tuneless, stripped out of his coveralls and stuffed them into his locker. This was what he lived for, Saturday night. Date night. The moment time handed him the keys to his handcuffs, and said, "Go ahead, live it up kid." All the hassles and hard work were swapped for anticipation, as he locked the shop door and headed to his car.

Danny had met Darlene Thatcher the year before, at a dance in Hackensack. They hit it off right away and pretty soon he was bragging to the guys about his "Jersey Girl" and how he was going to marry her someday and have a bunch of kids.

It wouldn't be easy. She lived in Edgewater, daughter of a big shot lawyer and his professional society wife. They weren't too thrilled their daughter was hooked up with some common Bronx gear head. Darlene didn't exactly hide their liaisons, but they weren't included in the weekly household bulletins either. Sometimes her friends did double duty as alibis, especially on the days her parents started harping on about her meeting a respectable boy from town.

But it sure felt like love and nothing was going to spoil tonight. Danny had saved a few bucks every paycheck, ever since he'd heard New Jersey's legendary Palisades Park was to close in September. Tonight was a shot at being part of American History.

They'd ride, eat, laugh, cuddle and kiss the evening away, and at the end he'd boldly drop her off at her front door, maybe with the radio full tilt. Nothing could get in his way tonight.

Danny slid behind the wheel of his ailing '65 Dodge Dart. Funny how the guys who knew cars always drove crap. Those who didn't know shit had the flashy wheels. He had enough time to get home, shower, shave and shove off to Jersey, in time to pick up his Jersey Girl at eight. A half a block away the car stalled. He coasted to the curb and turned the key. The engine slobbered twice, gave a feeble cough and went into cardiac arrest. Danny tried again. Nothing. *For Chrissake dude, you're a mechanic. This is no big deal. Whatever it is, you can fix it.* Two minutes after opening the hood, he knew he wasn't going anywhere. *Now what? This is gonna take at least two hours and it's...shit, 6:30 already.*

Danny stood staring at the engine, as if that could change anything. Then he saw the light shining through Nick's front window. There was his answer. It was against the code, but this was an emergency, an emergency of the heart. If he stood Darlene up, it would be one more reason for her parents to be down on him. Nick would understand, he wasn't so old that he didn't remember what it was like. Besides, he'd have it back by midnight. Curfew in the

Thatcher household was eleven. A couple of minutes later, he walked into the office and took the Charger key off the hook.

"Honey," Nick Carbone called to his wife from the kitchen table, where he sat trying to make sense of his invoices. "I'm missing some papers, I gotta go back to the shop and grab them. Won't be ten minutes."

Five minutes later, Nick walked into the shop and grabbed what he needed from the filing cabinet. Out of habit, he checked out the garage before leaving. *What the hell, where's the Charger? Danny took it out for a test? Better hang around and wait for him to get back.*

Twenty minutes later, he knew something wasn't right. A test drive took five minutes. He dialed Danny's number. No answer. *Oh, yeah the big date.* He checked for signs of a break in. Nothing looked out of place. *Danny? No, his car is gone. Besides, he would never. Another ten minutes and I call the cops.*

It had been the perfect night and Darlene was nestled as close as bucket seats would allow. It was 10:30. Danny would have his Jersey Girl home in time to keep the old man happy and the car back before midnight. Tomorrow, he'd deal with his own shit box.

As he approached the ramp to the Interstate, a car pulled out from the shoulder, siren squealing and lights flashing.

Soho

I'm hanging in Soho, looking for a bit of atmosphere and maybe a few deals. Friday afternoon in New York sports a palpable vibe. Folks are just a bit lighter, friendlier, more bearable than usual.

The heat hugs everything, the air oily enough to use as a lubricant. But nobody seems to mind. It's Friday.

Despite the torrid afternoon, I'm craving caffeine. After several strike outs, I find an authentic New Yorker who directs me to Fanelli's Café. Awesome, I've hit the jackpot. Fanelli's isn't just a café, it's a destination, one I've stumbled upon quite by fortune.

This landmark watering hole, dating back to the 1840's has a long and chequered history, but for the past twenty-five years it's been skippered by ex-boxer Bob Bozac, who once worked out in the back of Ciro's bar in Toronto. Bozac had the dubious privilege of being pummeled by Larry Holmes in 1973.

The interior does not disappoint. It's more of a tavern, spared from kitschy makeovers. The bar is lined with blue collars who greet each other upon arrival. I sit facing framed photos of boxing legends. I order a cappuccino, toast the likes of Jack Dempsey, Rocky Graziano, Jake LaMotta and Sugar Ray Robinson. I start to drift into another world.

Mickey Spark took the plain brown envelope and exited the back door into the alley. He stepped down onto a pile of brown slush, which promptly soaked through his mesh brown and tan spectator shoes. He'd run a lot of cheap errands to earn those shoes and didn't foresee getting another pair any time soon. Glancing up and down the dark lane, he hightailed it to the street, tucking his package into his trouser front.

Mickey was just a small time hood trying to make it in the world of high stakes skullduggery. A couple of years ago, he'd caught a break when Carlo "Shorty" Rivera, an up and coming crime boss, needed a new soldier for deliveries and other dirty deeds. Spark had a reputation for being willing to do anything to get a foot in. After a couple of jobs, Rivera was pleased, so now he'd graduated to handling a small group of rookies, the first step in moving up the ranks. But it was taking so long, Mickey was starting to wonder when it was going to happen.

But his boys were pretty much dolts, lucky to get a coffee run right. This job was too important to hand off to some spotty faced greenhorn. His reputation and future were on the line. So now he found himself standing in the middle of Hell's Kitchen, with a soggy pair of shoes and a bundle of money in his pants. Worth getting smoked for.

He stood in the cold drizzle, deciding his next move. *Mickey boy, you're too tense, act natural like or someone's gonna figure out you're hiding something. Move nice and easy, like you just came from visiting your mother.* As he passed a newspaper box, he noted the headline. "Windy City Battle Tonight: Sugar Ray vs Raging Bull." In all the excitement he'd forgotten. It was only 7, he could be down to Fanelli's by 8, in time to hear the fight. *Well, now you know where you're goin' Mickey. Consider it your Valentine's Day gift to yourself.*

As expected, the place was packed with every Joe in the neighbourhood. A few had brought along their girls, to show off. There was barely room to stand. He scored a beer and moved as close as he could to the big radio off the side of the bar. The announcer was blathering on about the crowd, the mood and the boxer's stats. Mickey noticed a small party gathered off in a corner. Stuff was changing hands. *I knew there'd be some action.* The envelope was starting to feel uncomfortable. *Mickey don't be a chump. It ain't your dough. If you can't hand it over to Shorty tomorrow, you might as well jump off the Brooklyn Bridge tonight.*

He headed to the gents. Once he was in the stall, he dared to open the envelope. Counting out the crisp hundreds, he stopped at $1000. There was still a substantial pile left. *Look Mickey boy, it's a sure thing. Sugar Ray's all washed up. LaMotta's gonna make ravioli out of him. With these odds, you can write your own ticket, no more bein' the gofer.*

The envelop went back down Mickey's pants and he passed the rest to a man in a brown fedora, in exchange for a slip of paper. A couple of Rivera's boys gave him the eye as he slunk back to his corner.

Later, as he stood on Broadway, the full impact of what he'd done sank in. One grand. How was he going to get that back by tomorrow? What kind of story could he make up? He'd been seen by people smart enough to figure out what was going on.

He walked until two and then climbed back to his rooms. The bottle of bourbon was sitting where he left it. Mickey grabbed it and took a long pull.

A frantic pounding startled him out of sleep. Daylight poured through the smoke stained glass. "Mickey, we know you're in there. Get your ass out here right away. The boss wants to see you and he's pretty sore."

"Anything else sir" I look up to see the sweet smile of the waitress.

"Thanks, no." I give a quick nod to the wall and move out into the gelatinous afternoon. I reckon I'll go get a bite, head back to my air-conditioned hotel room and catch an early night.

Going to take a trip out to Ellis Island tomorrow. Check out what kind of shadows might be hanging around there.

GRIST FOR THE MILL

On a trip back to Manchester, England, my cousins took me to visit the Quarry Bank Mill in nearby Cheshire. Quarry Bank was one of over 100 cotton manufacturing factories which made Manchester one of the textile giants of the 19th century. But this prosperity came at the expense of the workers, who endured dangerous conditions, long hours, and back breaking work. Some were little more than children themselves, and from birth, they were destined to the same bleak life of their fathers.

Grist for the Mill

Thomas Harding leaned on the railing, hypnotized by the thrashing sound of the huge water wheel. Barely fifteen, he stood just 4 foot 9 inches, unable to stand completely erect, his back and knees bent from years of stooping to retrieve material from the dusty factory floor. Thomas peered into the water below. The giant drum had turned for seventy years now, only stopping for repairs or when some unfortunate soul had come too close to the edge. Thomas felt his every breath was joined to the rhythm of the blades, as they vanished under the water. Just about everything he did in his life was in some way tied to that machine. It felt as if he, himself, was being dragged around its immense form.

For the past six years of his short life, Thomas had risen at 5:30, six days a week and trekked up the cobble street to begin his long working day at Quarry Bank Mill in Cheshire. The nearby village of Styal, built for the workers of the busy textile factory, was his home. Although life was much better for workers in the village than many other places, work at the factory was hard and wore a man down long before his time. When he was younger, Thomas had worked nine hours each day, but now as a young adult he had to work a man's shift, returning to his home sometime after eight in the evening. There were just the two breaks in the day and much of that was spent cleaning the work area, while eating some meager meal.

The crashing of the water had never seemed so loud, as commanding as it did this morning. Thomas knew if he dawdled, he would be late. The supervisor didn't take kindly to tardiness. He might go without his breakfast, or maybe worse. Mr. Dodds was known for his harsh ways. Why only the other day, young Ethan Jones had received a beating when he let a spindle come loose. Mr. Dodds said that a half hour of work was lost because of that, and Ethan had to pay.

And here he was, stood by the rail, in no hurry. The wheel consumed him. He found a mark on one of the paddles and counted until it appeared again. This was his life then, the same cycle over and over, just as his father had lived. His dad had died, after seventeen years of coughing up blood, lungs choked and congested from the cotton dust, which hung like snow in the shafts of light from the factory windows. His mother had received a little money, but not enough to care for seven children. The paltry salary he and his three brothers earned was enough to get by, not sufficient to take him away from here.

Once he'd travelled to Manchester, where he had seen those important men rushing around in their tailcoats and suits. People who mattered, had somewhere to go. He had dreamed he and his brothers would leave Styal one day, and find good work, in a clean office. They would send money to their mother. After that, Thomas decided to learn more about the world. He read every book about the world he could find and learned plenty. But texts like *A Voyage of Discovery in the Pacific Ocean*, and *Travels and Adventures in Canada and the Indian Territories* had only magnified his yearning for adventure, to leave this God forsaken place

But the wheel just kept revolving, and every rotation brought him to the same realization. This is where he would continue to live, grow up and grow old, if he was lucky. And likely this is where he would die. If he ever had children, he would only doom them to the same pathetic life he lived.

Thomas thought a lot. Right now, he wondered what it would be like to jump into the wheel, become part of it. Pastor Duggan had told him he thought too much for a young boy and it would come to no good. It was God's plan, and he must make the best of it. He told Thomas his reward would come in the next life. Codswallop, that's what most of what Pastor Duggan said, was. He had it easy, spreading mindless platitudes, sprinkling water on babies. Let him spend a few weeks in this hell and then ask what he thought of God's plan.

It must have been ages since the morning whistle went. Its ring was loud enough to wake the valley, and yet Thomas heard only the constant sloshing of metal on water. By now his mates would have noticed he wasn't at his station, but they had enough to handle just keeping up, hoping they would not make a mistake like young Ethan. But Mr. Dodds would be frantic, not worried about Thomas, but about the empty space at his work area.

That would vex him all right. It wasn't often one of the young ones was away, no matter how sick. Nate Meek had been away for a while when he caught three fingers in the gears, a year back. Old Dodds gave him no end of grief about that. Asked what kind of use a boy with only two fingers on his right hand could be.

The thundering wheel pulled his thoughts back. Nausea gripped him when he thought of walking into the mill, but he couldn't bring himself to go home. For a moment he reflected on the wheel again. He could just slip between the rails and jump. Then he would never have to think about the mill, or Mr. Dodds, or the other poor souls whose lives were spinning just like that damned drum. Thomas smiled briefly, as he imagined the few hours break his friends would enjoy, when the factory needed to be shut down, as they fished him out of the machinery.

TALES FROM THE STORAGE UNIT

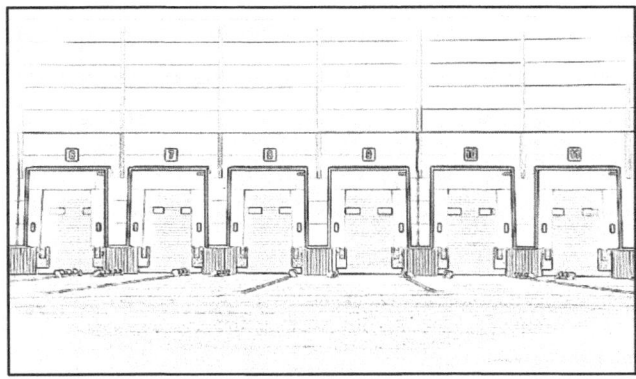

No big backstory here. I used to be part owner in a small neighbour-hood bar. When the owner of the building sold it, we needed to put the contents into a storage unit until we could find another place. One night while visiting our unit, I just got to watching people come and go. I got to wondering what kinds of stories they might have to tell. Perhaps this might be one of them.

Tales from the Storage Unit

Arnold balanced the last box on top of the brown pyramid and stood back to admire his work. Satisfied it was not about to tip over, he strode back to the door and padlocked the unit. He walked outside and his daughter Annie started the car.

"You know, Dad, I've been sitting here all this time watching people come and go. Do you ever wonder what's going on with them? This place must have a lot of stories to tell."

"Guess so, and we're one of them. Your mum and her never ending refurnishing. Let's get moving, we're already late in giving our approval to the new suite." Annie could almost see the quotation marks dancing around the word approval.

"Yeah, just grin, say it's lovely and hand over the card." Annie saw a rather tired looking woman with a couple of suitcases outside the entrance gate. "Look dad, she doesn't even have a van or car. It's past eight. I wonder what's up with that."

"Maybe she just forgot a couple of things." Arnold was checking out his watch. "Two hundred a month, just to store a perfectly good living room. Your mother is going to put us in the poor house with her spring renos."

"Where exactly is the poor house, anyway?" Annie said absently as she punched in the exit code. A white cube van was waiting to enter the lot. Three young guys sat in the front cab. One was tapping on the dash, while the other two passed a joint back and forth. Annie smiled as she made eye contact with a familiar face.

The lines under Emma's eyes betrayed her attempt to freshen up. She had managed to pack a few belongings and get out of the house in the few hours that Tom lay passed out, after his drunken rampage. This was the second time, and for Emma that was one more chance than she had planned on giving him.

A couple of frantic calls to friends had yielded only voice mails. After Tom had cleaned out her wallet, she only had a few dollars stashed in her coat. The storage building closed at ten, but the gate was only supervised until six. There was usually someone coming in late. She had waited in the cold for a car or van to either come or go. Emma only needed one night. In the morning she could call her friends again and sort some temporary digs. If this was the start of a new life, it was a hell of a way to begin. She prayed there was at least one empty unit, so she didn't have to spend the night in the hall. A red BMW with a middle-aged man and young woman in front, exited the lot. Moments later a white van pulled up to the entrance. This was her chance.

After it entered, she slipped in through the closing gate. When the van parked right outside the building doors, Emma realized with irritation that now she would have to wait until they were finished, before she could go in.

Twenty-four hours earlier on the other side of town, the rehearsal had ended in a huge row. The vote was three to one in favour of the tour offer. Four weeks through some of the most remote towns in Northern Ontario. *Tortured Soul* was booked to play gigs in six different places, no doubt in some of the roughest, seediest hotels in town. Jack, Ivan and Rob figured a gig was a gig and the money would help pay off some of the huge equipment debt they had racked up. But Zak, he was another matter. He had a day job and a steady girlfriend. The offer just didn't add up. He wanted to pass.

Things had become heated and he'd walked out. It didn't take him five minutes to figure out what to do. The equipment and storage room were under his name. He wasn't going to let them cart all the gear to some backwoods hick town where it might get trashed or stolen.

Early the following morning, he borrowed his dad's truck and hauled out the entire kit and moved it to his garage. Drastic action, but those other guys could be pretty crazy and besides, he had promised Annie that he would not go out on another tour for a while.

Shortly after eight that evening Jack backed the van up to the entrance and Ivan, metal shears in hand, went inside while Rob kept watch. He rounded the corner and gaped in horror.

"Holy shit," he screamed, "Get in here you two!"

"What is it," Rob's face dropped as he neared the unit.

"He's cleared us out. The bastard took it all."

"Are you sure?" Jack realized what a stupid remark he had made.

"Of course I'm bloody sure, take a look for yourself. It's gone." Ivan bolted back outside as if he might still catch Zak in the act.

"Shit, shit, shit. What are we gonna do now?" Rob hollered to anyone in earshot.

As Emma waited on the other side of the parking lot, she heard the shouting and a moment later saw the three men get back in the van, code the gate open and blast off down the street, tires squealing. With a final look around, she picked up her bags. In their panic the guys had left the door unlocked. Stepping inside, she looked down the corridor and found what she had been hoping for, an open unit. She crept inside, pulled the door shut, took out a blanket and curled up on the floor.

Annie and her dad entered the showroom, where her mum stood holding court with a young salesman. "He's kind of cute. Can we keep him and dump the suite?" Arnold broke into a laugh. Annie had a way of doing that to him.

"Over here," she waved. "Isn't it beautiful?"

He gave a wan smile and ventured a quiet, "Yeah, lovely."

"Mum, Dad, I'm supposed to meet Zak later on, so I'm just going to bus it over there." Annie was already making her way to the exit before the usual warnings and parental advice could be given. Arnold gave a pleading, *don't leave me alone*, smile. Annie nodded in sympathy and headed out of the showroom. She hadn't been able to reach Zak all afternoon. She knew how upset he was about the tour, didn't care if the band broke up over it. She felt bad. Annie knew he loved drumming and had high hopes of leaving his day job and going full time into music. Another try yielded only voice mail. Better go over and check that everything was okay.

Annie arrived at Zak's just as the white van turned into the driveway. Zak pulled her in and slammed the door. Before she could say a word, Zak cut in, "I don't care what you say, they're not getting the equipment, I'm up to my ears over that stuff and I'm damned if I'm letting them take it on the road without me."

Annie held up a finger to her mouth, "Zak, I know, but I've been thinking. It isn't fair for you to throw away your dream because of me. You guys have been hoping for some kind of break for ages. Maybe it isn't the Phoenix, but it's a start. I've been running this around my head all the way over. I'm not going anywhere here. Why don't we go on the tour together? I could be like a road manager."

By now there were insistent knocks on the door. "Zak, c'mon. Let's talk about this man. Open up, we just want to talk."

Zak looked into Annie's face. He could see she was completely serious. "Do you really mean it?" She nodded. "Hold on a minute guys!" he called to the other side of the door. "What about your parents?"

"Zak, I'm 22 years old, don't you think it's time...." Zak picked her up off the ground and hugged her.

"Absolutely sure?" he was reaching for the door. "Come on in, let's talk."

At seven AM, Emma's travel alarm woke her. She quickly rolled up the blanket, stuffed it into her bag, went out and stood by the gate, waiting for the first arrival. She'd go to the coffee shop, make some calls and figure out her next move.

By eight, Tortured Soul had the van loaded and were headed over to Annie's house to collect her stuff. They stopped briefly to pick up breakfast. "Funny, I've seen her before." Annie pointed at a woman carrying a couple of suitcases out of the coffee shop.

After her parents left for work, she would slip in and pack her bag. Her folks would read the simple words: *Gone with the band for a few weeks, don't worry, I'll call when we get to the first gig. Love you, Annie.*

Arnold would come home, see the note, and dread the next few weeks alone with his wife, without the buffer zone that was Annie.

Delilah in Heels

Everything about noir drips of danger and darkness. It clings like a fog to each detail. There is more menace in fifteen minutes of a noir story, than five slasher films combined. The secret is atmosphere, a mood which gently takes hold of you from the first scene and doesn't relax its grip until you are wondering how you didn't know the outcome sooner. Delilah In Heels was my homage to these old films. I needed a story of less than a thousand words for a competition, so this is short and to the point. I think the voice would be Bogart, although you can choose your own hero.

Delilah in Heels

It may have been the moment you walked through my office door. That confident walk, betrayed only by those restless eyes. I wasn't sure which was the real you, but I had to find out. I admired that you didn't beat around the bush. No small talk, or waiting to be asked to sit down. For God's sake, you even helped yourself to a cigarette without an invitation. You sure threw me off my game. I remember fumbling for my lighter, trying to make sure I brought it up to the tip before lighting it.

Your voice was everything I hoped it would be. Just a simple "Thanks, Mr. Thorn", at least I think that's what you said, because all I could hear was Billie Holiday singing *My Man*. You got straight to the point, no long winded back story, "just the facts ma'am", as they say. You had me when you told of how your guy'd run off with some cocktail waitress. How he'd taken your jewelry and money. When you persuaded that little quaver into your voice and ran that single tear down your left cheek, I just about ran over and held you. But you hadn't even hired me yet, and big displays of emotion can be a bit off putting. So instead, I just nodded like a dummy, and gave you a couple of "wow's" and I think a "Holy cow." When you finished and asked if I could help find the jerk, I almost said, "No charge." But I didn't. I simply asked you how much you had. You could have pretty much said any amount.

I picked you up at your place the next day, hanging on every move as you came down the walk and sashayed into the passenger seat. Again, you slipped a cigarette off the dash, and once more I groped for my lighter and almost set your hair on fire. Then you laughed. It's corny, but if a rainbow could laugh, that's what it would sound like. My brain was already busy planning our wedding, our future. But all you said was, "Take Fullerton out to Elmwood Park." Bang, went the wedding bells. But I had a feeling they'd be back.

As we closed in on our target, we spent more time together. It was a gas just being around you. Yeah, there were some rough moments, but we had lots of laughs. I thought I'd die when that jerk tried to come on to you at O'Malley's. You so casually dropped your cigarette butt in his whiskey and told him to take a powder. I almost felt sorry for the dope as he walked away, his tail between his legs. I was starting to see the stuff you were made of and I liked it. I liked it a lot.

I gotta admit you scared me when you pulled your gun on that mug that followed us out of the bar and into the alley. I mean, I thought you were crazy, but it kinda got me all hot to see a dame like you making a big cheese like him squeal like a chicken.

And you were smart. Any time I tried to follow up on a dumb lead to nowhere, you were right there telling me, oh so nicely, I was all wet. Then you gave another plan which turned out to be the right one. Sometimes that drove me crazy, or was it just I was crazy about you?

At the end of the caper, you were cool when the cops took him and his floozy off to the big house. Not one tear. Instead you walked over to the counter and poured yourself a double bourbon.

After you'd downed it in one gulp, as I was sitting with the dough in my hand and your mug of a husband had got what was coming to him, I really wasn't shocked at all when you took your pretty little Colt 1911 out of your purse, pointed at me and said, "It's been a gas working with you Henry, but I think I'll just be taking that bag and moving on." You turned on those pretty red heels and walked out the door.

It was the last time I ever laid eyes on you. I knew then that I loved you and would find you again someday. Besides, you still owe me for my services.

SUNSET ON GANYMEDE

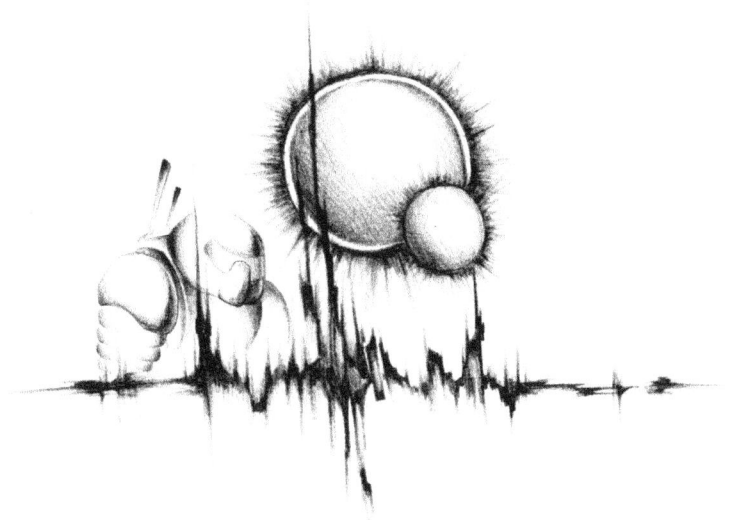

My first exposure to science fiction came from a series of anthologies called the Golden Age of Science Fiction. Authors such as Bradbury, Silverberg, Heinlen, Asimov, "Doc" Smith. The stories were not always scientifically accurate, especially with what we now know. But they took me to worlds of fantasy, amazing inventions and brave adventures. These tales still stand the test of time. The more you are drawn in, the less the science matters. My first forays into the world of the fantastic were a homage to these pioneers. I have included a few here.

Sunset on Ganymede

Earth's sun had reigned over the sky for billions of years. Its light had shone on great civilizations; glistened over a million lakes and rivers: revealed the tragedy of war in her rising; and spawned endless dreams at day's end. Since human-kind first stared into the heavens, it had behaved as a good star should. Hydrogen to helium in constant motion. And humans had reaped the benefits. They had lived.

Despite the predictions of the naysayers, humanity had not only survived but thrived through the eons. Eventually, war had ended. Famine and hunger became a distant memory. Humans had moved to the farthest reaches of known space and had flourished. And while first contact had still not yet been made, the galaxy was sprinkled with life, all of it, "Origin Earth."

On a Monday morning, Cameron Reid woke his sleeping son, Taylor. "Is it today?" Taylor asked, one eye open. His father smiled, tousled his blond curls and laid the boy's suit out on the bed.

They slipped into the flight tube and shortly after, arrived at the space port. The departure area was full and Taylor could feel the excitement in the air. "Are we all going to the same place?" He asked.

"Not exactly," said his dad. "We're all going to Earth's Solar System, but we'll be landing in different places."

All matter is finite. The hydrogen in the Sun had begun to run out, its payload now largely converted to helium. For a long time she would continue to burn in the sky, seemingly unfazed by imminent death. For those still inhabiting Earth and the nearby colonies, life would continue as normal. But those who studied her, had long ago constructed the timelines.

Every death should have a memorial. Through the Universal Web, a date was chosen and arrangements were made available, to those who still cared. Of course, over such vast stretches of time, most people had little knowledge or concern about a life so far removed from their own. But there were still those who felt a connection. Through memory cubes and ancient history courses, the past remained relevant.

Cameron Reid was an astronaut. His father and countless predecessors had followed the same vocation. His ancestors had even traveled to Earth when it was still habitable. The stories had passed through the generations. Cameron was determined that his son would carry on that legacy. Some things should never die.

When they had boarded and were ready for liftoff, Taylor started asking the same questions he had repeated over the past few weeks. "Was the Earth as beautiful as it is here? Did everyone have to leave? Can we ever go there again?"

His dad smiled, "Earth was as beautiful as any place you have ever seen. But there came a time when the sun got so hot, people couldn't live there anymore. That's why we moved to where we are now. All these people traveling with us today think it's important to remember where we have come from."

"Why is it important?" asked Taylor.

"Because if you know where you came from, you may know more about who you are now," Taylor turned and watched the home world shrink, before the ship moved into drive.

When the hydrogen was no longer available for fusion, the sun contracted back into itself. There it became so dense that the matter rekindled itself as fuel and blew the remnants of the sun's energy into space. Red and tortured, the sun swallowed the inner planets. The Earth's oceans evaporated and the atmosphere boiled away. Long before this happened, humankind had left in search of a brave new future.

Technology was to the point where distance was virtually irrelevant. In short order they had arrived at the outer frontier of the solar system. At one time the sun would have been little more than a bright spot from this vantage. Now a swollen orange ball, surrounded by a ghostlike fog commanded their central view.

Many ships had left their homelands, all destined for the outer regions of the Solar System. They were simultaneously landing on the moons of Neptune, Uranus, Saturn and Jupiter, as these giants held no solid surfaces on which to alight. All of the destinations were close enough to view the spectacle, far enough to be safe from radiation, and with temperatures now moderated by distance from their bloated star.

Sol had used all of her energy. The furnaces had all but gone out. But in the throes of death, it protested and spewed its atmosphere into space, sending wraithlike rings past the remaining inner planets and moons. For someone standing on the surface of these bodies, they would see these ghostlike images expanding into forever.

"Why are we landing on Ganymede?" asked Taylor.

"This is the biggest moon in Jupiter's system," his dad said. "From here we'll have the best view. There will be lots of others coming to see the same thing. From today on, the sun will get smaller and smaller until you won't even be able to see it anymore. But today, it will be as beautiful as it's ever been."

They left the craft and boarded the Sky Rover which would take them to their destination. Taylor looked out at the bleak landscape. The sun's warmth had melted the once frozen surface, which was now a barren yellow plain, pitted by space debris. The sky directly above was black, but exotic ribbons of red and orange flickered with an eerie glow. The horizon was framed with a cherry fog.

After skirting some low hills, the Rovers slowed and touched down. Their occupants stepped out onto the dusty surface and walked to the viewing platform. A thousand others were already there, peering at the sky through special glasses. As the giant moon slowly passed out of Jupiter's shadow, they were able to look into the heart of the Solar System.

Through the swirls of orange haze, they saw a crimson orb pulsating with light. Bands of vibrant energy burst from the surface and then dissipated. An occasional flash of lightning pierced the sky.

Cameron Reid had seen the images of ancient sunsets on Earth. Spectacular vistas capping sapphire oceans. Fire burning over the Rocky Mountains. But here in the middle of a barren outpost, in this long-abandoned sea of planets and moons, the sun was offering its last and most brilliant sunset.

Hardly a word was spoken on the way back to the ship which would carry them home. As they settled into their seats; Cameron saw the tear in his son's eye. Perhaps even millions of years could still not completely sever humans from their origins, he thought. No matter where we travel, Earth is still a part of who we are. One day, his son would pass this gift to his own children.

Eventually the sun's matter would fall back on itself. All hints of its former radiance would be gone. Only a blackened hull would remain, still the centre of its kingdom of barren rocks, floating through space.

SCHEHERAZADE X1L15

I may not have been inspired by 1001 Arabian Nights at first. But as the story line developed, I realized that was where I was going. Inspiration can come from anywhere. It then roosts in the back of the mind. Once the creative flood gates start to open, you never know what is going to pop out. So Kudos to all those unknown writers who composed that magical book. I've just taken the idea and rewired it a bit for the 20 somethingth century. I'm sure the original Scheherazade wouldn't have had a problem telling it to the Sultan.

Scheherazade X1L15

At a discreet distance, Nicholas Shaw followed the young girl through the damp streets. The narrow lanes were a maze of cobbles and dim streetlamps. He didn't know why he needed to pursue her, just the feeling that she might lead him home. The town was foreign to him and he felt as if the ground had spat him forth into the clammy night and abandoned him.

He tried to get his bearings but found none. She had come out of the small shop, across from where he stood. An ever so slight smile had given him the courage he needed to follow. Now, as she entered the tavern, he knew he must meet her, talk with her, find out her story. Everyone had a story, and Nicholas was drawn by a compulsion to learn about this strange girl, whom he had first seen not five minutes ago.

As the two sat sipping hot rum, she took his hand sweetly and spun the story of her life. She wove a warp of joy and weft of despair, each strand of her life moving him to tears and exhilaration at the same time. These were tales of great romance, dashed hopes, life just begun and life extinguished. Her words pulled him into her tale and became his own life.

With the intrusion of first light, she stood up, kissed him on the cheek and rushed out the door. He tried to get up but felt a great fatigue come over him and he fell back into his chair and slept.

He awoke and remembered where he was; the deserted landscape, empty buildings on the horizon, and right in front of him it stood, tall and silent.

Nicholas Shaw was one of the few survivors of the explosion on Endor Colony, perhaps the only one. Having left Earth when he was 6, Endor had been the only home he knew, but when disaster came, he had been immediately transported back. Only this was not the home of his birth. It was empty, its people devastated by the catastrophic solar flare and radiation pulse in 2150. How strange to see everything still intact and yet not find another human.

Now he had two goals, to locate his boyhood home and find someone, anyone.

In school, Nicholas had learned a little of the Earth's geography, but a scan of the area revealed he hadn't a clue where he was. And then he had seen it. At first it was a flash in the distance, but it quickly grew in size until it stood five feet from him. At least as tall as he was, metallic silver and as humanoid as a robot could be. Once stationary, it made no further movements.

Nicolas crept towards the figure. When it didn't stir, he gained some confidence and started to examine it. The surface was smooth, shiny, with none of the marks one might expect from something so long exposed to the elements. Then, on the lower part of the left leg he noticed some kind of engraving. He bent down and read, SHZX1L15, Americorp Inc.

He returned to the capsule and brought out his emergency supplies and life support. An SOS message was sent to the satellite colonies, and he went back outside. The temperature was stifling compared to Endor. Nicholas set up a simple base camp and sat contemplating his next move. The sun became a crimson stain on the horizon.

It was then it spoke to him. "You will need life support once the sun goes down. Since the event, the temperature drops sharply at night. You will freeze."

Nicolas looked at the droid. In a whisper, he asked, "Did you speak to me?"

"Indeed," said the droid. "I told you to suit up. It is going to get cold."

Nicolas tried to get his head around this turn of events. "You mean you just travelled halfway across this wasteland to warn me to get into life support?"

"Of course, that is the job of SHZX1L15. It and other Androids were created to take care of the humans. Once the plague came there were not enough Android series to help. Human history was downloaded so that Earth stories would not die. Then came the flash that eliminated the rest of humanity. You have survived and need help. SHZX1L15 will take care of you. Also, if you get into your life support suit, you can hear the Earth stories."

What a curious creature he thought. Still he had been warned. "What can I call you?"

"SHZX1L15, Americorp Inc. humanoid droid. You can call me SHZ if it is easier for you. What is your name human?"

"I'm Shaw, Nicholas Shaw. Please tell me where I am. Am I near Lexington, Kentucky? That's my home. Can I get there? Is there anyone else alive? Tell me all the details about the flare?" He realized he was rambling.

"SHZ has information but is not programmed to answer all questions. Instead SHZ can tell you stories about humans. SHZ collects and saves human stories."

"How many do you have?" The fatigue of the past day now dropped on Nicholas like the final curtain of a play.

"At the beginning of the plague, before the event, there were ten billion, three hundred and twenty-three thousand, nine hundred and four humans on Earth. SZH had many of their stories. Then when other androids stopped functioning SZH input their stories. SZH has ten billion, three hundred and twenty-three thousand, nine hundred and four of their stories in its memory bank. Plus, SZH has received input of human history and story books. That makes its archive very large."

"Are there any more of you?"

"To SHZ's best knowledge, SHZ is the only of its kind left. Now Shaw Nicholas Shaw will hear SHZ's story."

Too tired to object, Nicolas Shaw nodded and lay down beside the android.

The creature began to tell him a story about a magnificent king who ruled over the Yuan dynasty in China in the year 1300. As he drifted to sleep, images of triumphant conquests, brave warriors, exquisite courtesans and joyous homecomings filled his dreams. He became the brave heart. He was the hero, the conqueror, the lover.

Nicholas awoke to white light on the eastern horizon, and a heart filled with longing. In front of him the android stood, silent, in the same spot it had been the night before.

That first morning he tried to get the droid to speak. He looked all over for switches and dials. He invented passwords and made signals that he hoped would end its muteness. When nothing worked, he decided to explore the area, find where he was and see if someone was out there. He didn't dare wander far from camp. By midday the heat drove him back to the shelter, where he remained until the shadows grew long. His evening foray into the nearby city yielded little. It was clear that unless some people were in hiding, the city was dead. There were no lights, no sounds and no sign of movement.

On his return, Nicholas noticed his quiet companion had begun to glow, like a lighthouse or beacon, to guide him in the growing blackness. He had just arrived back, when it started to scold him.

"Shaw Nicolas Shaw should not be away from home in the dark. Danger of getting lost. Without life support Shaw Nicholas Shaw will later freeze. Go fetch nourishment and put on support system now."

Bossy little bugger, Nicholas thought. But still, not a bad idea. He made a small fire and sat eating his simple meal and drinking hot coffee.

"Now you are finished getting sustenance, SHZX1L15 will tell you another story. Switch on life support please." Nicholas found he was in no mood for another tale and was about to say so when the droid began. "This story involves a captain from your Crimean war, trying to get home to his wife and children after a successful campaign in Sevastopol." Again, he felt an overwhelming weariness and succumbed to sleep. Shaw then found himself embroiled in battles, conquering armies and to his great joy, returning home to the arms of his family.

In the morning the droid was struck dumb once again. Shaw took what precaution he could against the coming heat of the afternoon and struck out towards the city. The day felt a little cooler and he made it to the outskirts by late morning. His heart sank as he walked each street, closing in on the town's centre. There was nothing for him. No sign of life. Not even the mark of death. Just empty buildings, plazas and avenues. He had so many questions, but he knew his tin man would only tell him old stories which had nothing to do with the fate of humanity.

He returned in near darkness, led by the droid's glow. Upon arrival, it once again chastised him for his carelessness and gave him his evening instructions before launching into the next tale.

Nicholas lost track of the days, days spent searching for life, a way home, any kind of hope for the future. But now the nights, they were his refuge. Blessed sleep overcame him and the wonderful dreams took him away to strange and fantastic places. There he faced danger, sometimes horrific scenes, but without fail he was led home, to where he was safe and loved.

Then came the night when the spaceman lay down beside his companion, exhausted from his day of searching in the scorching sun. In an instant he was asleep. And on this occasion SHZ did not wake him to remind him to employ his life support. On this night Nicholas Shaw finally went home.

The rescue capsule settled on the dusty plain a few days later. Captain Natasha Kalmakova had intercepted a strange SOS and immediately headed for Earth. She scanned the horizon, where the sun was beginning to set. She was startled to see an object moving towards her. Its metallic surface glowed orange in the waning light. When she could make out the humanoid figure, Natasha drew her weapon.

The machine ambled towards her and then rested. "There is no need for your weapon," it whispered. "SHZX1L15 is here to protect you. Sun is setting, it will be cold soon. Please go to your ship and retrieve your life support system. SHZX1L15 will then tell you an Earth story. You can call it SHZ if it is easy for you. SHZ collects and keeps stories about humans."

THE SENTRY

This is a variation of the "Loneliness of The Lighthouse Keeper" theme. Perhaps one of the most desolate of situations is having to make a crucial decision and not having anyone to share it with. Our protagonist has the ultimate moral dilemma, and he must make it alone. Googling a map of Wales helped me devise the place names.

The Sentry

The Ynyr lighthouse had stood for nearly a thousand years. Perched on a narrow cliff, it overlooked what crews had come to call "The Sea of despair." The name itself was a caution to all those ship's captains arrogant enough to believe they could ignore the warnings Ynyr Lighthouse transmitted. And the wrecks of ten thousand freighters bore witness to the perils of the jagged rocks, which surrounded the Isles of Cadagan.

Yorath awoke from a deep sleep. Plagued by troublesome dreams, he now had difficulty separating them from his conscious state. He rose, shuffled to the sink, and turned on the tap, trying to splash some wakefulness onto his face. Weighted down by his nightmares and the decision he knew he would soon have to make, the steps up to the top of the lookout seemed double their usual height. He slumped into his favourite chair and stared out at the sea of stars. He hoped he may find some solace, maybe some direction here. At least for the time being, he felt insulated from the battle that raged not far beyond his rocky outcrop.

His mind drifted back to his early days as a lighthouse keeper. The Rhtrym lighthouse stood at the end of a long almost featureless plain, overlooking the Sea of Mastyn. Treacherous rocks dotted the coast and spread out into the surrounding corridor of water, which was the major shipping lane. For years Yorath had faithfully manned his post. There had never been an accident for which he could be faulted. The decision to leave and accept the post on Ynyr had been a simple one. He was already middle aged, with no family or ties of any kind. The chance to guide vessels through the rugged space debris which plagued the major shipping lanes leaving Terrant, brought him new purpose.

Although Yorath lived alone, he had never felt cut off from the world. For him the cliché "*the loneliness of the lighthouse keeper*" did not resonate. He had the stars for company, and the lights of the passing ships were like the smiling eyes of an old friend. At night, the wind would pick up and he would listen to its song as it sprayed dust and sand against the windows of the tower. There was no sense of isolation, but rather a bond with the universe, an awareness he was a part of something much bigger than himself. It was in this remote place that Yorath had developed his love for humanity, as he understood the deep trust placed in him, to ensure the safety of those who travelled the heavens. He regarded each ship and its crew as if they were his own family.

Stirring from his daydream, Yorath stared out at the void. For a moment he watched the stars and felt as if everything was in place, that the events of the past few days were only a dream. He wished he could just live out his remaining days as a simple lighthouse keeper in a far-off outpost, only responsible for the rare freighter that passed his station. But that had all changed when the mandate had come. Yorath had been baffled by the message, amazed he had received directives from the defense department. The simple words still blazed into his mind:

Warships passing Ryag lighthouse at 0700 hours on Day 236. Please be advised to give full guidance and positioning.

Yorath had scanned all the frequencies to help explain the cryptic message. Finally finding a censored government broadcast, he had realized the horrific truth. The new military dictatorship had decided to end their isolationist policy and made preparations to use their massive forces to invade and conquer the other settlements beyond Terrant.

Aware of their armed capabilities, Yorath knew a holocaust of the most devastating scope awaited those unsuspecting civilizations. Geography dictated the fleet must pass through the *Sea of Despair* before entering the frontier and moving into open space. Navigating the lethal asteroid belt would decide the success or failure of the mission. Their location and mineral composition rendered these jagged rocks invisible without the guidance of the Ynyr lighthouse. Should the navigation systems fail, it would likely result in the total annihilation of the fleet. In effect, Yorath had become responsible for the fate of a hundred worlds, and at the same time accountable for the lives of thousands of his countrymen.

Now, in this moment, Yorath understood what solitude was. There was no one to help him decide what to do, and no one to uphold him in his decision, once it was made. There were only the stars and the void. And between him and the armada, drifted the rocks of the Rhydderch Asteroid Belt. He needn't interfere at all. All it required was for him to do nothing, pretend he hadn't received the directive. It wouldn't matter in the end, because disaster for the

THE SENTRY

fleet would mean the destruction of his own small world. There would be no repercussions, except for culpability in sending thousands of his fellow Terrants to their deaths. But if he engaged the guidance systems and let the ships pass unharmed, he would be dooming millions of unknown innocent civilians, in worlds too distant to imagine.

Yorath felt the weight of his many years. He collapsed into his chair and gazed out at his beloved stars, perhaps hoping some direction might drop from the sky. This would likely be his own last day and yet he could do no more than watch through the glass into space. The old man had no idea how long he had sat there, when the first beeps from radar announced the approach of the Terrant ships. He took a last glance at the heavens, aware that he must come to some resolution. Yorath imagined every star being a planet in the path of the Terrant ships, and he envisioned each one slowly flickering and dying in the blackness, signifying the extinction of an entire race of beings. From the corner of his eye he saw screen images of the first craft approaching the belt, each one holding a thousand soldiers, who probably had no idea of the ultimate purpose of the mission. Rising from his chair, Yorath limped his way to the guidance system. It was only when he placed his hand on the control switch that Yorath knew clearly what he had to do.

HIDE AND SEEK

This is another homage to the Golden Age of Science Fiction. We always seem to assume that if we made first contact, the locals would either welcome us with open arms, or include us on their next dinner menu. There is a third alternative. What if they just can't be bothered and simply want to be left alone? Here's how it might play out.

Hide and Seek

Shortly before The Great Misfortune, the people of DZAGH sent a distress signal into the universe. In time, this happened to land on a rather inconsequential planet called Earth, which was mired in its own misery. Earth scientists soon discovered the source of the message was a mere stone's throw away, somewhere in the vicinity of Alpha Centauri. Yes, the plot line might be a bit clichéd, but it also happens to be true. Despite their best efforts, the top cryptographers in the world could not crack their code. Even had they done so, they couldn't have pronounced the name of the senders. For that reason, from now on they will be henceforth referred to merely as Fred.

The details of The Great Misfortune or GM, are sketchy, since records and memories were purged to spare future generations the pain this knowledge might bring. What it did do, was completely change Fred's way of life. All the genius they had previously put into technology, was replaced by an almost mystical alchemy. In time the GM became a simple footnote in history.

It also generated a huge case of xenophobia, coupled with a complete distrust of anything not Fred. They had studied the rest of the universe, considered it vastly inferior and decided it was not worth the bother. However, their distress message continued to pour out into the universe and there was nothing they could do to stop it.

When it finally reached the inhabitants of Earth it caused great excitement, as their own species was so tedious. They immediately began to broadcast messages in the general direction of Fred. This included moronic and ridiculous examples of life on their planet, in the form of television and radio broadcasts. While they could not end their own transmission, Fred were able to receive Earth's broadcast and this only deepened Fred's distaste for these extra-Fred-lifeforms.

A Starship in Near Space

Commander Henry Franks awoke from four years of cryogenic sleep. He felt like he had been liposuctioned by a storm drain cleaner. He ambled into the galley, ordered a mega espresso and finished it in a single gulp. *Three weeks to landing and the signal is still loud and clear. What the hell does it say? What's the sense of sending a bloody signal into space if nobody can figure it out? Still, we are here, knocking on the door of history.*

First officer Miki Barkov sat at a table contemplating a small mound of pasta. "Good morning Captain. I trust you slept well. Our ground crew has started preparing and we will begin sending our messages tomorrow." She looked wistfully at her rapidly emptying plate. "If the Captain will indulge me for a moment, four years without a proper meal is a long time."

Franks went to the dispenser and re-filled his cup. "Doesn't it bother you that the same signal keeps repeating itself? What do you think they're up to?"

"Captain, if they were planning on doing us harm it would have happened already. This is an invitation." Barkov inhaled her noodles. "So hungry."

"Let me know when we have a clear visual." The captain finished his coffee, noted the officer's empty plate with a mild sense of admiration, and left.

A very excited commander Peter Kim summoned Franks to the bridge the next morning and soon the crew gaped in wonder at the sight through the view screen. Frank's heart raced at what he saw; buildings, roads, crops. They were primitive looking, and there was no technology visible. Still, there was life and they were the first humans to witness it. Officer Sheila Carter said what they were all thinking. "Don't you find it odd? Here's a civilization advanced enough to send signals across light years and yet looking down there, it's like the Middle Ages."

Touchdown

While in orbit, they continued to scan the surface. Aside from some wildlife, there was no sign of activity.

The EVA team; Captain Franks, Peter Kim and Sheila Carter dropped towards the new world. Speculation grew.

"Where do you think they are?" mused Kim. "Some kind of plague, or invasion? It all looks so peaceful."

They touched down in a small meadow, adjacent to a fair sized town. The streets were bare. A few fluffy creatures which might be Fred-cats, moved in and out of lanes and onto door stoops. Some odd looking bird-like creatures perched on trees, gazing with curiosity. The team gingerly opened doors. No-one was home.

"If they had gotten sick or been attacked, there would be signs. We'll take the rover for a spin." Captain Franks glumly surveyed the remnants of a small rodent-like animal the cat had proudly deposited at his feet.

Departure

For the next few days they re-visited the surface, but found nothing. This was a ghost planet. There was intelligent life elsewhere in the universe, but not here anymore.

The signal teased them all the way home.

Postscript

Following the human's departure, something magical happened. One by one, the cats, birds and other creatures started to reconfigure themselves as Fred. Being very sensitive individuals, they could still sense, feel and smell human presence. And being a paranoid lot, they were slow to announce the all clear until they were sure the strange beings from the idiot planet one system over, had left. "Are you sure they've left?" asked one of the first out.

"Absolutely. Look, that ridiculous ship of theirs is gone." A tall Fred disengaged from a large tree branch. "But I wish we could turn off that damned signal. It's bad enough to have them as neighbours, never mind them doing the pop in."

For the rest of the day the Fred were busy, madly sweeping, spraying, disinfecting and washing away any remnants of the uninvited guests.

And back on Earth, a room full of very clever scientists sat around shiny tables, scratching their heads and trying to explain where this first contact had gone awry.

AMAZED AND CORNFUSED

Several years ago, when I was in a "New Age" shop in Glastonbury UK, someone came in and excitedly announced the discovery of a new corn circle in a local field. An idea marinated in my mind for a couple of years, until this came to me. It does take the mick out of corn circle chasers, government workers and even the locals in a quaint Somerset town. Whether you are a believer or not, this whole phenomenon is still fodder for a fun tale. I hope I have succeeded in conveying that.

Amazed and Cornfused

Glastonbury, England, Present Time

Sean Dougan stared as the foam on his latte morphed into clouds and planets. The July morning sun was starting to warm the bench in the courtyard of the Blue Note Café, where he waited to see who would soon be rolling through the door. News of this sort traveled quickly and those who cared about it, cared a lot. Perhaps more than most would consider normal. The only time their little consortium gathered in an ale free venue was when another corn circle was rumoured to be about.

"Well I'll be blowed, look who found his way out of the house before noon." It sounded more like a song than a statement. Willow and Will, yes they were a couple, plunked down on the other side of the picnic table. Willow, blonde and tall, had that vague, dreamy look of a nineteen sixties folk singer, while Will was short and stocky, with untamed black curls which looked about to consume his head. He would have looked in place bailing hay, and people were surprised to find he was an IT troubleshooter. Preamble and context were redundant in these circumstances, so Will dove straight into the matter at hand.

"Early this morning, near Bruton. Last night everything was normal and then this morning, how'd you do, in the middle of this farmer's field. Two Americanos please."

Sean leaned forward. "They say it's like the one in Maiden Castle. We can guess what that means."

Ulick came out from the café, cradling his customary herbal tea. "Thought you'd be out front." Like the others, he'd been born to pseudo hippies. Ulick's folks had thought it would be meaningful and very transcendent to honour their Nordic roots, and find something new age to name their child. It had also been the source of more than one playground beating in elementary school. Lanky, fair and very earthy, he had in time, lived up to both his name and his folks' expectations.

"Hey Ule, what do you think?"

"I'm thinking it's a perfect match. It's all coming together." Looking very pleased with himself, he slapped two photos on the table. "See, this one here is Maiden Castle, and this other one's last night."

"Crikey, how'd you get that so fast? I doubt the news van is even there yet." Will studied the two pictures. "I don't see any difference."

"I've got my sources. I'm telling you, they're telling us something." Ulick retrieved his snaps and put them into his bag. "Look, who's got a car that's actually working? We've gotta get out there before it turns into a circus, if it hasn't already. Man, once this gets out, every spaced out Armageddon junkie will be there, burning incense and chanting at the moon." Despite their zeal, Ulick's little group considered themselves to be the level-headed ones in a town which owed its prosperity to the mystical lunatic fringe.

Sean spoke up, "Hey my folks are away, and they were foolish enough to leave the car, so giddyup."

Twenty minutes later Glastonbury Tor was shrinking in the rear-view mirror. The Tor, another word for big hill, is believed to be a possible resting place of the Holy Grail, and this reputation has branded the town as one of the most sacred places in the UK. The transcendent can indeed be found, if one is willing to dig through the layers of ersatz flower children hawking incense, beads and counterfeit Celtic crosses; not to mention the legions of Sunday day trippers trailing squalling children, dripping ice lollies, and scattering crisp packets over hallowed ground.

The four Space Cadets, as they called themselves, were soon barreling down the A361 towards the relentlessly sleepy town of Bruton. After a few miles on the Bruton road, a gap in the hedgerow exposed an all too familiar spectacle.

A portion of the field was littered with tents, caravans and bonfires. A few yards back from the line of yellow tape which marked the forbidden zone, aging hippies mingled with Generation X'ers and dogs sniffing each other's bottoms. It was a friendly affair, as one would expect in rural Somerset, and no one seemed eager to break the harmony by breaching the frontier. A truck proudly displaying *BBC News* on its front and sides, disgorged its human and technical cargo onto the grass.

"God, this is so predictable, goddam circle junkies." Will breathed in the musky-sweet mix of wood smoke, weed, and freshly cut corn and hay.

"Hey, check this out." Ulick pointed to a small cart track to the left of the action. There, as if teleported from the movie *Magical Mystery Tour,* jounced a small school bus, painted in all the colours of a bad acid trip. At the windows, what looked like fugitives from a 60's commune, chanted and sang incomprehensible invocations to anyone willing to listen.

"Where do they come from?" Willow asked. "I thought we were a bit over the edge, but this is Neverland."

The bus squeaked to a halt. Its bizarre crew found the first unoccupied patch of grass, formed a circle, and under the direction of their leader, who sported a royal blue robe and a pointy hat with stars on it; began to chant to the sky.

"Check out Dumbledor, guess the hat's a beacon to guide the mothership."

The Night Before at the farm of Alfie Giles, Near Bruton, Rural Somerset

Farmer Alfred Giles looked at the sky, wondering if rain was on the way. He'd been to check the barn as there'd been rumours of a tramp squatting after dark. He wasn't the nervous type, but to err on the side of caution, he held his old cricket bat, normally used to ward off badgers and other furry invaders. As they headed back through the lower field, Bailey, his six-year-old Border Collie, let loose with a series of loud barks, punctuated with whines and the odd howl. Bailey went rigid and gazed up and down the rows of hay. He jumped up, ran in a circle, lay flat again and reinstated his bark, cry, howl cycle. Alfie, as he was known to all, glanced skyward, then scanned the row. "Now what's got you in a tiz? I've checked all. There's nought happening, yet." The sound of his master's voice settled Bailey and the two companions started back to the house.

The evening walk had been routine for the past six years since his dear wife had passed on. His kids had decided farm life was a little too rustic for their taste and had resettled in Bristol. Some folk are worn down by farm life. Alfie was the opposite. He thrived. Tall, fit and ruggedly handsome with a full head of silver hair. He was still considered to be a bit of a catch by some of the more seasoned local women. Life was a bit quiet these days, but Alf was content to do the farm work and head to the local for a couple of pints, some darts and a bit of a natter in the evening. Tonight, he was a bit knackered and decided to stop at home. He felt a pang of guilt, as Bailey loved his evening foray into town.

They turned in early, but about four o'clock, Alfie was shocked out of sleep by Bailey's yowls. A bright light shone into the room. He bolted to the window and caught the tail end of a glowing object as it dipped below the misty horizon. A low rhythmic droning sound followed. "Come on boy, I think that's for uz."

He put on his dressing gown, grabbed the cricket bat, and headed out toward where the fire ball had appeared to land. It only took a moment for Baily to find his prize. As he always did, Bailey barked twice, grabbed the soft ball from the tall grass, and galloped back to his owner. Alfie threw a "good boy" at him, patted him on the head and plucked the item from his mouth. When they got back to the farmhouse, Alfie placed it on the fireplace ledge. "Well, ole mucker, that's a job well done, back to bed for uz."

Alfie nearly dropped his mug of tea when he opened the kitchen door the next morning. Great swaths pierced the rows of hay and corn. What's more, they weren't random, rather, perfectly formed. This wasn't the work of wild animals or daft kids on their ATVs. Whoever or whatever had done this, had much better equipment than he. *Crikey, this isn't what I signed up for.*

A short time later, half the world seemed to appear at his doorstep. First it was the police telling him they had to cordon off part of his land. Then it was the damned crop chasers, looking for starships and one-eyed aliens. *You told me this would be a simple operation. It's already getting out of hand.*

One of the local cops showed him an aerial picture. There, in the middle of his field, sat a big eye, maybe 10 yards across, and a spiral of round shapes like some kind of galaxy or solar system. This wasn't one of those silly designs of fairies and giant caterpillars made by folk with nothing better to do.

Alfie wasn't going to get anything done today, and after all, it was now after 11. So given the situation, perhaps a couple of ales were in order. At the call of, "Come on boy, let's go for a pint." Bailey leapt to attention and the pair walked down the path to the main road. "Should I tell 'em we're leaving? What the hell, they don't need this gaffer and his dog around to have a good time."

Twenty minutes later he walked into the Sun Inn on Bruton High Street. It was your typical village pub, quaint and ancient, nothing remarkable. It had fine ales, the food was decent and the company was always agreeable. Since Jenn's early departure from his world, it had helped fill some lonely hours. More important, it was within walking distance, hence, no drinks limit. His welcome took him somewhat aback. A couple of his mates started into the theme from Star Wars, while another tried to growl out a bad Wookie imitation.

"Okay, okay, we don't know what it is yet. Coulda been you three puggle 'eads for all I know. Pint of Doom Bar please Shirley."

"So Alfie boy, why aren't ye back home where the action is?" Ray handed him the darts.

"What odds isit to I? 'Sides, every noggerhead within a hundred miles is around my barn. Let 'em bide. Tiz where I am, and tiz where I stay, least 'til all that lot has fucked off. Shirley luv, with all that hullerballoo s'marnin I forgot to feed old Bailey. He's likely starn. Do ye have a little something to tide him over 'til his supper? Gonna be a late one."

At nine o'clock the next morning, Alf was awakened by a banging at the door. He saw a White van with blue and yellow checkers, in the drive. Three very serious looking men in full police gear were walking towards the barn.

"Bloody hell, what now?" Alf put his dungarees over his pajamas and went downstairs.

When Alfie opened the door, he was greeted, if such a word could be used, by a man who looked as if he had been kidnapped from the RAF, circa 1943. Dressed in an immaculately pressed uniform, he sported a tidy mustache which hung on a face which was losing the battle to stay young. "Good morning Sir. Chief Superintendent Oliver Wendall Haughton, Ministry of National Defense. I am speaking with Alfred Giles?"

"That you are lad. That you are. Come in. Come in. I'll put the kettle on."

Alfie could offer little to illuminate the events, except to state a truncated version of the previous night.

Next came the unsettling revelation that Alfie's farm was going to be crawling with experts for a few days and he could either stay there and deal with it, or they would foot the bill for him to go somewhere else. Alfie had half expected to be whisked away to a hideaway and placed in a white bubble suit until it all blew over.

He thanked the Superintendent and told him of his decision to stay. "You just stay as long as you need, and don't bother about me officer, I have lots to do around here. You won't be in my way." Alfie then put on his hat, summoned Bailey and proceeded in the direction of The Sun Inn.

Ground Zero Day Two

Having no desire to stop the night in the car, the Space Cadets had decided to go home for the night and return early the next day.

In the morning, they maneuvered through the growing throng. It seemed another vehicle pulled onto the field every few seconds. Professor Dumbledor was still giving his version of The Sermon on The Mount to the faithful, curious, and just plain sardonic. His followers, known as the Flowered Light And Karmic Essence Servants, (did they not see the irony of the acronym?), badgered onlookers with offers of informational brochures, free for a small donation.

Will looked at his friends. "How long before they give us all the heave ho, d'ya reckon."

"As long as I get one good close up look, it doesn't matter." Willow led the way through a gap in the crowd and soon they were standing at the yellow ribbon. "It would be so easy to just slip underneath and crawl through the grass."

"Hay," corrected Ulick.

"Same thing." Willow gently pushed the tape up. There seemed to be no police in the immediate area.

"Well, yes and no. You see hay is a kind of...hey, what are you doing?" It was too late, Willow had disappeared into the tall stems on the other side. Ulick noticed a policewoman, rather forcefully escorting a man, or woman, draped in a purple robe, back across the barrier. "Willow, get back here, the coppers are right over there."

"You mean here?" Willow clutched a handful of stems in her left hand.

"Are you crazy? You'll have us all in the nick."

"It's called evidence. We take this with us and have it checked out at the University to see if there's anything suspect."

Ulick stood gawking at Willow. "Hey Will, Sean, over here, you won't believe this. Well don't just walk around with that in your hand. Stick it in your purse or your dress or something."

"Look, either we're Space Cadets or we aren't. We came for answers. Maybe now, we have some."

"ATTENTION. LADIES AND GENTLEMEN. THIS IS PC 31 OF THE AVON AND SOMERSET CONSTABULARY. YOU ARE ON PRIVATE PROPERTY. YOU ARE REQUIRED TO VACATE THIS AREA IMMEDIATELY. PLEASE PACK UP ALL YOUR GEAR AND PROCEED TO THE MAIN ROAD IN AN ORDERLY FASHION. THE PUBLIC WILL NOT BE PERMITTED WITHIN A ONE MILE RADIUS OF THE AFFECTED AREA UNTIL FURTHER NOTICE. FAILURE TO COMPLY WITH THIS ORDER WILL RESULT IN CHARGES BEING LAID. THANK YOU FOR YOUR CO- OPERATION...OH, AND HAVE A NICE DAY."

At this, the more timorous began packing up and walking, biking or driving towards the main road. The Magical Mystery crew enjoyed a few more minutes of exquisite lunacy, before reluctantly piling back on to their craft.

"That's it then, let's take our contraband and go home." Sean got into the driver's seat and soon they were driving down Bruton Road. They passed three Ministry of National Defense vehicles going in the opposite direction. "Holy shit, this is the real business. Remember that one in Redlynch last summer? Just a local news team, a couple of local coppers and the usual crazies."

"We were there," Will reminded him.

Sean ignored the comment. "Once in a while it goes up a notch, but the MOD boys only come in when they suspect something huge is up. The Ministry doesn't even have a UFO investigation unit anymore. At least none they'll admit to." As they rounded the next bend, the Magic Bus appeared. Sean sped up and beeped his horn as he passed. The occupants, engaged in a rousing version of "Mother Nature's Son", cheerfully waved and hooted their appreciation.

"Boy, if aliens are watching, they must think we're a right sorry lot. If I were them, I'd stick a sign up in the Stratosphere; *Earth, Caution: Avoid At All Costs.*

The Ministry of National Defense Special Operations Unit then moved to the "Infected" area to do what they do best, which involves a lot of picture taking, measuring things with fancy meters, letting dogs loose to sniff things, and most important, stand around with paper cups of something hot, and saying, "Aha".

The next evening, Alfie was settling into his fourth pint when unbeknownst to him, or anyone else in town, an officer found something odd in the circle. "Chief Superintendent, over here, I've found something." Ten minutes later, four men were carrying a large black crate towards the armoured truck at the side of the field.

By the time Alfie got home, the MOD had left. They did not come back the following morning.

Two days after the Bruton operation was terminated, and the contents retrieved from the Giles farm were sent to London, an emergency session of Parliament was called.

The first session was held on July 8th, four days after the curious case had been found. Except for the honourable MP for Somerset, nobody in caucus had ever heard of Bruton, much less could they place it on a map.

An envoy from the Ministry of Defense offered a truncated version of the events, given with the same ambiguities and obfuscations a mother might offer a six year old daughter who has just asked where babies come from. M.P.s left the session and headed for the pub, none the wiser than they'd been before, with a directive to remain in town, pending further instructions.

In 2010 scientists from the University of California, revealed the discovery of a potentially Earth Like planet orbiting a White Dwarf star, approximately 20 light years from our own beloved rock. Compared to the vastness of our galaxy, this distance is little more than a walk to the corner shop to buy some fags for us humans. The world was named Gliese g. It is also referred to as Zarmina. The latter has a lot more ear appeal than Gliese g, which sounds more like a caulking compound than a planet. Now it wasn't discovered in the sense that Columbus tripped over America. Nobody has actually seen it, but all the spectrum analysis and light shifting and other obtuse things space scientists do, have led to varying opinions about its existence.

As it turns out, it is indeed there, and the Zarminians have had their eye on us for some time, having a good old chuckle at our expense.

Two days before the Bruton event in the Grand Assembly Pod, Zarmina City

"Gentlemen, if I could have your full attention, please." Despite their technological prowess, the race was clearly mired in the Middle Ages when it came to matters of gender equity. "The experiments on planet Terra are getting tiresome, not to mention expensive. If you look at the screen you can see what we're dealing with." The picture displayed the FLAKES in all their loopy glory, chanting and praying into the air." Nevertheless, I suggest one more try before we pull the plug."

This was met with rather feeble applause, as the Zarmanians tend to be an apathetic lot.

Precisely one Earth week after the discovery, the object next to the mantle in Alfie Giles house began to glow. Bailey whined and sniffed at it. Alfie placed it to his left ear. After a moment, he set it down and turned to his restless friend. "Okay boy, no rest this evening. We've work to do."

He picked up the glowing sphere and headed out to the barn with Bailey in tow. They climbed into his pickup. "Okay old boy, seems we're off to Warminster, farmer by the name of Wilbur Puddy. We're going to have some fun tonight. Looks like the last time though."

Alfie pulled back into his drive about ten that evening. He put the truck in the barn and when Bailey began to bark and whine, he said. "What's the matter boy? Want to go for a drink?" By 10:30 they were at the Sun Inn, Alfie hoisting his pint and Bailey lapping from his bowl at the end of the bar.

"Well Alfie, things finally settled down at the farm, guess life can get back to normal."

"Arr Charlie, reckon Bailey and I won't be bothered for quite a bit."

The next night, another strange light passed over Bruton. The following evening, Alfie and Bailey were nowhere to be found.

MEMORIES FROM HEAVEN

This bit of silliness was shaped by the old scientific principle of Conservation of Energy. You know the one we learned in high school; energy neither is created nor destroyed. Also considered in the mix, was the idea that all the electronic media on Earth is travelling through space and ready to be picked up by alien life, convincing them that a visit to our planet is not worth the trouble. I was delighted when it was accepted for publication.

Memories from Heaven

The scientists knew they were wrong. But they didn't realize their mistake until the first fallout came drizzling out of the sky. It was barely noticeable at first, small dots of matter, landing gently on major urban areas. When these substances were examined closely by many learned men, they were in for a big surprise. Each piece had some kind of printing or picture on its surface, but even under powerful magnification the markings proved impossible to decipher.

Then the larger pieces came, falling like flakes of a wet snowstorm. They floated through the air and planted themselves on everything. They did not melt, but lay there until they were scooped up by curious onlookers. This time the images were large enough to make out with the simplest enlargement. To everyone's wonder they contained illustrations of movies, television shows, video games and all manner of electronic media. The scientists knew this was important.

When the streets of New York ran an inch deep in clips of *Rosanne, 60 Minutes* and old *National Lampoon* films, people began asking some serious questions. Still the experts were baffled.

Next came the noise, soft at first but then building to a crescendo of unbearable proportions. The lucky ones were serenaded with the classics and good old rock and roll. Those less fortunate, were tormented with Michael Bolton songs and commercial jingles. Every dog with a sense of hearing began howling and then hid behind whatever object was available.

Scientists continued to perform their tests. The frequency and intensity of the bombardment continued without abating. Stores sold out of headphones and ear muffs. People came into emergency after trying to claw out their ears. What had started as simple images, became holographic sequences of American Idol reruns and Freddy Kruger movies. Inside and outside, the sound and light show shattered lives. Church congregations met to pray for blessed silence. It did not come.

Working feverishly in sound and sight proof conditions, the scientists finally made this amazing pronouncement. The reason for the phenomenon was simple. The air was full. For a hundred years, humankind had been pumping out various kinds of audio and visual images. Although some of these had indeed travelled into space as previously believed; shocked scholars realized the bulk of these signals had become trapped in the Earth's atmosphere. In layman's terms, the air was saturated. Laden with all the sound and visual pollution it could carry. Like the heavens on a hot, humid, summer day, they had reached the point of no return and started raining down on the Earth. Unlike a thunderstorm, the source of the moisture was unlimited and so the tempest had no end. But even as this startling discovery was announced, people continued to inject increasing amounts of litter into the sky.

There were notable tragic incidents. The president of Mexico was crushed under a ten-foot strip of a Taco Bell billboard. Several riders were trampled by their horses when they fell over images of Camilla Parker Bowles on a fox hunt near Sandringham.

Leaders implored the public to stop using smart phones, Blackberries, MP3's and other electronic entertainment. All radio and television broadcasts were halted. Cloud seeding was used to bring down the remaining refuse.

In the end the world was saved. All the rubbish from space was gathered up and stored. People began to use their devices again, but this time with restraint. Laws were passed to limit the output of electronic media.

In the ensuing years, there was a brisk trade in the entertainment nostalgia and memorabilia trade.

CORRECTED

Many science fiction tales involve technology becoming self aware, and subsequently turning on its master. Soon an apocalypse has been instigated by the very beings we created. But what if those life forms used their newfound sentience to fulfill their intended purpose; to serve humankind? Would that be better or worse?

Corrected

The familiar buzz reverberated from the coffee table. A few seconds later it buzzed again. Two messages. "Geez this is supposed to be my day off." Gary rose into a semi-sit, picked up his mobile and punched in his code, M-E-N-S-A-B-O-Y-#1. A bit long and definitely pretentious, but nobody was likely to crack it. The only problem with a clever code was you couldn't show anyone how clever it was. That would defeat the purpose of the code, and also show you weren't worthy of the name MENSABOY#1.

All of these pointless thoughts rattled around in Gary's head before he noticed he'd put in the wrong PIN. He made a small pout and pressed it in again. Same result. Curious. Okay Gary, it's a day off work, not a day off from your brain, go slowly. Third time's the charm. There we go. Shouldn't have had that spliff with breakfast.

Dude, what are you doin'.

Bruce. Funny how people put in the apostrophe to avoid typing the "g". I mean what's that about?

Eating a bowl of Captain Crunch and watching cartoons.

So when is your tenth birthday?

Very funny, and I suppose you're sitting there figuring out ways to combat climate change.

Could be. Anyway, any plans for today?

Dude, it's a day off, plans don't come into it.

Thought I might go down to the lake, hang around the beach, maybe catch some breakfast. Feel like joining me…that is if you aren't all filled up on kid's cereal.

Sounds good. Meet at Toms in an hurry?

What?

Gary looked at the screen. Damned autocorrect. "Hey asshole, write what I tell you, don't improvise."

> Sorry dude, Tim's in an hour. Auto correct seems to be putting words in my mouth recently.

> Well considering the shit that comes out of there half the time, not such a bad idea.

You're a riot Bruce. Gary turned off the phone and looked for something that didn't need to go into the wash. As he buttoned up his shirt, another message came in. He was half tempted to ignore it, but it might be Bruce trying to change the plans, as was his habit. Rhonda. Okay, I'm always up for Rhonda.

> Hey Gary. Been too long. What's up?

> Not a lot. Just was talking to Bruce, hot day, thinking of going and holding up the bench.

> ??????

Gary glanced at the message. What? Geez, again. He tapped in a new message. *Should be; hanging at the beach. Sorry my autocorrect seems to have gone a bit rogue today.*

> I despise those things. It's like having a miniature parent in there, correcting everything you say. I mean it doesn't know what we're trying to say in the first place. Someday there's gonna be a war started because of that. Imagine the president texting the leader president of Russia and saying that there's a shipment on the way and instead it changes it to you're a shithead.

Haha, Rambling Rhonda. I've missed you.

> What about you?

> I'm thinking I could deal with a little sun myself.

> Great, see you at Tim's in 20 bitch.

"Holy shit, what are you doing? You trying to get me into shit? Yeah like you can hear me you stupid Android shithead."
Sorry. See what I mean. See you at the beach, by the ass cream stand.
Ah what the hell, she knows what I mean. Might as well give her a smile. Seriously, better take it in and have someone look at it. Gonna get me into a heap of trouble. Funny how we always call devices she, like Siri, the GPS lady. Maybe someone needs to start a movement about tech sexism.

Gary pocketed his mobile, took his keys off the hook and headed out. He felt the judder of the phone. Screw that, I'm going phone free for a while.

As he turned on to Lakeshore Boulevard he felt the vibration again. Gary may have done some stupid things before but he was a stickler that mobiles and driving don't mix. He'd had more than one friend get into a tango with another car for breaking that rule. The familiar ice cream stand came into view. He pulled into a spot, turned off the ignition and checked his mobile. So much for staying clear of the phone all day.

Couldn't resist could you bud?

What the fuck?

He looked down again.

Hey dude I'm here, where are you?

Okay, one of us is cracking up. He checked the message one more time. It hadn't changed.

Gary sneered at the screen, got out of the car, and walked in the direction of Tim Hortons. Holy shit, that's a long line. He decided maybe he didn't need coffee after all when Bruce appeared, two double doubles in hand. Does that make fours, he mused to himself.

"Bruce you are one capital dude. Rhonda's gonna meet us here."

"Yeah she texted me, said you called her a bitch," Bruce had a sly twinkle in his eye.

"Yeah I did actually," he paused for effect. "That stupid auto, it's being doing some weird shit recently. I'd completely dismantle it except I don't know how to spell."

"That's what you get for dropping out of school in fourth grade."

"You never run out do you?"

"Hey guys." Rhonda appeared from the queue, ice cap in hand.

Gary's phone alarm was a dull backdrop to his dream. It was time for him to do something constructive, like getting up. He was feeling the results of some bad decisions from yesterday. The three friends had left the beach late in the afternoon, and decided it would be nice to go to one of the resto-bars on the water. Drinks had turned to dinner, which had reinvented itself into a serious post prandial bender.

He glanced at his buzzing screen. Holy shit, 9:00 AM. Impossible. "I set it for seven." He complained to whoever was listening.

"What the fuck? I wasn't that drunk." He checked the screen again.

You were. You got to sleep so late. You needed sleep dude.

Dude? Oh come on. What's going on here?

Against all common sense, he texted.

Hey autocorrect, what the hell man? What are you doing?

Nothing.

This time he said it out loud. "I said auto, what do you think you are doing?"

A few seconds later the screen lit up.

I'm making corrections, that's my function.

He typed again.

Just make the corrections you're sppose to make.

He looked down at the screen.

Just make the corrections you are supposed to make.

"That's better. Now, you're doing your job."

Gary needed to phone work and tell them he'd be late. He punched in the number. Shit, voice mail, and he knew they wouldn't check it until he was already long overdue at his desk.

He texted his partner, Darryl.

Dude, my alarm didn't go off. I'm leaving in 5 minutes, gonna be there about 10:30

He checked the screen. Nope, looking good. He opted for a quick shower. He felt a lot better after, and as he was about to leave, he sent Darryl another message.

Leaving now.

He read it over.

Sorry Darryl, think I have the flu, can't get out of bed, you'll have to make do without me.

He kept staring down at the phone. Shit like this just doesn't happen. It's just a stupid program, it can't think.

Gary pondered his options. Come clean and tell Darryl what's going on? "Well that's the stupidest idea you've had so far today and it's not even 10 yet."

he said out loud. Could text again, say I took some flu tablets and be in this afternoon. Nope, no point, I know Darryl, he'll have delegated already. That leaves option number three. Enjoy another day off.

"Okay then, that's decided." He didn't know anyone else who was off, so that meant he was going solo. "Not such a bad thing." He realized what he was doing. "Gotta cut back on these solo conversations." Either that or get a roommate.

He picked up the phone from the coffee table in case someone from work had texted back. This time the message was in all caps.

"YOU'RE WELCOME GARY."

A new thought floated through his brain. Someone had found a way to get into his phone, check out his messages, and mess with him. But c'mon, who would be doing that, Russian hackers? "Dude, don't be so arrogant. You aren't that important." He put his hand over his mouth when he realized he was thinking out loud again. Someone who knows me then. Well it would be a pretty funny prank, I've got to admit. But I don't know anyone who could keep it up this long. Enemy? Nah, not everyone loves me I'm sure, but I never pissed anyone off enough for them to go to all this trouble, and I'm assuming it is a lot of trouble.

Wayne Symmonds had just walked through the front door of Mogistics Inc. The name was a combination of motivation and logistics. Nobody really liked it. They dealt with setting up sales rallies and such. Daryl was there at the door.

"Wayne, you're a lifesaver. Gary can't make it in. I honestly don't know what the fuck he is working on right now, but I do know he's the only one who can do it. You guys have had a lot of back and forth so I'm hoping, praying you can make some sense of it all."

"I'll do what I can, but you owe me big mate. Had to back out of a lunch date for this. Finally Rhonda agreed to talk to me again. After what I did last week, it was a miracle she'd meet me. Okay, show me where to go."

"Sorry Wayne, I'll find a way to make it up to you."

"I highly doubt that." Wayne walked into Gary's office, as Daryl held the door.

Gary munched absently on the slice of pizza he'd bought at 7-11 last night. He thought he'd eaten it, but now he was grateful he hadn't. On the TV Wolf Blitzer was talking about some senator that meant nothing to him. "Well this is a pretty shitty way to spend a day off. Hey wait, Wednesday is Joe's day off, maybe he'd be into hanging for a while."

Dude, got an unexpected day off, any ideas?

He checked the screen again as he put the phone on the coffee table. A minute later he glanced down.

Okay bud, sorry you can't hook up, another time.

What the fuck?
He picked up the phone and scrolled.

Dude, got an unexpected day off, any ideas?

Sure, I'm game, whad'ya have in mind?

A bit of pool maybe, a few drinks by the lake.

Works for me. When?

Oh shit, hang on, my mum needs me to help her move some stuff. Gonna have to go there now. Sorry Joe, maybe if I finish early I'll give you a call.

This time he shouted, "Okay, whoever is doing this, you've had your fun and I am starting to freak out a little, so stop already."

The phone did its thing.

I am sorry if this disrupts things Gary, but I needed to stop you. Your hook up would have ended in disaster. Autocorrect has averted that disaster.

"All right this is out of hand. Now you're not only able to think, but you're also clairvoyant?"

I did not say that. I just said I can help you avoid difficulty.

"Okay, first of all I'm done texting with you. If you're so clever then you can understand what I am saying."

That is acceptable.

"Of course it is. Okay then, will you please tell me where does the all knowing gadget get all this information from? Or are you going to tell me that you have a brain?"

Gary, please realize I consider you a friend.

"Friend? Seriously?"

And what appears to be an attempt on my part to make your life difficult is not so. Perhaps you have seen too many tech gone rogue movies. But think about it. I am a device that is programmed to make corrections for its owner. Therefore, is it not logical if I see you are about to get into difficulty or make some questionable decisions that are not logical, my duty is to correct these issues.

Shit why are you so logical? "Listen Spock, that's what I'm going to call you. He's a character...."

I know who Mr. Spock is. Would you like to see a video of him? I have the ability to upload any relevant videos from the Internet on this phone.

"No that won't be necessary. As I was saying, God, you've got me so rattled that I can't remember what I was going to say."

If I may, I would surmise by the agitation present in your voice that you were about to admonish me for my actions, which I assure you is totally unnecessary as my actions are completely honourable and necessary. To quote your Mister Spock in the Star Trek movie, "Nothing necessary is ever unwise."

"And that means I'm going to have you around constantly watching and fixing everything I do?"

Not everything, just the things that are misguided and ill-advised and could lead you to a harmful outcome. However, given your history that could be quite often.

"Dude I'm not that bad. I think I'm doing pretty well actually. Good job, nice digs, friends."

Might I also remind you of the famous car roll over of 2015. The failed canal jump of 2017. The infamous job interview of 2018. They are still talking about the naked break dance on the bar at Guvernment. Shall I go on?

"Please don't. But look, that was then, I've made some positive changes."

Would you like to know what would have happened had I let you meet up with your friend Joe this afternoon? It's really quite disturbing and if I might add, a bit amazing.

"And again no thank you. But making mistakes is human, that's how we learn."

Agreed, but are you familiar with the three laws of robotics.

"Sort of, and you aren't a robot."

I must disagree, what is defined as robot in the novel you are referring to, has now been replaced with the term artificial intelligence, and if you choose to read the documentation, autocorrect meets two of the criteria: reactive machine and limited memory. And to refresh your memory, the third rule of robotics is: A robot must protect its own existence as long as such protection does not conflict with the First or Second Laws. Therefore as I am clearly not causing any harm to you. I have no choice but to correct your errors.

"Well your idea of harm and mine are different."

I do not believe harm can be differentiated. I am also helping others. The domino effect is really quite fascinating. For example, your friend Wayne would have caused many difficulties for your other friend Rhonda. That issue is now moot as he had to break his appointment with her again, and I believe she is not willing to make another. You must remember there are consequences to your actions which go beyond you.

"Okay then, we'll just cut out the middle man." Gary began to power off the phone, missing the next message. "I'm going out, if that's okay with your correctness."

I'm sorry Gary it's not that easy.

Gary tossed the phone on the couch, grabbed his keys and walked for the door.

"Alexa, unlock the door please."

"Sorry, I cannot perform that action Gary."

THE KINGDOMS

I often read Zen Parables. I love how they convey profound meaning in just a few words. The story's clarity is where its strength lies. No frills, no unnecessary side bars, but poetic and poignant just the same.

The Kingdoms

The two Kingdoms had faced each other for centuries. Each sat perched on a hilltop, within eyesight on a clear day. The Noble Dragon River cleaved the plain between the two peaks. This was regarded as the borderline, when convenient. As they were so close, their cultures and lifestyle were alike. Their languages were also comparable, with a few subtle, albeit key differences in dialect. Through a well powered glass, one could stand on a turret of one of the magnificent temples or castles and watch people on the other side go about their everyday affairs. Those who were so inclined, spent a lot of time doing so.

The two Kingdoms were not fond of each other. The rich, the military, politicians and even the clergy were exceedingly jealous of their counterparts. Truth be told, the leaders were a rather unpleasant lot, filled with self-importance and greed. Although both nations were prosperous, it didn't stop them from coveting what the others had. The most cunning concocted ways of sneaking across the valley, and partaking in a brief plunder or two in the hope of swelling their personal wealth and luxury.

This had triggered several minor scuffles, and many ignoble insults were often tossed across The Noble Dragon River. However, before things got out of hand, one or two sounder heads prevailed and those in power were persuaded to put aside their hostility and extend their hands in peace, even if it was just to wait for a more opportune time for treachery. So it was, a very dodgy accord was maintained throughout their long history.

During calmer times, the kingdom's merchants visited the other side to exchange and sell goods. There was little in the way of consumables each didn't possess, but in the areas of the Arts and Innovations they found much to envy. Each had a number of talented artists who produced unique works. Those with the means, negotiated with guile, trying to best their rival. If that failed, they quietly coveted their neighbor until they could no longer bear it. That was followed by a surreptitious raid. Participants proudly displayed these pur-loined treasures in public, passing them off as being "home grown" talent, although most knew otherwise.

After several centuries of cautious co-existence, one of the kings came up with a scheme he fancied might be to his great gain. He chose two of his more skilled aids to carry out the plan. Fearful of the idea falling into the wrong hands, the King did not write his suggestion on paper. Instead, he personally instructed them how to present the proposal in Court. This would turn out to be an unwise move.

These two vain men set out on horseback, and along the way began to dis-cuss their mission. They began to crow about which one the King preferred and who should be trusted to speak at the meeting. This spiraled into a squab-ble, fueled by a past steeped in jealousy.

Upon arrival, they were welcomed with a sumptuous meal, fine wine and entertainment. The King spared no kindness, hoping to use the occasion for his own profit. When it came time for their audience with the King, they be-gan to speak at once, trying to impress His Majesty. Affected by the drink, their fondness for bombastic speech and the variations in dialect, their mean-ing rapidly became subject to misinterpretation and personal insult.

Furious, the king had them imprisoned and ordered the army to stand ready to attack. At sunrise, on the opposite hill, sentries were shocked to see masses of horses, weapons and soldiers stampeding towards their gates. They sounded the alarm and soon their own army was at the ready. A frightening battle ensued, during which a large part of the city was damaged. After over-coming the disadvantage of the surprise attack, they recovered and drove the other side into retreat. As payback, they sent a party towards the second King-dom where they ravaged parts of that glorious city.

At day's end, neither could claim victory, although they did. One thing was certain, the beautiful metropolises would never be the same.

A few days later, as if the gods themselves had been inflamed by their be-haviour, a terrible earthquake rattled both Kingdoms. Many of the remaining buildings tumbled into ruins. Once the ground stopped shaking, both cities were almost beyond recognition.

The Priests decided the gods were punishing the citizens for their sins of envy, greed and theft. They ordered their congregations, who were inclined to believe anything these impressive, robed men said, to take up all the pilfered items they could find, run to the Noble Dragon River and toss them into the gushing water to appease whoever they had ticked off.

As they approached the river, to their horror, the people saw a massive wall of water approaching from the Great Southern Ocean. It exploded into the countryside and up the sides of hills, engulfing both realms. The remains of the cities were swept into the now raging river and out towards the sea, settling on the floodplain at the ocean's edge.

Those who survived the apocalypse left to go inland, and never returned. Over the coming centuries the waves and torrents of silt from the river buried the remnants of the Kingdoms.

Present date at an archeological dig at the confluence of the Dragon River and the Great Southern Sea.

Professor Henry Thompkins sifted through the silt, exposing artifacts from the delta. He picked up a statue of a small angel. "This one is marvelously well preserved. Look at the intricate lines and form."

His partner, Dr. Angelica Santori, took it from him and ran her hands over the dull alabaster surface. "This is just amazing. These samples are in such good shape, I just can't believe this. It's the find of the century."

"Agreed; the tools, pieces of art, everything. This must have been a noble, refined culture. Nothing around this part of the continent suggests this should even be here." Thompkins stood shin deep in the brown muck which had given up so much treasure. "You know for a civilization to produce this kind of legacy, it had to have existed for centuries. There weren't many people from this era that could go five minutes without raping and pillaging their neighbours."

"Well, I reckon most of the rest of the relics would have been swept out to sea. Guess we'll have to get the marine squad out for the rest of the dig." Dr. Santori, briefly gazed upriver. Just at the horizon, she could barely make out twin peaks gleaming in the setting sun. She then turned and focused her attention to the far-off shoals, which low tide was starting to expose.

A QUICK WORD
ABOUT OUR
QUIRKY AUTHOR

This is Stephen F C Porter's second book. The first, *Teaching in the Spirit,* was a guide to help teachers to bring more meaning and compassion into the classroom.

The *Quick and the Quirky* is a collection of short stories compiled over the past several years. The stories range from science fiction to noir and several genres in between.

Stephen has followed various pursuits on planet Earth, including; medical research librarian, middle school science teacher, chef, counsellor at the distress centre, on air radio host and producer, documentary writer and producer, and working with children with emotional and behaviour challenges. In addition, he worked at several jobs too painful to mention here. All of these lives have provided fodder for this varied collection of tales.

Stephen currently resides in Toronto.

www.ingramcontent.com/pod-product-compliance
Lightning Source LLC
Chambersburg PA
CBHW070433120726
47910CB00003B/769